HARP
MAIDEN
Web of Secrets

HARP MAIDEN

Web of Secrets

JACKIE BURKE

LINDON BOOKS

First published by Lindon Books in 2021
9 Raheen Park, Bray, Co. Wicklow
Web: www.grindlewood.com
Email: jackieburke@grindlewood.com

Paperback   ISBN: 978 1 78846 203 7
eBook – ePub format   ISBN: 978 1 78846 204 4
Amazon paperback edition   ISBN: 978 1 78846 205 1

Produced by Kazoo Independent Publishing Services
222 Beech Park, Lucan, Co. Dublin
www.kazoopublishing.com

Kazoo Independent Publishing Services is not the publisher of this work. All rights and responsibilities pertaining to this work remain with Lindon Books.

Kazoo offers independent authors a full range of publishing services.
For further details visit www.kazoopublishing.com

Cover artwork © Rachel Corcoran, 2021
Printed in the EU

BOOKS BY JACKIE BURKE

HARP MAIDEN SERIES
Harp Maiden
Harp Maiden: Web of Secrets
Harp Maiden: Ladder of Charms

GRINDLEWOOD SERIES
The Secrets of Grindlewood
The Secret Scroll
The Queen's Quest
Zora's Revenge
Othelia's Orb

ABOUT THE AUTHOR

Jackie grew up with her sister and three brothers in Dublin. An avid reader and writer since her early school days, she only recently began writing children's stories, having dreamed of doing so for quite some time. *Harp Maiden: Web of Secrets* is the second book in Jackie's second series for children, following the hugely popular Secrets of Grindlewood series.

The magical, mystery tale of the *Harp Maiden* was inspired by Jackie's other great love, music. She is also greatly inspired by her love of nature, gardens, forests, wildlife and of course magic! Reading, hill walking, music and baking are just a few of her other many interests and hobbies. Jackie divides her time between writing and giving creative writing workshops to children in schools and libraries around the country. She lives with her husband in Bray, County Wicklow. They share their home with a big fluffy cat called Millie.

CHAPTER ONE

The applause was like thunder. Evie felt her cheeks flush as she took her bow. Her first concert playing the flute had been a great success, better than she had dared to hope. In the wings of the stage her governess Julia was clapping and smiling warmly. Evie stood up straight again and smiled at the audience. Finding her parents among the crowded hall was easy as her father had insisted they sit in the front row. He was standing now, clapping louder than everyone else. Beside him Evie's mother beamed with pride.

Then Evie heard that awful word – 'Bravissima!' It was a voice she knew well.

Her eyes darted to the wings, trying to hold her smile for the audience until she was escorted off the stage. Where was her escort, her tutor? He should have come on stage immediately after Evie took her bow. A feeling of dread shot through her as her eyes locked on the approaching figure.

'Where is my tutor?' Evie mumbled, panic rising, her breath quickening. 'Where is Mr Reid?' She felt stuck to the spot, her legs suddenly like lead and the happy smile evaporating from her face. 'That's not Mr Reid, that – that's Mr Thorn!' she cried. 'But it can't be! Something is terribly wrong! That man ... he, he's supposed to be dead!' She was shouting now, almost hysterical. 'No! No! He can't be here!'

Evie covered her face with her hands, not wanting to believe what she was seeing. 'What's happening to me?' she blubbered into her fingers.

Her distress only worsened when she glanced up again, rubbing her eyes in disbelief. Evie stared at the man, the demon who had possessed the eccentric maestro and kidnapped her just a few months before. Another shadow emerged from behind the stage props, bulky and awkward. It was Olga, the tall, bullying housekeeper, another demon who had also taken human form in the demons' quest to find the magical harp – now Evie's harp. Olga was different from Thorn, taller, stronger, volatile and very dangerous – an ogress-demon.

Olga stood beside Thorn, dwarfing him. The same evil smirk Evie remembered stretched across her broad, ugly face. Evie looked frantically about for her governess, worrying for her safety, but she was gone. Turning back to the audience, she stared. They were still smiling and clapping like nothing had happened, like it was normal. Yet Evie knew something dreadful had happened and she feared it was about to happen again.

'They can't help you, Evelyn,' Thorn said, walking slowly towards her. 'I will always be your tutor, only me. You and the harp belong with me. Why didn't you play it today? Your flute is no match for the harp, not a magical harp.'

Evie couldn't find the words to reply.

'I see Mr Reid has abandoned you already,' Thorn continued. 'Forget about him. You and I have important work to do, as you well know.'

Evie gulped, almost wilting on the spot, and trying hard not to retch. Would no one come to her aid? Could the audience, her parents not see this too?

'You heard him, girl, you're coming with us,' Olga said, stepping out of the shadows. 'We're not finished with you yet.'

A spotlight shone brightly over Evie's head. It made her feel hot, even more uncomfortable. The applause stopped and Evie felt everyone was waiting for her to reply, give some explanation. Looking at the suddenly strange sea of faces, the fifteen-year-old flautist, having just performed her first solo in the local town hall, didn't know what to do.

As she tried to make sense of it all, Evie remained stock-still, centre stage. She began fidgeting with a pendant around her neck. Looking down, Evie didn't recognise it. She didn't normally wear a pendant, did she? Where had it come from? The stone was large, too large, and so very dark, inky-black. It felt increasingly heavy around her neck, distressingly so. The hall was getter hotter and stuffier, too, as her confusion and fear became almost overwhelming.

Then, with a jolt, she remembered: the Black Ruby of Yodor, the powerful, magical ruby that Olga had hidden away, hoping to present it to her brutal master, Volok, in exchange for power and favour. It had been lost in the great fire at Dower Hall when Evie had escaped her captors. She had hoped to go back and look for it, yet here it was around her neck.

'It can't be,' she gasped, and almost swooned. 'The ruby is still among the ruins, it has to be. Unless ...'

'I'll take charge of that,' Thorn said, moving quickly forward.

He reached for the ruby and Olga roared at him.

'No! It is mine! I promised it to Volok.'

Evie stumbled backwards, clutching the ruby as the two demons lunged for it. She screamed, ducked, spun around, and continued struggling and twisting in the melee, trying to hold on to the prize. Why did she want to keep it? Was the Black Ruby so very important? Evie couldn't remember. She was outnumbered and greatly outmuscled by the two demons, and still no one was coming to help her.

'Enough!' Olga roared as she batted Thorn away with a tremendous punch. She grabbed Evie by the neck with one large hand, and lifted her off the ground. Then she wrenched the pendant away from her neck with her other hand.

'THIS – IS – MINE!' she roared into Evie's face, then dropped her to the ground like a doll.

CHAPTER TWO

Evie sat bolt upright and gasped deeply for air. One hand clutched at her throat, the other was clutching at the bedspread. She lay back on her pillow, staring into the darkness.

There was a gentle knock on the door.

'Evie, are you all right?' Evie's governess opened the door a couple of inches and peeped into the room. 'I thought I heard a cry. Did you have another bad dream?'

'Yes,' Evie said. 'Sorry for waking you.'

Julia lit the candle on the bedside table and sat down on the edge of the bed. Tilly, the housemaid, appeared at the bedroom door.

'Is everything all right, Miss?' she asked. 'I was sewing late and thought I heard a noise.'

'Fine, thank you, Tilly,' Evie said, embarrassed. 'Please, everyone go back to bed.'

'We will in just a minute,' Julia said. 'Tilly, would you mind fetching Evie a glass of warm milk, please?'

'Of course, Miss,' Tilly said, and hurried off.

'What was it this time?' Julie asked.

'The Black Ruby again,' Evie said. 'It was on a pendant around my neck – at the concert. Thorn and Olga were there.

Olga nearly strangled me to get it.' Evie rubbed her neck as though it still hurt.

'These dreams will stop,' Julia said. 'It's only been a few months since that nasty experience in Dower Hall. All those horrid memories will fade in time.'

'What comes next worries me more than what has already happened,' Evie said.

'Such as?' Julia asked.

'All that I must do, and do well,' Evie said. 'And what the demons are planning, wherever they are.'

'I keep hoping they all died in the fire,' Julia said.

Evie gave her a doubtful look. 'You know we can't be certain of that,' she said. 'They only found two bodies, Thorn and Lucia. Poor Lucia. I wish she were here to counsel me, tell me more about her time as a Harp Maiden.'

'You were probably lucky to meet her at all,' Julia said.

'How do you mean?' Evie asked.

'She told us the new Harp Maiden only takes over when her predecessor dies,' Julia said. 'It was Thorn who identified you as the next Harp Maiden. If you hadn't gone for the audition at his house, you might never have found the harp and never discovered that you could play it. Being in Dower Hall, however frightful, also allowed you to meet Lucia.'

'Because she was one of the demons' prisoners too,' Evie mumbled. 'You're right, at least I met her and she told me a few things, but not enough to help me now. Like how do I choose who to help with the harp's magic? How do I stop the demons? How do I protect the harp for the rest of my life, while keeping its magic a secret?'

Julia nodded but didn't reply straight away. She didn't

have the answers, and it was a grim list of questions. 'Perhaps you're feeling a little nervous about the upcoming concert,' she said after a moment, trying to change the subject. 'It will be a big occasion for the whole town.'

'Maybe,' Evie muttered, still distracted by her thoughts.

'You played very well at the last rehearsal,' Julia continued. 'Mr Reid has been a very supportive music teacher. All his students have improved since he arrived, but especially you, Evie. And remember, you will be playing the flute at the concert, not the harp. Try to keep your worries as far from your mind as possible and just enjoy the performance.'

'I will,' Evie said. 'I am looking forward to the concert, but you know the flute had a part to play in all the drama in Dower Hall too.'

'That was purely chance,' Julia said, 'and an extraordinary stroke of luck. Your flute made our escape possible.'

'I want to be a good Harp Maiden,' Evie said, 'not just to satisfy my pride, but for Lucia's sake, and for all the Harp Maidens who went before me. Many of them probably suffered dreadfully, perhaps for their whole lives, all for possessing this amazing gift.'

Julia was about to reply but turned instead towards the door. Tilly arrived with a tray of warm milk and shortbread biscuits, Evie's favourite. She placed them on the other bedside table beside Evie's book, *Little Lord Fauntleroy*.

'Master Freddie adores that book, Miss,' Tilly said.

'Yes, he can read it by himself now,' Evie said. 'I really should let him keep it. Only …' Evie paused.

'Only it belonged to Master Ben,' Tilly said. 'We all miss your little brother, but it is nice having a youngster running about the house again. He was so excited about his tenth birthday. He made us all laugh. We still talk about it downstairs.'

'It was a lot of fun,' Evie said, smiling and relaxing a little, remembering Freddie's excitement at his party in February. 'I think I will give it to him … yes, I will, tomorrow.'

'Give me what?' Freddie cried as he bounced into the room followed by a rather dishevelled and sleepy-looking Professor Wells, Evie's father.

'Are we having a midnight feast?' he asked as he took one of the biscuits. 'Freddie woke me, thought he'd heard voices. Is everyone all right or am I interrupting something?'

Evie frowned, noticing her father looked at Julia for the answer to his question. His bushy eyebrows always wriggled ridiculously when he lifted them, which was every time he asked a question. But then Evie had to smile; her father was usually so jolly it was impossible to be out of sorts for long when he was around.

'Evie had a bad dream but she's fine now,' Julia said. 'All forgotten.'

Freddie grabbed two biscuits then scrambled onto the bed and snuggled in beside Evie. 'I used to have bad dreams,' he said, 'but I have better dreams now that I live here.'

'That's good to hear,' Evie's father said. 'You three had quite the adventure last New Year. It's no wonder you have lots of muddled-up thoughts spinning around in your heads that wake you up with a fright! Keep busy, that's what I always say, and keep reading books! Now, everyone back to bed before we wake anyone else, especially the mistress. Thank you, Julia, and thank you, Tilly. Come along, Freddie.'

Julia popped her head around the door before she closed it. 'We'll talk more tomorrow, Evie. Good night.'

Evie nodded and blew out the candle. She was glad her parents had never probed too much about their ordeal. They accepted the shortened version of events that Evie had told them: she had been kidnapped by an eccentric maestro who was obsessed with her musical talent, aided by his formidable housekeeper and rogue of an assistant. Though all of that was true, the full story was more sinister. Explaining how she had been held prisoner at Dower Hall by demons who wanted to use a harp that only Evie could play would have been too much for them to bear or even believe. Julia's kidnapping and Freddie's imprisonment had terrified Evie, forcing her to give in to their demands. Although knowing the consequences could be horrendous, Evie had to play the harp, release its magic and free their demon lord, Volok, from his curse: imprisonment inside the wooden frame of the harp.

Evie tossed and turned in her bed remembering it all. Julia might have died of pneumonia that New Year's Eve night if they hadn't managed to escape. Freddie, an orphan, had been kept a prisoner in Dower Hall for years. Evie was so glad her parents had adopted Freddie. Everything had worked out so well in the end. But it wasn't really the end, was it? She had so much to learn, so much to do, and the danger wasn't by any means over.

Only the three of them – Evie, Julia and Freddie – knew what really happened during the last months of 1899, and on that fateful New Year's Eve and early New Year's Day under the bright full moon. Ironically, the day the demons brought their master back into the world with the help of the harp's magic was also Evie's fifteenth birthday -- 1 January 1900.

Despite her best efforts and Julia's reassurance, a terrible guilt hung over Evie because she had been forced to play a major part in bringing Volok back into the world by playing the harp. Not a minute went by when she didn't dread what his plans might be and what she would have to do to stop him. But she was the Harp Maiden and it was her duty to take up this quest. Something told her the Black Ruby was at the heart of it, so it was no surprise she was haunted by it in her dreams.

CHAPTER THREE

Evie took her new role very seriously. As Lucia had warned her, being the Harp Maiden came with grave responsibility and many concerns. Evie worried constantly about how she would keep it a secret her entire life, and equally, who would be deserving of the harp's magic. There would always be so many worthy causes; how on earth was she to choose?

Her first list of deserving candidates had been ridiculously long and repetitive. Looking at a later, shortened version written in her new diary – a gift from Julia – she had to admit that even then not all of the candidates on the list were in dire need. Evie realised it was going to be quite a challenge: first to *find* those in real need, then to *choose*. Only one wish could be granted on the night of each full moon; only one person could receive the harp's magic on that night.

Evie relived in her mind her first wish over and over. It occurred in the small hours of New Year's Day when they were trapped in a snowstorm having made their escape from Dower Hall. Making that first wish for rescue sealed Evie's fate as the new Harp Maiden. That was how it would be for the rest of her days. She would live a secret life – undoubtedly a privilege, but at times it would be her burden too. Indeed, she could already feel the gathering weight of this new and extraordinary responsibility.

At the next full moon, 29 January 1900, Evie chose to heal her father of arthritis. It had plagued him for the last few years, and with all the snow that winter it had worsened. As it threatened to greatly restrict the professor's career and in particular his adored archaeological expeditions, Evie made a wish for the brilliant Professor Wells. She knew he would be lost without his work, his lifelong passion for history, ancient civilisations, and the discovery and identification of lost artefacts.

On 26 February Evie wished for her mother. Mrs Wells had succumbed to a deep melancholy that had haunted her for the two years since Evie's little brother Ben had died. Everyone put Clara's improved mood down to having Freddie around, their newly adopted 'nephew', and undoubtedly that was true too. Now, Evie's mother was back to her cheerful ways, but with a 'slight tendency to worry about everything', as Evie's father would joke.

The night of the March full moon arrived. Evie liked to talk through her preparations with Julia, though she insisted on performing the actual task alone.

'You know I am only too happy to go with you,' Julia said.

'I know,' Evie said. 'But I think it's better if you stay here and cover for me if anyone suspects anything.' She also thought, but didn't say, that she was concerned about Julia's health. Her governess had been frequently unwell throughout the winter months and had admitted that she had suffered a bout of tuberculosis prior to her time with the Wells family. Her lungs had been weakened by it, and she was prone to catching influenza and other nasty infections. Evie noticed a weary look about her governess that was lingering, and it troubled her.

Julia nodded, the expression on her face one Evie had become accustomed to – understanding mixed with concern. Evie knew that Julia had resigned herself to the fact that in all matters concerning the harp, Evie was in charge and Julia must let her decide how it would be. It didn't mean they agreed on everything, however, and Evie hated when they argued, or when Julia wouldn't accept as necessary Evie's determination to face up to all aspects of her new role, even the dangerous ones. Though she was deeply grateful for having both Julia and Freddie to confide in, Evie intended to take on the darker responsibilities of being the Harp Maiden alone.

At the March full moon, Evie planned to help her friend Grace with a wish. Grace's poor eyesight and the frightfully thick lenses in her spectacles interfered with her ability to read music at night, when candles threw awkward shadows across the pages. Evie was excited she could secretly help her best friend, a talented pianist, but she was forced to change her plans at the very last minute.

Dinner was over. Evie entered her father's study to get two sheets of parchment: one for writing the wish and one as a spare, just in case. She was surprised to find her father there, not smoking his pipe in the drawing room as he often did after dinner.

'Evie, my dear, come in,' her father said. 'I'm researching the last couple of artefacts found in your overturned cart, the stuff that Drake stole from Dower Hall. He had a surprisingly good eye for antiques, the scoundrel.'

'Did you find anything interesting?' Evie asked.

'Perhaps. I'm still working on it,' her father said. 'Did you want something, dear?'

'Just some parchment. May I?' Evie went straight to a drawer in her father's desk.

'I see you have discovered where I keep it,' he said, smiling at her as he removed his spectacles.

'I might have borrowed a page or two,' Evie said, a little embarrassed, 'to write on, I mean, to add to my new diary, the one Julia gave me.'

'Help yourself, dear,' her father said. 'Just don't let me run out, will you?'

'Of course not,' Evie said.

'Writing to a pen pal or an admirer, perhaps?' her father asked, his eyes twinkling.

Evie felt her cheeks flush. 'No! Why? What makes you say that?' she asked.

'Parchment is special,' her father said. 'Only used for special occasions nowadays, or for special people. Or for work.'

'I … I like writing on it,' Evie said. 'It feels nice, special, for my special diary.'

'I understand,' her father said. 'Take whatever you need, any time.'

Evie took two sheets of parchment and hurried out of the room. She didn't want to lie to her father about its purpose. Avoiding a direct answer was about as much as she could bear. She was at the top of the stairs when there was a hammering on the front door. The butler, Mr Hudson, opened it.

Evie heard only bits of the conversation, but enough to

know it was an emergency. A frantic neighbour was telling Hudson about a dreadful accident: someone had fallen from a horse and probably broken their back. Could Professor Wells send someone in his carriage to fetch the local doctor? Evie came down the stairs to see Hudson rush to the study to tell Evie's father. The professor came out immediately, grabbed his coat and hat and hurried out the door, Hudson right behind him.

'Who was injured?' Evie asked, standing in the hall.

'Mr Baldwin,' Evie's mother said. 'I hope he'll be all right. He has a young family, I believe. Hudson knows them.'

Evie's mother returned to the drawing room as Evie slowly mounted the stairs again, her thoughts whirring.

At one o'clock in the morning, Evie crept downstairs and entered the parlour. She lifted the harp from the table in the bay window and silently left the house by the back door. She was well wrapped up against the chilly, starry night. Before passing through the back-garden gate, Evie grabbed some of the dried twigs she and Freddie had collected over the previous week and tied them in a bundle. She pulled her satchel from her shoulder and stuffed them inside. Then she checked one final time to see she had everything else she would need: the two sheets of parchment, a special pen and some ink to write the wish, which she now felt obliged to change, and a box of matches. With the harp's magic she would be able to heal Mr Baldwin, and though disappointed for Grace, Evie knew it was the right thing to do.

The bright moon lit the way as Evie headed to a secluded part of the local park. She couldn't risk performing the ritual in her own back garden, nor could she travel too far at night. The nearby park seemed the best option.

Evie set the harp down in a small clearing behind a thick copse of trees and knelt beside it. She set about building her little fire, wondering how long she would be able to use that same secluded spot. If someone found evidence of the fire, there would be questions asked and she would have to find another location. She brushed the thought from her mind for the moment and continued with her preparations.

After untying the twigs, Evie surrounded them with the same stones to contain the fire that she had used before. Carefully, she wrote down the wish and waited for the moon to reach its peak. She took off her gloves and put them in her satchel. Nothing must be left behind by accident; no evidence except the ashes from the fire, which hopefully no one would notice once she kicked them away and hid the stones under a bush. Evie strummed the harp lightly to warm up her fingers. The sound was soft and wouldn't travel far. A sliver of cloud drifted over the moon. Evie stopped playing to watch its passage as it crossed the bright silver disc then continued on its way.

The moment arrived. Evie lit the fire with a match, nurturing it carefully. Once it took hold, she laid the parchment on the flames to burn the wish, then began to play. At every full moon, Evie felt happy, satisfied. She was making a positive difference to someone's life every time she made a wish, releasing the harp's magic. Very soon, Evie thought, smiling to herself, good fortune will shine on Mr Baldwin and his injuries will simply disappear.

CHAPTER FOUR

Evie slept heavily the night of every full moon. After the anticipation and tension of the secret ritual she was tired out. On waking the next morning, she immediately thought of Mr Baldwin and hoped it wouldn't be long before she heard he was fully recovered.

After breakfast, Evie waited for Julia in the parlour. Sometimes her parents would sit in to enjoy her music practice, but today they were going to see the local tailor to have Professor Wells measured for a new suit. He had a number of important conferences to attend over the coming weeks. Evie's mother had already made arrangements for a new evening gown to be made.

Evie jumped as the parlour door opened, pulling her out of her reveries. Julia hurried in, her skirt rustling around her.

'Goodness! Did I startle you, Evie?' she asked.

'Sorry,' Evie said. 'I was thinking about … everything.'

'We'll talk more as soon as we're alone in the house,' Julia said, her voice low. 'I sent Tilly into town first thing to purchase some more parchment for you.'

'Thank you,' Evie said. 'Father knows I've been dipping into his stores. I think he suspects something.'

'Oh?'

'He thinks I'm writing to someone – a pen pal, maybe a boyfriend.'

'Really? Who?'

'I don't know! No one,' Evie said uncomfortably.

'Perhaps it's a good thing,' Julia said. 'It might keep him off the scent.'

Evie was silent.

'What is it, Evie?' Julia asked. 'You seem upset.'

'I hate having to choose who will receive a wish and who will not,' Evie said. 'It doesn't seem fair that anyone's fate is up to me, that I decide what may or may not happen.'

'Did everything go all right last night?' Julia asked.

'It was perfect,' Evie said. 'I was glad to be able to help Mr Baldwin. He had a dreadful accident, as you heard. It's just … I had intended to help Grace. Having to change my mind at the last minute left me feeling confused.'

'Choosing who to help must have been a dilemma for every Harp Maiden,' Julia said, taking a seat beside Evie.

'I want desperately to help my family, my friends and people I care about,' Evie said. 'But the wishes are precious. I have to use them for those who need them most. How do I *ensure* that? If I hadn't heard about Mr Baldwin in time, he might have died. There must be so many people who need help, and not just here in Hartville but everywhere!'

'You can only do your best,' Julia said. 'Perhaps we could look further afield, as you say, beyond Hartville. It doesn't mean you will ignore everyone you know, but I suppose you can't keep your gift close to home forever, unfortunately.'

'Why unfortunately?' Evie asked.

'Because the more you move around, the greater the risk

that your secret will be discovered,' Julia said. 'But at the same time—'

'At the same time, how will I help more people if I don't look elsewhere?' Evie finished the question.

Julia nodded.

'I need to be *free*, that's how,' Evie said with a burst of passion. 'Not constantly watched by my parents or my governess because I'm only fifteen.'

'Evie!' Julia cried, surprised at her uncharacteristic rudeness.

'I'm sorry, Julia. I apologise,' Evie said. 'This is going to be more difficult than I thought. I never imagined I would have such power over people's lives, and despite that power I feel helpless.'

'You are not helpless,' Julia said. 'You are new to it, that's all, and you made three good choices so far. When is the next full moon?'

'The twenty-third of April,' Evie said.

'Right.'

They were both silent for a moment.

'Your new music teacher, Mr Reid, might be able to help,' Julia said, 'without actually knowing it, of course.'

Evie noticed a rare mischievous gleam in Julia's eyes, but her governess waited until the penny dropped.

'The concerts!' Evie cried.

Julia nodded.

'Mr Reid wants to organise more if the first concert goes well,' Evie said. 'We would be travelling, visiting different towns. I might hear of more people who need the harp's magic.'

'Exactly,' Julia said. 'I'll talk to him. I'll offer to make the inquiries myself.'

'Perhaps I should ask him,' Evie suggested enthusiastically.

'Hmm, I don't know,' Julia said. 'It might surprise him, even arouse suspicion.'

'We could stay overnight,' Evie said, her thoughts racing ahead. 'That would give us more time to look around and ask around.'

'I could do that while you are rehearsing with the other students,' Julia said, then she was thoughtful for a moment. 'It won't always be easy, though,' she muttered. 'The concerts will have to be timed with the full moons or we will have to find an excuse to go back on the right date.'

'My parents must not attend all the concerts,' Evie said. 'I'll have to put them off somehow.'

'That could be tricky too,' Julia said. 'Though they do have a lot of engagements coming up. Perhaps—'

'Someday,' Evie interrupted, dreaming out loud, 'I will travel not just for a day here and a day there but for longer and further, maybe to foreign countries too. Lucia did for a while.' She sighed, wondering how she would manage to do that without having to make up excuses and lies. Her being the Harp Maiden had to remain a secret.

'You have plenty of time to think about it,' Julia said.

'Four weeks to choose who will receive a wish,' Evie said. 'I just hope I make the right decision every time. And I haven't forgotten about Grace.'

'You will be the wisest of Harp Maidens,' Julia said. 'Soon you will instinctively know what to do. As for travelling, why not? Once you are eighteen, and I could be your chaperone.

I'm sure your parents would agree. But for now, you need to get accustomed to this new responsibility, try to feel comfortable about it.'

'Will you trust me, Julia, and support my decisions?' Evie asked. 'I need to know because I hate arguments and I've made up my mind about something else.'

'Oh?'

'I'm going back to Dower Hall to look for the Black Ruby.'

'But how, Evie?' Julia asked. 'How will you hide what you are *really* doing? Finding the ruby in that rubble would be a miracle, not to mention dangerous. And what about … them?'

'The demons,' Evie said. 'Yes, Olga and Volok must have been looking for it. I so hope they haven't found it already. I know they are still alive, Julia, I know it. That's why I have to find the ruby. I can't let them have it.'

'But you don't know what it can do,' Julia said. 'It might just be a status symbol, a mere trinket, or something best left alone.'

'Or it might be unbelievably powerful,' Evie said.

'Now you are scaring me,' Julia said.

'Whatever it is,' Evie said, 'I must find it before anyone else – demons, looters, thieves, anyone.'

Julia stared at her. 'You already have a plan, don't you?'

'I do,' Evie said proudly. 'But I would like to know you will cover for me if I need you to, and *not* give me away because of your fears. Can you do that, Julia?'

'Of course,' Julia said, 'but I will still point out the risks you are taking.'

'All right then,' Evie said. 'We will talk again about the

concerts after you chat to Mr Reid. Now, I've been doing some research.' There was a new excitement in Evie's voice. 'I've been browsing through some of Father's books on archaeology, history and ancient mythology.'

'Goodness! Did you find anything useful?'

'Not yet. There are a lot of books.' Evie rolled her eyes. 'I might have to ask Father for help.'

'Impossible!' Julia shrieked. 'Evie, you can't!'

'I won't tell him why,' Evie said. 'We both know I can't do that.'

'You mean you are going to *lie* to your father,' Julia said. 'Once you do that, Evie, you will find yourself caught in a tangled web. One lie leads to another, and then another. It never ends!'

Evie squirmed a little. 'I'll tell him something true but not the *real* reason for my interest,' she said. 'If he could somehow point me in the right direction, it would save me so much time.'

'This is your decision, Evie, as we just agreed,' Julia said. 'And I will always respect your new role, but I beg you to leave the ruby alone. You have enough to concern yourself with the ritual, and not go hunting for an ancient artefact as well. Such a task will be so difficult and fraught with danger.'

'A moment ago, you said the Black Ruby might be a trinket, an unimportant status symbol,' Evie said, a wry look on her face.

Julia sighed.

'Won't danger always be a part of being the Harp Maiden?' Evie asked gently. 'I have to keep the harp secret and safe, use it wisely and protect its magic from everything that could harm or misuse it. Well, don't I?'

'To a point,' Julia said. 'Well, yes. But those demons are *very* dangerous. Look what happened to Lucia.'

Evie glared at her governess.

'I'm sorry. I take that back,' Julia said. 'What happened to Lucia was horrendous – years of imprisonment, torture and death. But you understand my fear.'

'I do, but can I *rely* on your support, Julia?' Evie pressed. 'Even when my task is terribly dangerous? When I have awful choices to make or crazy things to do? I don't want us to be on opposite sides.'

Julia paused, then said, 'You can always depend on me, Evie, always. But you will have to listen to my protests too.'

Despite some difficult discussions, Evie knew that deep down Julia understood that there was no turning back. Evie's fate was already sealed. Evie didn't like to admit that she wanted an ally as she grew accustomed to her new role; she didn't like to appear weak, or even admit to herself that she felt so unprepared. It was a role she had been thrown into, but now wanted to take on completely, not in some half-hearted way. Freddie knew all about Evie's secret too, and Evie knew the time would come when she would need his clever ideas and common sense. But he was only ten years old and Evie hoped he would have a more normal life, at least for a while, now that he was part of her family.

Her decision made, Evie now had to come up with a good excuse to return to Dower Hall so she could search for the Black Ruby. But the ruined manor house was almost three hours' carriage ride away, and that was only one of the many obstacles that lay ahead.

CHAPTER FIVE

Evie's father was delighted by his daughter's renewed interest in his work as an historian. As a little girl, Evie loved to hear him tell her about his amazing adventures and travels, combined with a colourful repertoire of myths and legends, tales he would exaggerate to enthral her, claiming they were all true, or at least partly so. Then Evie's interest in music took over and remained. She was chuffed to see the surprise and delight on his face when she came into his study asking to look at his old books.

'Have you anything on ancient amulets, and also demons and sorcerers?' Evie asked.

'Amulets, demons and sorcerers indeed!' Evie's father said, grinning from ear to ear. 'I have always been fascinated by such things and hoped you would develop a keen interest too, though your mother never wanted me to press you. You know, some people said I was crazy to waste time on things that aren't real, when there is still so much real history to uncover. But I said, "My friends, sometimes the unreal can lead us to the real, to the truth. Sometimes, we must investigate the most unlikely stories in order to solve a mystery." I am thinking of writing a book on the subject, so if you find anything juicy that I might have missed, make sure to tell me.'

Evie gave a little cough to hide a giggle. Her father was so excited, his spectacles were dangling perilously close to the end of his rather long nose.

'Come, look over here,' he said. 'Let me introduce you to the newest additions to my collection.' Evie's father led her past several floor-to-ceiling bookcases, stopping at the last one along the wall. He tapped the middle shelf. 'These are very special books. They were expensive to find and even more expensive to buy. People are always so secretive about the occult, that is demons, rituals, dark magic and so on. I had to go through some irregular channels and unsavoury people to obtain these treasures.' His eyebrows rose very high and his eyes twinkled mischievously. 'For goodness' sake, don't tell your mother!' he whispered. 'It'll be our secret!'

Evie's heart fluttered as she thought of all the secrets she was already keeping. She wondered about her father's secrets, what strange and exotic characters he had met throughout his career, and what deals he might have struck to increase his private collection of books. She felt rather pleased that he might be keeping secrets too. It made her feel a little less guilty.

'Henry! Where are you, dear?' Evie's mother called. 'Hudson is waiting at the door.'

'I'm in the study, dear.' Evie's father walked to the door, then paused. 'Some of these books are very old *and* very delicate,' he said softly. 'Be gentle with them. They are my most prized possessions.'

'I'll be very careful,' Evie said. 'Enjoy the opera.'

He waved a hand with a flourish over his head. 'I'm sure your mother will!'

Evie heard the front door close as she stood staring at the vast array of books.

'And to think I had to struggle through so many books before I found the courage to ask!' Evie whispered to the shelves. 'I should have spoken to him sooner. Well, let's see what I can find now.'

She moved the sliding ladder into the corner, secured it and climbed up. Some of the books on the higher shelves were musty, their scent reminding her of Thorn's collection in Dower Hall. Others were worn and flimsy as her father had said. She decided it would be sensible to look at those in good condition first, as she could flick through the pages quickly without worrying about damaging them. The delicate books would need greater care.

Evie had already visited the local library a number of times to try to find the information she wanted. She hadn't yet dared to ask for anything in detail but kept her inquiries general, not wanting to alert the curious librarian. It had already become quite a chore trying to answer the librarian's probing questions without really answering at all. Wouldn't it be just perfect if all the information she needed was right here at home? she thought. And wouldn't it be even nicer if her father was in on her secret? He might be able to tell her so much more than she would ever find in books. Evie wondered if she would ever have the luxury of telling anyone else her secret. She sighed and began to scour the pages.

The hours ticked by as Evie moved from book to book, stopping occasionally to light more candles. The new electric light became unreliable in the later hours of the evening, flickering, dulling and brightening, sometimes going out altogether. Her father always kept lots of candles in the study in case he needed them, not liking interruptions caused by sudden blackouts. Candleholders of every style, shape and size filled every spare space on side tables, shelves, her father's enormous desk and even the mantelpiece.

It was in the oldest and most faded books that Evie finally found something of interest, but they were only passing mentions of Volok, Nala and King Udil of Yodor – Evie had read about them in Thorn's study too. There wasn't enough information, nothing new, and yet she shivered seeing those names again.

Evie sat back in an armchair, thinking. She had never known that demons and dark magic were of interest to her father; she thought he only dealt with facts and historical events. Was he an expert in other things too, like the occult? She shook her head and sat up straight. What she really needed to know was why the Black Ruby was important and why Volok wanted it so badly. 'Find it, Evie. Find it!' she said crossly.

She glanced at the clock on the mantelpiece: it was eleven o'clock. Her parents would be back any minute and she did not want her father to find her still in the study. As quickly as she dared, she turned some of the most crumbling pages, scanning each one. 'At last!' she gasped. 'A mention of the Black Ruby.'

Though sitting, Evie jumped and nearly dropped the book when her parents came through the hall door. She noted the book and the page and quickly began replacing the books on the shelves.

Her father peeped around the study door as she was

descending the ladder. 'I thought I saw light,' he said. 'Having fun?'

'I lost track of time,' Evie said. 'Did you enjoy the opera?'

'Oh, yes, very nice,' her father said. 'Your mother loved it, but she's gone straight up to bed. If I weren't so tired myself, we could look at some books together now.'

'We can do that again,' Evie said. 'I'd like that. Whenever you have time.'

Evie returned to the last book she had been reading once she heard her father climb the stairs. She had to know just a little more. What she read next disturbed her greatly, so much so, she would not tell even Julia or Freddie what she had found. Evie wondered whether Olga knew what the Black Ruby could do, or was she only interested in impressing Volok, her beloved demon lord, caring little about the consequences? Now that she had discovered its true purpose, Evie knew she had to move quickly. If the ruby fell into the demons' hands it would be disastrous, catastrophic. For what else could it mean for a magical artefact to bring a demon back from the dead?

CHAPTER SIX

The following night before going to bed, Evie knocked gently on Julia's bedroom door. Her thoughts were in a great jumble in her head, and she needed to tell her governess a little of what she had read if only to unburden herself. After repeating her intention to return to Dower Hall to search for the ruby, Evie explained a little more.

'I found some information in one of Father's old books,' she said, 'about the different types of demons, how they have a range of abilities, purposes and goals. Many of the myths and legends are mixed in with the historical facts, the truth blurred but woven into the same stories. The truth is there if you look properly, though I think it will take me a while to find all of it.'

Evie continued before her governess could protest. 'I have to figure out where the demons are hiding, what they intend doing – and somehow I have to stop them.' Julia took a breath to speak, but Evie wasn't finished. 'The demons might need the harp's magic to complete Volok's recovery, or maybe he just sees it as another talisman to add to his collection. Either way, it's the Black Ruby that is really important to him right now. Do you remember Volok's reaction when Olga said she could get it for him?' Julia only managed a nod. 'He must be planning something big and probably awful. I don't understand why Olga kept the ruby from him, when she had it. She must have meant to give it to him sometime. Then she lost it when the house collapsed in the fire, and now, well, no one knows where it is. And I keep thinking about those spooky trees lining the long driveway up to the house and the thick, dark forest behind Dower Hall. I believe they were guarding something, at Olga's command. There is a riddle concerning those trees, Julia. I simply have to unravel it.'

Evie paused at last, deep in thought.

'I'm sorry, Evie,' Julia said, raising a hand so Evie would allow her to make her point. 'What you're planning will be more dangerous than when we were held captive in that cellar fearing for our lives. Please, concentrate on the harp and finding good causes, good people to help. I can assist you with that. I'd be happy to. *That* is your role, not all this terror and danger.'

Frustrated, Evie was afraid she would reveal the secret power of the Black Ruby to prove just how urgent it was to find it. Instead, she took a deep breath and politely said she knew Julia must be tired. It was late, and they would talk again at a more convenient time. As she left the room, Evie knew she would need to think of better arguments to convince her governess, and not to burst out with her ideas so emotionally. That never seemed to work. And there was a new and nagging question buzzing in her head: should Evie confide in Julia at all? The whole business with the harp and everything connected with it seemed to stress her governess terribly. Perhaps it wasn't fair to involve Julia; perhaps Evie expected too much. That thought made Evie feel surprisingly uncomfortable, and a little disappointed in herself. Why did she need anyone's support? She was the Harp Maiden. She should know what to do and just do it.

Walking back to her own room, Evie heard her parents talking downstairs in the drawing room, the door slightly ajar. She crept down a few stairs and sat down to listen, her curiosity getting the better of her as usual.

'You know, Clara, I think Evie may become an archaeologist one day, or better still, an historian like me,' Evie's father said, sounding pleased.

'Or perhaps a famous musician,' Evie's mother said. 'She is as talented on the harp as the flute now. But we must let *Evie* choose, Henry. Please don't put any pressure on her.'

'Of course, dear.'

'I'm surprised she has the time to read your books with all her other studies, as well as the extra music practice for the concert,' Evie's mother said. 'What sparked her interest in your work at this particular moment?'

'I don't know,' Evie's father said. 'She has always been a very inquisitive child, and it's good to see her busy with lots of interests and pastimes. We don't want her dwelling on that awful business last winter.'

Evie could just make out her father's reflection in a mirror across the hall. He was frowning, his brow deeply furrowed as he puffed on his pipe.

'True,' Evie's mother said. 'But I don't want her exhausted or becoming ill. Did you notice how Julia has been ill a lot these last few months? I wonder if we are asking too much of her too. I worry about them both. Freddie, on the other hand, seems to be thriving.'

'Nothing fazes that boy. He will make a fine young man,' Evie's father said. 'Julia's health is bound to improve over the spring and summer. And Evie likes to be busy. Let's see how far she takes this interest in my work. I promise to follow her lead – no pressure to engage any further. Now, time for bed. I have another busy day tomorrow. I will be writing a sharp letter to the telephone company. We really should have had a telephone installed by now. I hope it won't take as long as the electricity did.'

'I thought we were going to have electricity brought upstairs first,' Evie's mother said.

'First the telephone, dear, then the upstairs electricity,' Evie's father said. 'Such marvellous inventions! How I love progress!'

As her parents stood up to leave the parlour, Evie crept upstairs. For the next couple of hours, she lay awake wondering how long she would be able to keep her secret. It was a relief that Julia and Freddie knew, but telling anyone else didn't sit well with her at all. Not yet, anyway. She wasn't sure if she should trust, or burden, anyone else. And it was a burden; it probably would be until she got used to it. Or so she hoped. Already, she felt it was hanging over her like a cloud, affecting everything she did, everything she thought. It had to be her priority now, but increasingly she felt her secret was ensnaring her. And it wasn't one secret, it was many. Together with the excuses and lies she would inevitably have to tell, she had created a tangled web that was only going to become increasingly sticky and complicated.

*

Evie spent time in her father's study whenever she got the chance. Some of the books were so faded it took ages to decipher any text. Many were written in ancient languages that were no longer used or had morphed over the centuries into modern Greek, Turkish, Persian, Farsi and Arabic, among others. She marvelled at how many languages her father could speak fluently: French, Italian, Latin, Arabic and Russian, and several more that he knew well enough to translate with the help of a dictionary. After she had spent an hour in her father's study, Evie had a French lesson with Julia. Almost immediately, she found it too difficult to concentrate and put down her textbook.

'Thorn was an artistic type of demon, less violent than the other two,' she said. 'He might have even liked music and therefore his host, the real maestro. Poor, unfortunate man.'

'How awful,' Julia said, closing her own book, and grimacing at the thought of bodily possession. 'Did you find something in the study about that?'

'Yes, odd but interesting facts,' Evie said. 'Some demons have a stare that can transfix a person. I think Volok is one of those. I remember his stare. I felt completely stuck, unable to move or think. It was very scary, like being trapped in a weird bubble or sucked into outer space.'

'He is a dangerous brute,' Julia said. 'I keep worrying that he may be stronger now, but I hope the botched ritual left him weak, or better still dead.'

'What if there are more demons out there?' Evie said, her mind wandering again. 'What would they be like, and where could they be?'

'I would rather not know,' Julia said. 'Evie, listen to me. I agree with you on so much, but please, please give up the idea of hunting down these monsters.'

'But don't you see?' Evie cried. 'I *have* to protect the harp from everything, including the demons. Who else will? And I have to do it alone, because who would believe me if I told them the story and asked for their help? They'd say I was crazy, and nothing would be done. No one can do this but me!' Julia raised a hand, but Evie ignored her. 'We should include Freddie in our discussions from now on. He may know more than he realises. He might remember something Lucia told him that will only come to mind if he talks about it. He was in Dower Hall, after all, and for a lot longer than we were.'

'But he is only a boy,' Julia said. 'He has already been through so much.'

'You know I don't want to upset him,' Evie said. 'His life was dreadfully cruel in Dower Hall, but to survive he had to be clever and brave, more than other boys his age. What he has seen and heard most people could never even imagine. I need him, Julia. This is too big for just the two of us, and I don't want you stressing over it because then I feel stressed – and that's not helping.'

'I see,' Julia said, clearly miffed.

'In time, we will have to trust more people,' Evie continued. 'Maybe not yet, but we do need Freddie. I've been thinking about telling Grace sometime too.'

'Grace?' Julia said. 'Why on earth would you do that?'

'Because she's my best friend and I trust her,' Evie said crossly. 'She helped save our lives because she sensed something was wrong and raised the alarm. I think she knows there's a lot I haven't told her about that night and our escape from Dower Hall. And if I'm going to heal her eyes, I should really explain how. Oh, don't worry, Julia. I haven't decided yet.'

'All right,' Julia said, standing up. 'Let's leave the lessons for now. I think we both need a break.'

Evie also stood, but she was feeling flustered and uncomfortable instead of relieved. She had aired more frustrations and concerns than she had intended, and half regretted it. She looked hopefully at Julia.

'Every action has a consequence,' Julia said, gathering up her textbooks. 'Please don't rush any important decisions, not until we talk this over some more.'

Evie nodded and went upstairs to her bedroom. She sat down on the dainty cushioned chair by the fireplace, her special place for brooding. The fire wasn't lit but Evie didn't feel cold. The irritation caused by Julia's comments was still keeping her warm. She looked around her elegant bedroom. The walls were covered with pale pink and white hand-painted wallpaper, depicting a pretty scene of songbirds and flowers. The deep rose quilt on her bed was warm and lush, the two puffy, white pillows soft and scented. Her matching closet and dressing table were beautifully carved from expensive mahogany wood. They gleamed, thanks to Tilly's dedicated polishing. Evelyn Wells was certainly a privileged young lady, with no right to be so cross or frustrated. On top of her good fortune, she had now been given the gift of magic.

Evie opened the window and gazed down at the garden.

Spring had well and truly arrived, and the cherry trees were budding. In a few weeks they would put on a spectacular display of white and pink blossoms. Up on the red-tiled roof of the house, out of Evie's sight, a blackbird was singing its heart out. How beautiful, she thought. Feeling somewhat soothed, she returned to her favourite chair. She wondered if all the Harp Maidens before her had had such a stuttering start to their role. Or was Evelyn Wells the only one who found herself caught in a web of secrets, lies and endless worries?

CHAPTER SEVEN

Grace had promised to call on Saturday afternoon. She accompanied Evie on the piano while Evie practised her solo flute pieces for the concert in eleven days' time – Spy Wednesday, the start of the Easter break. It was such a nice spring day that the girls decided to walk around the garden afterwards. The daffodils were at their very best, a blaze of brightest yellow, and some snowdrops and hyacinths were still in bloom creating a lovely contrast. The two girls sat down on the double swing, surrounded by the bobbing heads of the daffodils and a few early tulips. Then Grace told Evie her news.

'My father is returning to Dower Hall on Monday,' Grace said. 'He's taking several constables with him, an architect and an engineer too. They're going to examine what's left of the old manor house. He thinks they'll probably have to knock it down, but your father persuaded him to try to salvage anything of value first. I can't see how there could be anything left after such a devastating fire.'

'*My* father?' Evie cried. 'He never told me he was going to Dower Hall!'

'He probably didn't want to upset you,' Grace said. 'My father needs your father's expertise, as antiques are not his speciality.'

Evie immediately began to hatch a plan. She stood up

from the swing and turned to face her friend.

'Grace, do you think we could go too?' she asked.

Grace stared back, her eyes looking enormous behind her thick lenses.

'I know it might sound odd,' Evie said quickly, 'but I really want to go back, if only to see the place in ruins.' Evie looked away, knowing it was only half the truth, barely half. 'It would be … helpful, and sort of, um, healing to see the house reduced to a pile of rubble and ash.'

'Wouldn't it bring back awful memories?' Grace asked. 'I was nervous even telling you about it.'

'No, not anymore,' Evie said. 'In fact, I think it would be a good idea.'

'I must admit, I wouldn't mind seeing the place after all you told me,' Grace said. 'I'll ask my father when he comes to collect me. Perhaps we could bring a picnic and have a day out, of sorts.'

'Your father is collecting you?' Evie asked.

'Yes, any excuse to chat with your father,' Grace said. 'Actually, he had some business in the town. He said he would call here afterwards, around five o'clock.'

'That's great!' Evie said, then realised Grace was watching her. 'I mean, it's great that our fathers get on so well.'

'They're almost as good friends as we are,' Grace said.

But Evie would have preferred if her father wasn't going to Dower Hall as well. It was bound to make it more difficult for her to search for the ruby.

'Are you sure you want to go, Evie?' Grace asked, sounding a little concerned. 'Your brow is wrinkling like it does when you're worried.'

'You really notice everything!' Evie said. She laughed. 'I was just thinking that my father might fuss. But maybe Julia and Freddie would like to go too. All of us together, back to the scene of the crime.' They could provide some useful distraction while she looked around, Evie thought but didn't say.

As soon as they went inside, Evie confronted her father, and he explained.

'In his role as the local magistrate, Jeremiah Finch wrote and asked me to accompany him and his constables, and some other experts, to take a look at the ruins. He thought my expertise might come in useful and I jumped at the chance. You never know what we might find in an old manor like that.'

'I see,' Evie said.

'Yes indeed,' her father said, contemplating. 'Important archaeological items, remnants of valuable antiques, perhaps something really interesting if we're lucky. The curator at the museum also wrote to me. He said that Dower Hall was rumoured to be an art collector's paradise, so there may well have been other items of value too.'

'Really, Professor?' Grace said. 'In among all the ruins?'

'Well, hopefully,' Evie's father said. 'Sadly, after what you told me, Evie, we will be fortunate to find anything at all. But it's worth a try.'

'Grace and I would like to go too,' Evie said. 'A day out – with a difference.'

After plenty of reassurance, Professor Wells agreed that Evie could go, Freddie and Julia too, but Grace would have to ask her father, Mr Finch.

'I expect Freddie will be very excited,' Evie's father said. 'He loves exploring our garden, the park, the whole neighbourhood. This will be a big adventure. Julia will need to keep an eye on him, on you all, but especially Freddie.'

Evie didn't protest. Her father was normally very modern in his thinking, but occasionally he would revert to being an overprotective father, forgetting that Evie was not a little girl anymore; she was fifteen.

'There's no need to make a fuss,' Evie said.

'Your mother may disagree,' Evie's father said. 'But I'll do my best.' He smiled at the girls and left them to chat.

After a series of discussions with Evie's mother, it was settled, and Mr Finch wasn't too difficult to persuade at all, on condition that everyone would 'observe all rules of safety'. He would organise a bigger carriage to take the larger party. It would follow a police wagon full of enthusiastic young constables who were eager to visit a crime scene. So many people, Evie thought, too many. How on earth will I search for the ruby without being noticed?

Later in the evening, Evie asked Julia and Freddie to join her in the parlour.

'Julia, at Dower Hall, will you distract Grace and keep watch in case anyone gets too close?' she asked. 'That way Freddie and I might get a chance to search.'

'I will try,' Julia said. 'But I cannot control what the policemen do. They will have instructions from Mr Finch.'

'Tell me what the Black Ruby looks like again,' Freddie said.

Evie pulled a piece of folded paper from her pocket. She opened it out and showed him a drawing she had made.

'It will be hard to spot,' Freddie said. 'It looks just like a lump of coal.'

'It does,' Evie said. 'But it's a ruby so it will be shiny.'

'Let's hope the sun is shining,' Freddie said. 'That will make it easier to see.'

'What if someone else finds it?' Julia asked, wringing her hands nervously.

'No one else knows about it so they shouldn't be looking for it,' Evie said. 'And if someone does stumble across it, I'll say it's mine, that Lucia gave it to me.'

'What if a constable finds it but doesn't tell you?' Julia said.

'They would be obliged to show it to Mr Finch,' Evie said. 'And, like everything else they find, it will be shown to my father.'

'Then you will have to steal it from your father, or tell him all about it,' Julia said.

Evie tried to ignore Julia's awkward questions and Freddie's questioning looks. She pressed on. 'I also want to look at the trees. I'm so sure they were guarding something and perhaps they still are.'

'You do remember how they tried to kill us the last time we were there,' Julia said irritably.

'If the demons are gone, and the Black Ruby too, there is no need for the trees to be on guard anymore,' Evie said. 'But if they are protecting the ruby, they'll be as spooky and peculiar as they were before.'

'Unless they're guarding something else,' Freddie said.

'Yes,' Evie said, her mind whirring again. 'Then I'll need to know what that is too.'

'Honestly, Evie!' Julia said, then started to cough, a harsh, barking sound.

'We can do it,' Freddie said. 'We'll find the ruby and you can look at the trees. There has to be a reason why they're so strange.'

'You make everything sound easy, Freddie,' Julia said, croaking a little. 'But remember, Olga could be hiding there, or Volok, or both of them.'

'Freddie, how should we search without letting anyone know what we're doing?' Evie asked, watching him keenly. His eyes were bright with excitement, no trace of fear or doubt at all.

'We'll just say we're exploring,' Freddie said. 'I love exploring. Uncle Henry does too, even though he's old. He won't mind what we're doing once we say we're exploring.'

Julia smiled and Evie laughed.

'Don't forget, we still have to keep what we're doing a secret, even from Uncle Henry,' Evie said. 'No one must know, or even suspect.'

'They won't, and they won't bother us,' Freddie said. 'They'll be busy doing their own stuff. You'll see!'

CHAPTER EIGHT

The party headed off on a fine spring morning: Evie, Freddie, Julia, Grace, Mr Finch and Professor Wells, Evie and Freddie excused from their lessons for the day. Their carriage followed the police wagon carrying ten constables, the engineer and architect. Evie was glad to hear from Mr Finch that the journey wouldn't take nearly as long as she thought. One of the constables had found a quicker route to Wick's End than the one taken back in January.

'Grace remembered the way almost perfectly,' Mr Finch said. 'But those coachmen had tried to fool you by taking you on a long, winding route to ensure that no one remembered the location of the manor. They wanted to be certain you could not be found, Evie. Or so they thought.' He looked proudly over at his daughter sitting opposite him.

With the new shorter route and the ground unusually firm after a spell of dry weather, they arrived at Dower Hall in a little over an hour.

'We really weren't that far away at all,' Evie muttered to herself, again her thoughts whirring, forming yet another plan.

'Everyone is to wait in the carriage until Mr Finch has spoken to his men,' Evie's father said.

They watched through the insect-spattered windows as Mr Finch issued his instructions, directing the constables to different parts of the ruins. The engineer and architect hurried straight towards the once-imposing, now-lopsided hall door. Evie watched as they pulled out their notepads and measuring instruments, scouring the façade of the house, discussing points of interest and areas of imminent risk. Overall, the manor house was a pathetic remnant of its former self.

Hopefully the Black Ruby lies somewhere under all that rubble, Evie thought. I hope none of the constables finds it. Would they even recognise it as something important, out of place among all that debris? She shuddered, her heartbeat quickening as she waited impatiently. It was a jewel, after all, a large and rare one. Anyone might be tempted to keep it.

'Now – my goodness, you are keen!' Evie's father said, when he finally opened the door and stepped out, Evie almost flying out behind him. 'I thought Freddie would be the first to jump out!'

'I need some air,' Evie said. 'It was very warm in the carriage.'

'All right, now please be careful,' her father said, frowning. 'I would prefer if you four stayed over on the grass at the side of the house. Have some lemonade and cherry cake from the basket. It should revive you, Evie. I must accompany Mr Finch now. You are in charge, Miss Pippen!'

'Yes, Professor,' Julia said.

'Yes,' Evie said. 'Tea and cake, then some exploring.'

'Exploring, hurray!' Freddie cried.

'Don't worry,' Evie added. 'We'll only take a *little* look

around. We couldn't come all this way and have Freddie disappointed.'

Professor Wells hesitated. 'I don't want trouble of any sort, but I also don't want to spoil your day out. Your mother was concerned this visit might upset you. I had to tell her not to worry. I was right, wasn't I?' He looked from one to the other.

'We're all fine,' Evie said. 'Aren't we, Freddie?'

'Yes! Fantastic!' he cried, hopping up and down, raring to go.

'And you, Julia?' Evie's father asked.

'Fine, thank you,' she said, though she looked the palest shade of pale.

'And Grace, dear?' Evie's father turned to her. 'We mustn't forget your heroic part in all this.'

'Oh! Thank you, Professor. I'm very well,' Grace said.

Everyone turned at a roar from the engineer, followed by a loud crash. The heavy studded front door fell off its buckled hinges.

'And stay well away from the house. What is that silly engineer up to?' Evie's father added, scrunching his brows into another frown.

'Aww!' Freddie said. 'I wanted to go inside.'

Evie was disappointed too, knowing she might need to search everywhere.

'Don't worry, Professor,' Julia said. 'I will keep a watchful eye.'

'Good. Excellent. Thank you, Miss Pippen,' Evie's father said, and marched quickly over to where Mr Finch was observing the remains of the manor house.

The little group set up the small picnic. Freddie immediately scoffed down some cake, then he went chasing around, diving into hedges to see what he could find.

'We'll never be able to keep Freddie still,' Grace said.

'Not to worry,' Evie said. 'He's dying to find rabbits and hares, hedgehogs and foxes, even frogs if there's any water around. He loves everything!'

Evie turned to watch the men for a moment, glad to see they were too busy to notice what her little party might be doing. She looked at the trees that lined the drive to the front lawn. They didn't look particularly threatening today, but there was something about them she still didn't like, something odd, creepy. Suddenly Evie noticed one of the constables hanging back, casting furtive glances their way. He was tall and thin, sallow-skinned, his dark hair cut very short, barely visible under his police hat. His expression was formal, serious. Evie hoped he hadn't been instructed to keep an eye on them.

'I wish Father wouldn't,' Evie muttered to herself.

'Wouldn't what?' Grace asked.

'That constable,' Evie said. 'I think my father has asked him to watch us.'

To Evie's surprise, Grace laughed.

'I'm sorry, Evie,' she said. 'I don't know about him being a spy, but I forgot to mention that he is my second cousin, Samuel Banks. He's a new recruit to the police force and was sent to our local station just a few weeks ago. He was very excited about coming here today to see a real crime scene – his first. I think he's interested to meet you, Julia and Freddie, if you don't mind. He hopes to become a detective. I think he may want to ask you a few questions.'

'You mean he wants to practise being a detective?' Evie asked.

'Sort of,' Grace said, apologetically. 'Is that all right?'

'Of course it is,' Evie said. 'We can chat with him later. He has work to do now, and so do we.'

'We do?'

'Um, yes, exploring,' Evie said. She could have pinched herself for almost blurting out her real reason for being there.

'Freddie has well and truly started his explorations,' Julia said, with a knowing look in her eyes – a look which Evie noticed Grace had seen too.

'Come along, then,' Evie said. 'We should join him.'

She marched over to a hedge where Freddie was stuck trying to reverse out of a prickly, bushy section. He was already an absolute mess, covered in tiny bits of garden debris, multiple scratches and even patches of mud. He giggled as Evie hauled him out backwards, then ran off to the side of the house. Evie and Grace hurried after him.

The three of them stopped and stared. The entire back of the house was gone. They stood looking at the big gaping hole that had been the kitchen, the parlour, the music room and some of the upstairs bedrooms. All around them broken and charred pieces of household items lay strewn about, having been blasted out of the house in a series of explosions.

'You were really in there?' Grace whispered.

'Yes,' Evie said, 'though we got out before the fire completely took over, before the bigger explosions.'

'You saved Julia and Freddie despite the danger,' Grace said, clearly impressed.

'Evie came up with the escape plan,' Freddie said. 'I got out first, through the secret passages with a hammer!'

'That was very brave, Freddie,' Grace said.

Both girls smiled at him.

'You saved me again when you found me in the snow, after the cart crashed,' Freddie said, looking up at Evie.

'Incredible!' Grace said, though Evie had told her that part of the story before.

'Don't be silly,' Evie said, her conscience pricking her, and sensing that Grace hoped Evie would tell her more.

'What a sight!' Julia said, joining them. 'It is indeed a miracle we got out of there alive.'

'Now that we're all here,' Evie said, 'let's see if we can find anything interesting.'

'A treasure hunt!' Freddie cried.

'Exactly,' Julia said, glancing at Evie.

They rummaged around for a while. Freddie was keen to collect almost anything, bits of broken china and glass, buttons, parts of old boots, and one long piece of wood from a picture frame that he whipped around like an imaginary sword. Grace looked around with mild curiosity, but Evie was scouring the ground, hoping to spot something dark and shiny. She kicked at a few pieces of burned wood and broken pottery with her boot. It felt like a hopeless task, frustrating and tiresome, but she was determined to persevere for as long as possible.

After quite a lengthy search, Evie began to think it more likely that the ruby might be inside the house, as that was the last place she had seen it. But there had been so many explosions it could be anywhere. Olga could have found it.

No, no, it has to be here, Evie thought, hoping. But it wasn't going to be easy to venture into what was left of the house, not with her father and Mr Finch around, not to mention all the constables. She would have to return, and she had just thought of a plan, though it might sorely test her friendship with Grace.

Evie didn't want the visit to be wasted, nor had she forgotten her second goal. 'I think I need the bathroom,' she announced.

'I'm sure we could stop at an inn on the way back,' Julia said impatiently. 'Can't you wait? It is rather unsuitable here, and we are not alone.'

From Grace's expression, Evie knew that her friend had also noticed Julia's irritation.

'No, I can't,' Evie said firmly. 'I'll be back in just a moment.'

Evie walked quickly away from the group towards the edge of the forest, then hurried in among the trees.

'Don't get lost,' Grace called after her, but Evie barely heard her. She had to know if the trees were still behaving as weirdly as when she was held captive. If they were, she was sure it could mean there was something else going on, something else they were guarding. She shuddered as the thick forest foliage quickly blocked out any warmth from the sun.

Evie moved around the tall, gnarled trunks, watching carefully, stopping to listen now and again for any familiar sound from when she had been there before. She felt that same creepy sensation, one of being watched. She looked up, almost expecting faces to emerge from the old lumpy bark:

gloomy eyes looking down at her, blinking in surprise, broad nostrils quivering, roughened brows frowning, but most of all, large gaping mouths ready to call a warning. But to whom? Was it her vivid imagination or did she sometimes see similar ugly images in her dreams, her nightmares? Images of Volok and images of other, unknown faces on the bark of those weird trees.

Branches began to swish and sway from side to side. At first, it was a gentle rustling higher up in the trees. Then stronger movements happened lower down, gathering pace until the branches were hitting her, flicking at her arms, thwacking her back. Suddenly, a long, curved branch whipped low and whacked her behind her knees, knocking her off her feet. Were they warning her away, or warning someone else that she was encroaching on a space she should not be in? Evie had always assumed the ogress was commanding the trees, but perhaps Volok was their master. Someone was making them do this, someone or something. It certainly wasn't normal.

Evie felt surer than ever that both demons were alive. She could feel it in her bones, she could sense it there among those trees. Where were the demons if not here, close by the house, their recent past?

Confirmation of her suspicions came sooner than expected. A roar. Then another. It was unmistakeable – Olga. Evie couldn't let her come closer to the ruined house and find everyone. In the next instant, she made a decision. It was bold, reckless, but she simply had to – Evie ran towards the roar.

She didn't know what the rest of her plan was, she just kept running, knowing Olga would hear her and smell her too. She had to lure her away from the house, but to where? She really didn't know.

The ogress reacted quickly. Evie's heart lurched in her chest as soon as she heard Olga's heavy steps somewhere behind her.

Evie decided to run for as long as she could and try to tire Olga out. It flashed through her mind that she might get lost — that is, if she didn't get caught. It was difficult holding up her skirt, running as fast as she could, changing course abruptly, zigzagging her way through the forest while dodging the now whipping branches. A few times she heard Olga roar in frustration. The ogress was bulky and awkward, and Evie's nimble feet were sending her pursuer on a not-so-merry dance. But Evie couldn't keep this up for much longer.

Quite by accident, Evie reached the clearing where one of the rituals had taken place the previous winter. It didn't provide much shelter but at least she had her bearings now. Then she had an idea. As she quickly broke pieces of old bark from a dead tree trunk, she could hear Olga's snarls, and her huffing and puffing as she neared. 'Quickly, Evie! Time to hide!' she told herself.

Looking frantically around, Evie squeezed herself into a clump of dense, tall ferns growing behind the same dead tree trunk. With the top of the trunk rotten and gone, there were no branches left to attack her. Olga slowed, stomping purposefully towards Evie's hiding place, her breath loud and laboured. Evie leaned out and threw a piece of wood to one side, then another, and more at intervals, trying to lure Olga in a different direction.

Peering through the foliage, Evie could see Olga sniff the

air for scent and the tips of her ears twitched, straining for sounds. Silently, carefully, Evie threw another piece of wood, but further this time. Olga seemed to take the bait. She turned and began to move to where the missile had landed, but then she stopped. Oh no! Evie thought, was it really too much to hope for? Evie held her breath and didn't move a muscle. She couldn't hear anything except her own heart thumping wildly in her chest. Surely Olga couldn't hear that too!

To Evie's great relief and surprise, Olga suddenly gave up the chase. Something had distracted her, and Evie didn't care what it was. She watched the ogress lift her head, roar rather strangely and head away, back into the thickest, darkest part of the forest.

Evie didn't move until Olga was out of sight. As she scrambled out of the ferns, she noticed how all the trees had stopped moving. Glad, though again somewhat puzzled, Evie brushed herself down as best she could. She took one last look behind her then hurried back to the others.

CHAPTER NINE

Everyone except Freddie was quiet on the way back. He was still full of beans, delighted with his day out, glued to the window, pointing out and remarking on anything of interest, a stream, a broken fence, sheep in a field. Grace nodded politely, commenting occasionally. Julia was dozing, while Evie was deep in thought, wondering about the best way to approach her new plan.

They arrived back to Evie's house in the early evening. Everyone suspected something was wrong when they saw Evie's mother standing at their front door waiting to meet them. Evie's mind went into overdrive fearing Olga might have come to the house, or worse, Volok. They hurried inside, Grace and Mr Finch too. Evie's father closed the hall door behind them, and then Evie's mother spoke.

'I'm afraid we have some sad news,' she said. 'Tilly's mother died this morning.'

'How dreadful,' Evie's father said. 'I didn't realise she was so ill.'

'Tilly was sent for shortly after you left,' Evie's mother said. 'Later I received this note, confirming that she had passed away.' She handed a note to Evie's father. 'I said we would help with the arrangements.'

'Yes, certainly,' Evie's father said as he read the note.

Evie was stunned. If she had known how ill Tilly's mother had been, she could have made a wish and saved her. But she hadn't known; she was too busy worrying about herself and all she had to do. Too busy to actually talk to Tilly for more than half a minute. Evie felt overcome with guilt.

'Are you all right, dear?' her mother asked, looking at her curiously.

Evie nodded, unable to find words. Her mind was in turmoil, her throat tight. She had got it badly wrong; she had made the wrong choice. Of course she would have chosen to help Tilly's mother before Mr Baldwin. Though he was just as deserving, Evie didn't even know Mr Baldwin. Her mother had said he had a young family, but this was Tilly's mother. Good grief! How could she even think like that? Everyone was important, every single human being. So if she had known about Tilly's mother, who was really more deserving of the wish and the magic?

Julia put her hand on Evie's shoulder. 'There was nothing any of us could have done,' she said gently.

Evie turned to look at her governess, struggling to hold back tears.

'It's all right, my dear,' her father said. 'You're bound to be more sensitive to upsets after your recent ordeal. Why don't we all sit down in the parlour and have some tea?'

'I'd rather lie down, if you don't mind,' Evie said.

'Are you sure you should be on your own, dear?' Evie's mother asked.

Evie nodded and walked slowly up the stairs.

She wasn't tired; she didn't need rest. Rather, Evie needed

to figure out how to avoid such a nightmare again. She felt responsible even though she wasn't. And Julia was right: there was nothing she could have done. Poor, poor Tilly, Evie thought. She knew their maid had been very close to her mother. But that's about all she knew. She had never really asked Tilly about her life outside of her work in Evie's home. Evie slumped down on her bed, put her head on her pillow and wept.

Julia and Freddie came up to see her ten minutes later.

'We know why you're so upset,' Freddie said quietly.

'You couldn't have known, Evie, none of us could,' Julia said. 'Something like this could happen again, but you are not to blame. You won't always know who has the most pressing need. You can only make your decision on what you actually know at that very moment.'

'You'll never be able to save everyone,' Freddie said.

'No, but I'd like to,' Evie said.

'This is one of the burdens Lucia spoke of,' Julia said. 'Not only will you have to choose, but there will always be someone deserving of your help who you may miss entirely. Try not to let it upset you. It's just the way it is.'

'I feel so guilty,' Evie mumbled through her tears. 'I never thought ...'

'I know,' Julia said, putting her arm around her. 'Do you think you could come down in a moment? Grace and her father will be leaving soon.'

'Oh, I've been so rude to Grace,' Evie said. 'I'll come now.' Evie rose from the bed, grabbed a handkerchief and loudly blew her nose, much to Freddie's amusement. They left the room and went downstairs.

Grace gave Evie a hug as soon as she entered the parlour. Evie was glad of it, though another wave of guilt swept over her, knowing she was keeping the true explanation of her upset from her best friend.

'I didn't know you were so close to Tilly and her mother,' Grace whispered to her. 'I'd like to come to the funeral with you, if you think it would help. I assume you'll be going.'

Evie nodded. 'Thank you, Grace. You are the best friend anyone could have.'

After a few minutes, Mr Finch thought it was time they went. As they said their goodbyes, Evie could feel everyone's eyes on her, still concerned by how upset she was. For most of the evening, she felt her parents were watching her, her mother annoyingly trying to make light conversation. Evie caught her father frowning mightily, as he always did when something puzzled him. He must suspect something, Evie thought. Both of them are suspicious now, my father and Grace. I'm sure of it. If they aren't, they surely will be when I return to Dower Hall a second time.

Next morning, Evie woke feeling tired after a restless night. She thought about the day before, and smacked a hand on her pillow, her sorrow turning to anger and frustration. Julia was right about something else: she had to come to terms with her new role. Her life was different now. As the Harp Maiden, she would have difficulties to face, and she wouldn't always make the right decisions, but she would have to live with the consequences. This was only the beginning. She had to learn from her mistakes, stop snivelling, grow up and get used to it – starting right away.

CHAPTER TEN

Tilly's mother was buried two days later in the local cemetery. Walking back home after the funeral, Evie was surprised when Grace suggested they go for a carriage ride on Sunday – to Dower Hall.

'We could bring a full picnic this time,' she said. 'The weather is still nice, and it could be a lovely day.'

'You really don't mind going a second time?' Evie asked.

'I know it means a lot to you, though I'm not entirely sure why,' Grace said.

Evie didn't say anything.

'I thought you might like to go without our fathers fussing about, as well as having all those constables there,' Grace said.

'Yes, yes, I would,' Evie said, rather too quickly. She immediately saw that Grace had noticed her eagerness. 'How will we organise it?'

'Well, Samuel is still keen to speak with you, Julia and Freddie,' Grace said. 'We didn't get the chance while he was on duty last time. So I suggested to him that we go again when he's off duty. He's going to organise a carriage for us. It will be a better chance for you to talk, if Julia doesn't mind coming as chaperone again.'

'That would be great,' Evie said, thinking that if her governess went, their parents couldn't complain – and Julia would understand Evie's real interest behind the visit.

'I've already made it clear to Samuel that it's only a picnic and all of us are just friends,' Grace said.

'Yes, of course,' Evie said. 'Freddie might want to come. You know how he loves adventures.'

'I don't see why not,' Grace said. 'He would certainly keep Samuel occupied.'

The girls giggled.

'Samuel won't tell anyone else where we're going, will he?' Evie asked. 'I'd prefer to keep that to ourselves. I don't want anyone thinking I have some strange obsession with the place.'

'I'll ask him to promise,' Grace said. 'I told him the outing would mean a lot to you, so he would be doing me a favour, as your friend. Anyway, I know he's interested to look around again himself, so it suits everyone.'

'Thank you, Grace,' Evie said. 'It does mean a lot to me. It's just, well …'

'You can tell me when you're ready, Evie, though I admit I am curious,' Grace said. 'There is something else I was going to ask you.'

'Oh?'

'You seemed very upset by Tilly's mother's passing,' Grace said. 'I know you're very fond of Tilly, all your family is, but did you know her mother well? Her death seemed to hit you very hard.'

'I was shocked that she died so quickly,' Evie said, a little flustered. 'We knew she had been ill, but not that she was so close to the end.'

Grace nodded, though she didn't look convinced. 'Well,' she said, 'I'll let Samuel know that a picnic is arranged for Sunday.'

'Thank you,' Evie said. 'I look forward to it. We have concert practice on Saturday afternoon, so I'll see you then too.'

'Don't forget to bring lots of treats in your picnic basket!' Grace said.

'I will, and Freddie will insist,' Evie said. 'Oh, I've only just remembered – my parents are away this weekend. They're going to an archaeological conference. That decides it – Freddie will have to come. Are you sure that will be all right?'

'It'll be fine,' Grace said.

Samuel looked a little peeved when he and Grace arrived. Evie, Julia and Freddie were waiting to be collected at the hall door.

'You don't mind such a big party, do you, Samuel?' Evie said gingerly. 'Grace was so kind to suggest the outing, but my parents are away, so my governess has to come too. And we can't leave Freddie home alone. Our butler isn't very good at keeping a ten-year-old occupied!'

Samuel could hardly refuse. He politely agreed and after helping everyone on board, he climbed back into the driver's seat. He would remain there for the entire journey, holding the reins, guiding the horses, while Evie, Grace, Julia and Freddie sat inside the carriage chatting and laughing.

He must be very keen on being a detective or very curious about Dower Hall, Evie thought. Or perhaps he's keen on

Grace; they're only second cousins, after all. Evie smiled to herself. She liked the idea that Grace might have an admirer. But she was so keen to reach Dower Hall, all thoughts quickly melted away, and she began to focus on the task that lay ahead.

They had two picnic baskets between them, filled with freshly made sandwiches, a selection of cheeses, dainty cakes and biscuits, and bottles of lemonade. Samuel was impressed at the spread of food, hungry after the drive. Freddie, as usual, was starving and extremely excited.

'Lots of time to explore and no need to hurry home!' he cried.

'Exploring, yes,' Julia said, glancing at Evie. 'But remember what your Uncle Henry said: "No getting into trouble!" and even more importantly: "Miss Pippen is in charge!"'

'And as I am a constable, I am always in charge!' Samuel said. 'No escape, young Master Freddie!'

Both Evie and Grace quickly disguised their chuckles with delicate coughs.

'Some lemonade, girls? Samuel, some more?' Julia asked, opening another bottle. 'Freddie, you have had a lot already. Slow down, will you? Where are you off to now?'

'There's a fox over there,' Freddie said, and ran over to the hedge, returning quickly after the fox ran away.

'What do you hope to find when you go exploring, Freddie?' Grace asked.

'Treasure, of course!' Freddie said. 'Lots and lots of treasure!'

'That's the spirit,' Samuel said. 'You never know what

you'll find around an old ruin. I think it's quite safe on the outside, but not so on the inside. Everyone must be careful. Right, Freddie?'

'Yes, Constable Banks,' Freddie said as he chomped into another ham sandwich.

A treasure hunt indeed, thought Evie. Clever Freddie to think of a good cover story. But was the Black Ruby a treasure or a threat? Fortunately Evie had thought of a clever excuse of her own, knowing the moment would come when she had to explain what she was hoping to find on this big treasure hunt.

CHAPTER ELEVEN

E vie hated lying, so she decided to bend the truth a little and pretend that she had lost a necklace, one with a big dark gemstone.

'Lucia, the old lady who died in the fire, gave it to me,' Evie explained. 'I would prefer if my parents didn't know that I lost it, at least not before I find it again. If I find it. They would think it very foolish of me.'

'Your secret is safe,' Samuel said.

Julia spluttered into her glass of lemonade.

'We'll help you find it,' Grace said enthusiastically, getting to her feet. 'We have plenty of time to look today.'

They wandered through the rubble all around the house. At first it was mildly exciting, but after a while it became rather repetitive. No one found anything of any interest and even Freddie diverted his attention to the local wildlife for a while before returning to the hunt. Several times he thought he had found the ruby, only to be disappointed. Everyone noticed Samuel's loud sighs as he became increasingly bored.

'I'm going to take a look inside,' he said. 'Police work. Please don't follow me. It wouldn't be safe for civilians.'

Freddie looked like he was about to sneak after him, when Evie put a hand on his shoulder, and whispered. 'Let him go,

Freddie. Samuel will only get cross if you follow him and we don't want to make him suspicious.'

Freddie nodded, then in his excitement, he started to ask a question that he shouldn't. 'What about Grace, does she know?' His voice trailed off and a look of horror crossed his face.

'I think we should leave the detective work to the police,' Julia said, coming to the rescue. 'There are plenty of areas we haven't searched yet.' She rolled her eyes at Evie and shook her head. 'I'm going to sit down on the picnic rug for a few minutes. I'm feeling a little tired.'

'Yes, all right,' Evie said. 'You do look very pale.'

Freddie mouthed the word 'sorry' to Evie. She ruffled his shock of blond hair. 'Come on,' she said. 'Let's see if you can find it, then.'

'It's very unusual for a gemstone to be black, especially a ruby,' Grace said. 'I've never heard of one like that.'

'Neither had I,' Evie said. 'I should have asked Lucia more about it.' She rummaged among the debris, desperately hoping she might get lucky. But she didn't.

After another hour of searching, Julia re-joined them. 'I think we should be heading back,' she said. 'That dark bank of clouds is heading our way. We could be in for a drenching.'

'Really? Just a little longer,' Evie said, unable to disguise her desperation.

Grace looked at her, surprised.

'I must find my necklace,' Evie said. 'I feel so awful about losing it.'

'No one could blame you, Evie,' Grace said. 'Especially not during all that … trouble.'

'Quite so,' Julia said. 'And we won't tell anyone you lost it.'

Evie looked up from her search and glared at Julia. 'It will be difficult to look again, unless' – Evie looked imploringly at Grace – 'unless Samuel wouldn't mind. Would he?'

'Goodness! I'd forgotten about Samuel!' Grace said. 'Where is he?'

'He returned to the picnic area a little while ago,' Julia said. 'He had lots of questions for me about our kidnapping.'

'Oh, yes, sorry,' Evie said. 'I promised we'd chat about that.'

'He has probably finished off all the food by now,' Julia said.

'Oh dear,' Grace said. 'Perhaps this outing wasn't so interesting for him after all.'

'Either way, it really is time we got going,' Julia said. 'Freddie needs a good scrub in the bath. Just look at him!'

Freddie had somehow managed to cut both his knees, scratch his hands, get mud all over his trousers, his coat sleeves and his nose, and his shoes were possibly beyond recovery. Evie almost laughed at the sight of him, but she groaned instead at not finding the ruby. Catching Julia's glare, she knew they had to leave.

'Yes, all right. I'm sorry my personal mission took over,' Evie said. 'I'll go and apologise to Samuel.'

Evie led the party back to the picnic area where Samuel had indeed eaten everything. He was lounging on the picnic rug looking rather glum, but sat up straight as the others approached, remembering his manners.

'Samuel,' Evie said, getting straight to the point, 'I am

very sorry for taking so much of the afternoon to search for my necklace. It was selfish of me, and I hope you will accept my apology. We are very grateful to you for taking us out today. It has been lovely, and I know Grace told you earlier that it meant a lot to me, and it really did.'

'Not at all,' he said generously. 'I was happy to help, and I admit I was interested to come here for my own reasons too. I'm sorry you didn't find what you were looking for. Neither did I. There really isn't much left of the manor except rubble and rubbish, inside and out. I'll go and prepare the horses if you are all ready to leave.'

He stood up and walked over to where the horses were grazing contentedly, waiting to be hitched up to the carriage. Evie looked at Grace, then Julia. 'I am sorry. I never intended to take over the day like this. At least Freddie had good fun, judging by the state of him.'

'It was brilliant,' Freddie said, beaming from ear to ear. 'But I'm hungry again. Pity Samuel ate everything.'

The girls and Julia couldn't help laughing.

'I'll go and chat to Samuel,' Grace said.

'I'm sorry you couldn't find the ruby, Evie, but perhaps it's for the best,' Julia said, after Grace was out of earshot.

'It is definitely *not* for the best,' Evie said, her frustration returning. 'Coming here again won't be easy, as it's too far to walk!'

'Finding the ruby was always going to be a long shot,' Julia said. 'It could take many days of searching and, there would be no guarantee that you'd find it. Unless ...' Julia started muttering to herself.

'What is it?' Evie asked.

'Nothing, just a fleeting thought,' Julia said. 'I am trying to help you, you know.'

Evie tried to ignore Julia's terse reply and glanced over to where Grace and Samuel were standing, chatting. Samuel was smiling and talking animatedly, not appearing to be in any rush all of a sudden. It was kind of Grace, Evie thought, to try to cheer him up by giving him some attention. She thought her friend looked rather animated too; perhaps they did like each other. Then Evie remembered something, her curiosity grabbing a hold of her again.

'Julia, there is one more thing I must do,' Evie said. 'I need to take a look at those trees.'

'Didn't you do that the last time?' Julia asked.

'Not properly,' Evie said. Ignoring Julia's protests, she turned and ran quickly back to the forest behind the house.

This time, Evie was determined not to be surprised by swishing branches and imaginary faces. She noticed how none of the trees had been damaged by the raging fire, nor the explosions. Strange. There was no scorching, no blackening of leaves or bark, even on the trees closest to the house. They stood as tall, straight and ominous as ever, looming before her. This time, however, Evie didn't feel nearly so afraid. Despite the near windless day, the trees stirred, then began to sway. Without hesitating, Evie ventured boldly in.

With a sudden impulse, Evie ran ahead into the deepest, darkest part of the forest. Something was drawing her, something was there, she felt it. She stopped abruptly, shocked, yet it was what she had suspected. Olga again. The demon-ogress was still wearing remnants of the housekeeper's tattered clothing and some new items she must have found, a skirt tied with a rope, and a cape draped awkwardly around her huge body. She was in one of her rages. Evie watched as Olga broke off a large branch and thrashed it repeatedly against the trunks of several trees.

'Where is it?' she hissed. 'Find me the ruby. It has to be here. Find it! I command you! Find it!'

Evie stood stock-still, watching, listening. She stared at the trees swishing and swaying, stronger now and in all directions. Were they obeying Olga's command? Were they searching? How could that be? Or were they trying to drive her away? Evie sank behind a very tall tree that had no low branches that might hit her. She peeked out to watch Olga, but also kept an eye on the whipping branches above and around her just in case. She tried not to breathe too loudly despite being at least a hundred feet away from the ogress. They would all be in mortal danger if Olga discovered her now. Then Evie saw with some relief that Olga was marching away from her, stomping her way through the forest.

At least she hasn't found the ruby, Evie thought with some relief. That means it could still be among the rubble – but is it inside the remains of the house or outside? I must come back here and find it before she does.

Evie desperately wanted to stay and find out where Olga was going, but she knew the others were waiting for her. They might come looking for her soon and she couldn't let that happen. Olga's superb hearing might pick up their voices as they approached. What to do? Leave? Stay and find out more?

As ever, curiosity won out. Watching Olga almost disappear out of sight, Evie didn't think about it any longer – she followed.

The ogress didn't turn left or right, she kept walking

straight through the trees, smashing a pathway with the branch in her fist. Evie kept a good distance, treading as carefully as she could. Suddenly, she emerged from the cover of the forest to a strip of meadow that sloped down to the edge of a deep gorge. Evie gasped. It was so unexpected, as if the trees had simply fallen away into a giant chasm. Instinctively she ducked into the long grass. Without good cover, she would need to keep an even greater distance.

After a moment, Evie half stood, looking frantically around to see where Olga had gone. She began to panic when she couldn't find her, thinking the ogress might have doubled back in order to pounce on her. Then she spotted the bulky form at quite a distance, appearing and disappearing behind bushes and boulders, marching around the edge of the gorge. Then Olga began to disappear from view, heading lower before disappearing into the rockface.

What a good hiding place! Evie thought. Out of sight and awkward to reach. Perhaps she's been living there since New Year's Day. She could have been looking for the ruby all that time, and she still didn't find it.

Completely forgetting about her friends, Evie ran on along the top of the gorge.

Chapter Twelve

Evie stopped at the yawning mouth of a cave. Large rocks loomed in a disorganised pile around the entrance – good for hiding. Evie knew that Samuel had to return the police carriage he had borrowed by six o'clock, which meant they had to leave by four-thirty to be certain it was back on time. It was at least three-thirty now and progress would be slow if the rain came. She glanced up at the sky. Daylight was closing in as dark clouds gathered overhead. Julia was right again; they were in for a downpour soon.

Evie crouched outside the cave, thinking, her guilty conscience invading her thoughts. Samuel was bound to be cross at being delayed, and in trouble if they were late. Grace would be annoyed with Evie, too, for taking advantage of Samuel so soon after apologising to him. Evie would have to make it up to them somehow. Freddie wouldn't mind a delay; he never complained about anything, except being hungry. But he *was* hungry, he had said so. Julia would be anxious, and probably cross, but Evie simply couldn't leave yet, not when she was so close to finding out more.

Still crouching behind a boulder, Evie peered around the side, trying to see if there were good places to hide inside the cave as well. There were, and she went in.

Despite the wide opening and the cavernous roof inside, the cave felt airless, and smelled strongly of rot and decay. Bat droppings littered the floor and most of the walls. Water dripped from somewhere, an ominous, regular drip, drip, drip, as if timing how long Evie had before she was discovered. She could hear Olga shuffling around somewhere further in. The ogress was kicking stones and letting out the occasional roar. Evie hesitated, trying to judge where to go. There, she thought, down the left side. She moved quickly and quietly along the cave wall as far back as she dared, keeping low behind as many fallen boulders and rocks as she could. Occasionally, she glanced back at the entrance, knowing it was also her only exit.

The bad smell worsened further in. It was so strong Evie hoped it would disguise Evie's own scent. It was surprisingly dark, the light not reaching in very far, nor reflecting well off the murky walls. Olga was sitting on a rock, sucking on a bone. What bone? Evie wondered with a shiver. Olga lifted her head a moment, but only belched. After a couple of minutes, the stink became too much to bear, and Evie thought she might throw up. She swallowed hard, twice, three times, placing a hand firmly over her mouth to be sure.

Olga gave the bone a last look, then tossed it away. Evie ducked as it clattered across the rocky floor to where, she now saw, several other bones lay scattered and discarded. Still in a crouched position, Evie hoped to take another look when she heard Olga move. Which way did she go? Towards her? Away from her? In that moment Evie realised the complete folly of her decision to enter the cave at all. It was ridiculous at best, incredibly dangerous at worst. What had Evie thought she could discover? She couldn't remember. Curiosity again.

Then Evie heard an unexpected noise, a creak. She risked a quick look. Olga was sitting on a different rock now, a wooden casket on her lap. The ogress placed it in front of her on another flat rock, which looked oddly like a table. She bent forward and opened two richly carved doors on one side of the casket. Evie strained to see what was inside, but it was impossible given the angle. She needed to get closer. But then Olga spoke, and Evie stayed exactly where she was.

'Wake up, sorceress,' Olga said. 'I know you can call the Black Ruby. How do I find it? How? Tell me! Do not waste any more of my time. I cannot bear all this searching!'

A voice replied. 'You cannot call nor command the ruby.'

'You are lying!' Olga roared.

'I have never lied to you,' the voice said. 'I have always believed your threats.'

'Good,' Olga said. 'SO – TELL – ME!'

'There is nothing to tell,' the voice said. 'You may find the ruby if you look long enough. Then again, you may not.'

'Bah!' Olga snapped the casket doors shut, rose from her seat and stomped around in circles. Scowling, she looked even more terrifying. Evie wrapped her arms around her knees, not knowing what to make of what she saw and heard: Olga making demands of a talking casket. She had used the word 'sorceress' too. A wild thought flashed through her head. Could it be? No! But could it? Evie began to think she had just stepped into a horrible nightmare. Another one.

Sounds of movement. Evie peeped again, then watched as Olga disappeared into the back of the cave. Slowly and carefully, Evie moved nearer to the casket, dismissing all the sensible voices raging in her head, saying, 'Don't go any closer!' and 'Get out now!' Finally, Evie was in a position to see what was inside. She paused, looking into the distant darkness of the cave to see if the ogress would emerge. But she didn't, and Evie felt her courage return, her curiosity bursting.

Evie bent down beside the casket still perched on the rock. It was very dark wood, ebony perhaps, intricately carved, with tiny red and purple gemstones studded around the locks. Evie touched it gently with her fingertips; they tingled on contact. She stroked the carving on the front of the casket like she was stroking the harp. To her amazement, the two doors opened just a sliver. Gently, Evie pulled them back, trying to avoid any creaking.

It hadn't been a trick, nor her imagination. Evie took a sharp breath as she gazed into the casket at a woman's head. She had long dark hair, golden-brown skin, and features that revealed she had once been exceptionally beautiful. Evie was momentarily stunned. She only knew of one sorceress: Nala, from the fifteenth century, mentioned in her father's books, Thorn's books and Lucia's diary. Lucia had spoken about a sorceress called Nala who had enchanted the harp. The same Nala had studied and identified the power of the Black Ruby. But all that was so long ago. How could this be the same person?

Evie heard sounds coming from the back of the cave. It was time to leave. She was about to close the box when the eyes in the head opened and looked at her. Evie almost screamed but the eyes softened, and the face showed a relieved yet pleading expression. Evie felt torn, she had to leave, but she wanted to stay. She whispered so softly she could barely hear her own words: 'I'll come back. I promise.' And with that message, she closed the double doors on the casket without waiting for a reply.

Slipping back between the boulders, Evie headed for the mouth of the cave, stopping once, briefly, to catch her breath and steady herself. What a discovery! How could it even be possible? Only with magic, she thought. Extraordinary magic, dark and evil beyond anything she had ever heard or read about. Though the discovery excited her, it was still a shock. Her thoughts drifted as a wave of nausea shuddered through her again, and her legs began to feel heavy and awkward. She urged herself on. Out there beyond the forest were her friends and the carriage that would take them home. They had had a picnic. What a normal thing to do! And yet here in this cave there was a talking head, a head without a body. Nala's head. Nala, the sorceress from the fifteenth century. Ridiculous and crazy as it sounded, after all that had happened in the last few months, Evie knew in her heart it was more than possible, it was real.

Pulling herself together, Evie retraced her steps, carefully avoiding any obstacles. Outside, it was almost as dark as inside the cave, as the first drops of rain began to fall. She ran as hard as she could, fumbling her way back along the top of the gorge and on through the forest. The impact of what she had seen was finally hitting her, driving her on in a sort of excited panic. She hurried past the ruined manor to where the anxious party were waiting, huddled together under a tree for shelter while they watched for her.

'Where have you been?' Julia cried. 'We've been so worried.'

'I was just about to go and search for you,' Samuel said,

sounding like a cross constable.

Freddie hugged her. 'I thought you were lost,' he said.

'We all did,' Julia said, eyeing Evie crossly.

'I am so sorry,' Evie gasped, trying to catch her breath. 'Once again, so sorry, everyone. I, um, didn't feel well, and I couldn't bear to be ill in front of you all. I, um, I went into the trees back there to – avoid embarrassment. We can leave now. I think my stomach has settled. I'll explain the delay if you're in any trouble, Samuel. I'll take all the blame, I promise.'

'Are you sure you're all right?' Grace asked.

'Fine now, thank you,' Evie said, trying to look contrite. She could see they really were worried, as well as annoyed with her. They boarded the carriage in silence, Evie struggling to come to terms with her peculiar experience. Although desperately needing to talk about it, she had to keep this to herself. It made for an unsettling journey home.

CHAPTER THIRTEEN

Not long into the return journey, one of the horses began to whinny loudly. Samuel brought the carriage to a halt and jumped down to take a look. Evie pulled down the window.

'What's the matter?' she asked.

Samuel was examining one of the horse's hooves. 'This one has lost a shoe,' he said. 'We'll have to find a farrier. He can't make it back without a new shoe or he'll go lame.'

'Didn't we pass a sign a moment ago?' Grace asked.

'Well spotted,' Samuel said. 'The sign was for Crompton village. There's an inn there, and a farrier too, I think.' He approached the window. 'We passed through that village when I was out this way before, the first time we looked at the ruins back in January. We might as well take a break, get something to eat at the inn while the horse is being reshod. I'm guessing Freddie is still hungry. Well, Freddie?'

'Starving!' Freddie said enthusiastically. 'Can I take a look at the horse? Is he in a lot of pain? Will the farrier be able to fix him?'

'Samuel, how long will this take?' Julia interrupted.

'It will depend on how busy the farrier is,' Samuel said. 'Could be as little as half an hour, but longer if he has other horses to see to first.'

Samuel guided the horses gently to the turn in the road which led to Crompton. Luckily, it wasn't far. By the time Samuel organised the injured horse with the farrier and left the other horse and the carriage at the stable yard, it was raining heavily. Everyone hurried into the inn.

The Crompton Arms was old and a bit dingy, but it had a welcoming fire blazing merrily and it was surprisingly busy. Samuel led the way, the rest of the group following a little uncomfortably. It wasn't the type of place they would normally visit. A few locals sitting at wooden tables fell silent and stared, unused to visitors, especially ladies and children. Samuel suggested a quiet corner table, away from as many prying eyes as possible, then he went to speak with the innkeeper.

'Should we really eat here?' Grace asked in a whisper.

'We don't have anywhere else to wait, and it's probably the only inn in the village,' Evie said. 'Freddie is dying for some food, and I'm rather hungry too.'

'You didn't eat much of the picnic,' Grace said. 'I hope Samuel won't be in trouble because we are running so late.'

'Don't worry,' Evie said. 'I meant what I said. I'll take full responsibility for the delay and make sure Samuel isn't blamed.'

'Who knows when we'll get home now?' Julia said crossly.

Evie glared at her governess. She didn't need more reminding of how she had messed up their day.

'It's all right,' Grace whispered. 'No one could have known the horse would lose a shoe. We can blame the horse for the delay. It'll be fine.'

'I hope the food is good,' Freddie said.

They each looked around, trying to see what other patrons were eating.

'Well, I'm sure other travellers have eaten here as well as the locals,' Julia said quietly, trying to reassure herself as much as the others. 'Though I expect it will be different from what we're used to.'

Samuel returned, looking relieved. 'I've ordered lamb pies for everyone,' he said. 'I hope that's all right. I saw the innkeeper's wife serving another table and the pies looked surprisingly good.'

'Thank you, Samuel,' Evie said. 'The owner and his wife look quite jolly, even if some of the customers don't.'

'They have to keep their customers happy if they want them to come back,' Samuel said. 'There is a good crowd in this evening. Let's hope it'll be good fare.'

'I'm a customer and I'm starving,' Freddie said.

They all laughed. It was typical of Freddie to highlight the most important point. When the food arrived, everyone was surprised how hungry they were despite all the picnic goodies, and they enjoyed the meal.

'Why is everyone still watching us?' Grace asked softly. 'We can't be that strange, can we?'

'We're not local,' Samuel said. 'This is a rural village and people can be suspicious of strangers.'

'Perhaps we should say hello and try to chat to some of them,' Evie said, her mind buzzing with ideas again. 'It might reassure them.'

'No,' Samuel said firmly. 'They won't like being asked questions. We should eat and leave.'

But Evie wasn't deterred. After all, the locals might

know something about Dower Hall. Perhaps they had been scavenging through the rubble. Maybe one of them had found the Black Ruby. Suddenly Evie felt very alarmed. If someone had found it, how would she get it back? Stealing from demons was excusable; stealing from local people was not. She stared around the room, gazing from one character to the next: who might it be? Then her thoughts were interrupted.

'Excuse me. You folks aren't from around here, are ye?'

Evie turned and looked up. A local farmer – judging by his attire – stood looking at them, twisting his tweed cap in his hands nervously. He was in his sixties, strongly built but not overly tall. He had a kindly face, untidy grey hair, and he needed a shave.

Samuel stood up. 'No, sir, we are not,' he said. 'One of our horses lost a shoe and is with the farrier. We will be leaving shortly.'

The man nodded. 'I saw you drive out the gates of Dower Hall earlier. You should be careful going up to that manor. Nutters used to live there. Everyone around here avoided the place and they still do, even though it's gone now.'

'What do you mean by "nutters", sir?' Samuel asked, sounding like a constable again.

'We were having a picnic and exploring,' Freddie said.

Evie stood up. 'Excuse me, did you know the people who lived there before that terrible fire?'

'Not really,' the man said. 'Did you?'

'A little, I mean, I—'

'I am a police constable, sir,' Samuel said, interrupting Evie. 'I and my station colleagues examined the site after the fire and again recently.'

'Strange place to go for a picnic, then,' the man muttered, eyeing Samuel suspiciously.

'We are all friends,' Evie said.

'What is your interest in Dower Hall, sir?' Samuel asked.

'Used to be a kind lady who played the harp,' the man said. 'She would visit these parts now and again. Though that was a long time ago. Saved my niece when she was sick.'

'What has that got to do with the manor house?' Samuel asked.

Just then, Evie spotted two younger men, possibly the man's sons by their looks, leave their stools, walk over and stand behind him. Immediately, everyone felt uneasy. The younger two didn't say anything, but their stance was a little threatening.

'Sometimes I used to think I heard harp music coming from that house,' the man said. 'Sound travels quite a distance over these fields. I thought maybe the lady had come back. I hoped she had. Been missing a long time now. I inquired just the once but was told to go away – or else.'

'By whom?' Samuel asked.

'The lady, your friend, was her name Lucia by any chance?' Evie asked.

Julia glared at her. Samuel sighed loudly, not appreciating the interruption. Grace and Freddie stopped eating and stared at Evie. It was an awkward silence.

Evie watched the man keenly as he looked around the table, trying to size them up.

Samuel tried to regain attention. 'Ahem,' he coughed. 'The dead woman, Lucia,' he said. 'How well did you know her, sir?'

'Dead? Dear me, no.' He paused, twisting his cap in his hands again. A minute passed before he could speak, his face twitching with emotion. 'Aye, Lucia was the lady I knew. What happened to her? Was it the fire?'

'Yes,' Samuel said. 'She perished in the fire.'

'And you're sure it was her?' the man asked.

'She was identified,' Samuel said.

'Who identified her?' the man asked. 'She had no family.'

'I did,' Evie said. 'I knew her. I told the police.'

'What do you know of the other occupants of that house, sir?' Samuel asked. 'We are still looking for the housekeeper. Was she the one who sent you from the door?'

'Aye, but I don't know anythin' about her, nor anyone else who lived there,' the man said. 'I used to see a man drive a cart in and out sometimes, that was all. It seemed a quiet place, strange. I only knew Lucia a little bit really. She was a private lady, a special lady.'

'Very special,' Evie said. 'We know she played the harp. I play it too.' Evie looked him straight in the eye. He wanted to talk; she knew he did and so did she. 'Please, join us, Mr, um ...? It would be nice to share some memories of Lucia.'

'Just for a minute, then. These two are my boys, Danny and Martin,' the man said. 'We've got farm work to finish before sunset, so we won't delay. My name's Charlie, Charlie McGinn.' He turned to his two sons. 'Leave us to chat a moment, boys.' Danny and Martin nodded and walked back to their table and Charlie pulled up a chair beside Evie.

Samuel sighed loudly again, annoyed at what would no doubt be another delay. 'While you're getting acquainted,' he said, 'I will go and check on the horse. Then we must be on our way.'

'I'll come with you, Samuel,' Grace said.

'Thank you, Grace. I hope it is not still raining. Please take my cloak …'

Samuel and Grace headed for the door.

'Whatever you have to say can be said in front of Julia and Freddie,' Evie said, noticing Charlie's hesitation. 'They knew Lucia too.'

Charlie didn't know a lot about Lucia, but he did know she could help people, heal people and she played beautiful music on a small, plain harp. 'It was like magic when she played,' he said. 'Good things always happened when she was around. She would promise things would get better, and they did. There aren't many people in the world like her.'

Evie listened keenly to Charlie. Julia sat looking at her hands, tense and uneasy. Freddie tucked into his second apple pie and custard.

'She was very protective of that harp,' Charlie continued. 'She said it meant everything to her. I guess it was a family heirloom, or something.'

'Probably,' Evie said.

'People came after her, bad people,' Charlie said. 'They threatened her, even tried to kidnap her a couple of times, tried to steal her harp. Me and my boys put a stop to that. Then some years ago she just disappeared. I thought she had had enough and left, though I always worried that those ruffians might have got to her. Do you know where she's been these last fifteen years?'

'I, um, I'm only fifteen myself,' Evie said, avoiding the question.

'Before that, we looked out for her,' Charlie said. 'She

brought us happiness and good fortune while she was here, so we didn't mind helping her in return, no matter what she needed.'

'Did she tell you anything about herself?' Evie asked. 'Anything unusual?'

Charlie gave Evie a questioning look. 'Like what, Miss?'

'Please, call me Evie. Did she tell you why she was here? Or where she came from? Where she used to live? Did she tell you any secrets?'

'Evie!' Julia said, giving her a warning glare.

'My, you have a lot of questions,' Charlie said. 'Are you sure you were her friends?'

Suddenly Evie realised that she didn't really know much about Lucia at all. They had spent all their time talking about the harp and planning their escape. 'Yes, we were her friends,' Evie said. 'It's just we – we didn't have much time before she—'

The door slammed. Evie looked over and saw Samuel and Grace bustle into the inn. They were drenched. Samuel waved over and called, 'The horse is ready.' He approached their table, Grace following. 'We must go before the weather worsens. It's turning into quite a storm out there.'

'I agree,' Julia said.

'I'll settle the bill,' Samuel said. 'Please be ready to leave when I return.'

Evie spoke hurriedly. 'We were Lucia's friends, Charlie, though we didn't know her for very long. I think there are items that belonged to her in among the rubble of that manor house, and I wanted to take a look today to see if I could find anything.'

'What sort of things?' Charlie asked.

'Personal things, mementos,' Evie mumbled, unsure whether she should mention a jewel or not. 'Books, ornaments, other things.'

'Books won't have survived a fire,' Charlie said. 'And ornaments will have been smashed to pieces.'

'There was a pendant though, with a large dark stone,' Evie said. 'Nothing valuable, you understand, but Lucia wanted me to have it to remember her.'

'Evie, we must go,' Julia said firmly, the warning glare still in her eyes. She stood up. 'It was nice to meet you, Mr McGinn. Please excuse us as we are already very late.'

Samuel and Grace were waiting by the table now, rain still dripping off their coats and forming small puddles on the floor. Everyone was looking at Evie, wishing her to leave immediately. But Evie was looking at Charlie, trying to gauge if she could trust him or not. She glanced up at her friends to see Julia pale and frowning, Grace looking tired and puzzled, and Samuel very impatient. Only Freddie didn't seem to mind, and he came to Evie's rescue.

'That's right,' Freddie said to Charlie, breaking the silence. 'I was there when Lucia gave Evie her private papers and her special diary.' He looked directly at Evie. 'She would want you to have her other things too. She told me so.'

Evie waited nervously for Charlie's response. As he looked at her, she could feel him weighing up what he thought of Evie, her friends and what had been said.

'If me and my lads have some spare time, we'll take a look for you,' he said.

'Thank you, Charlie,' Evie said. 'I would be grateful

if you would keep this private, and I can pay you for your trouble.'

'There's no need for payment,' Charlie said. He leaned closer to Evie and whispered. 'I will do anything for the Harp Maiden, even now that she is gone. If there was something that Lucia wanted you to have, I'll do my best to see her wish granted. I owe her that much at least. Though I might need some proof that you were friends.'

Evie was taken aback. Had Charlie actually said those words, Harp Maiden?

'Proof?' Evie whispered, pulling herself together. 'Well, I could show you the diary she gave me. Would that do?'

'It would, another day then,' Charlie said. 'And don't worry, Lucia's secret is safe with me and my two lads. She trusted us for many years, and I think perhaps she trusted you too.'

Evie told him how to reach her should he find anything, then she hurried after the others. Grace was already in the carriage and Samuel was sitting in the driver's seat getting another soaking. Freddie climbed in, but Julia wanted a private word with Evie. They stood on the porch of the inn as the rain hammered down.

'Are you absolutely mad?' Julia whispered angrily. 'You just told a complete stranger about the ruby even though we don't know who – or what – he is. It was a terrible risk, Evie.'

'Lucia trusted him,' Evie said. 'She made a wish for Charlie's niece and he protected Lucia in return. You heard what he said.'

'How do we know he is telling the truth?' Julia asked, almost hysterical.

'I believe him,' Evie said.

'Do you? Just like that?' Julia stared at Evie, her eyes wide with alarm.

'Yes. I do. I can't explain it, I just feel it,' Evie said. 'And I never told him that I am the Harp Maiden now.'

'You told him you play the harp,' Julia said. 'If he knows even a little about the Harp Maiden's role, he will figure it out. He could have been working for Thorn for all we know.'

'He wasn't, he isn't,' Evie said, raising her voice too. 'We know it was Drake who organised the kidnappings, and Drake is dead. So is Thorn. There is only Olga and Volok left.'

'Indeed,' Julia said. 'Then perhaps this Mr McGinn is working for them!'

Silence.

Then Evie spoke more gently. 'I don't think Charlie knows the whole story, but I have to trust him because I must find the ruby before anyone else does.' She almost blurted out the discovery of the talking head and the ruby's ability to resurrect another demon, but checked herself just in time.

'What is to stop Charlie keeping the ruby if he finds it?' Julia asked.

'His promise to Lucia and his promise to me,' Evie said, knowing it was a poor reason.

'What promise?' Julia cried. 'Oh, Evie, you are being so naïve!'

'Well, who else can I ask to look for it, when I cannot?' Evie's voice rose defensively. 'I have no idea when I will be able to return.'

In the sheeting rain, Samuel strode over, his cloak billowing around him.

'I really must insist that we leave *now*,' he said. 'It will be dark before we return and Grace's father will be worried, as will my sergeant. The roads will turn into a mire in this rain, slowing our progress even more. Please, *please* get into the carriage. We have had more than enough delays already.' He turned and marched back to the horses, climbed into the driver's seat, and sat there, staring despairingly ahead.

Julia brushed past Evie and hurried over to the waiting carriage. Evie took one last look behind her to see Charlie standing at the door of the inn. He nodded to Evie in acknowledgement, but she was left wondering just how much he knew, whether she could trust him, and if she would ever see the Black Ruby again.

CHAPTER FOURTEEN

Everyone was tired, cold and a little cranky by the time they reached Hartville. They said brief goodbyes outside Evie's home. Samuel was already bracing himself for a stern conversation with Grace's father and his sergeant, though Grace assured him she would explain the delay, as did Evie. Evie's parents had not yet returned from the conference, which was a relief – no need for explanations.

That night Evie lay in bed, her head and heart in a muddle. She felt a mixture of hope and excitement that Charlie might become an ally, but also worried that Julia might be right, and that she had made a dreadful mistake by mentioning the ruby at all. Julia had spoken sense, but Evie's heart was telling her she had to trust him. Or was that just wishful thinking? Evie tossed and turned for most of the night, plagued by bouts of wakefulness in between disturbing dreams.

Julia was a little cool with Evie at her lessons on Monday morning. Evie tried to ignore it. She knew she had been out of line on Sunday, and she noticed that her governess looked particularly tired. Keeping Evie's secret was a strain on Julia too. Flute practice usually soothed them both, so Evie decided to apologise afterwards, later that morning, but not any sooner. She was still feeling a little miffed herself, and her stubbornness simply wouldn't let her.

Rehearsals were to be doubled in the days before the first concert which was scheduled for Wednesday evening, 11 April. Evie's music teacher, Mr Reid, was very excited about it, and about the fact that his son Matthew was due home from boarding school for the Easter holidays.

As Mr Reid would be collecting Matthew from the train station that afternoon, Julia would be taking the students for the rehearsal. Everyone had heard by now that Matthew was an accomplished pianist, as his late mother had been. Matthew would be joining them for rehearsals and would be included in any concerts while he was at home. Evie and the other musicians were eager to meet him.

Just before she departed for the rehearsal at the town hall, Evie received a letter. Curiously, she didn't recognise the handwriting. She opened it quickly.

'Who is that from?' Julia asked, as she buttoned her overcoat.

'It's from Charlie,' Evie said, surprised but excited. 'He has a notebook that belonged to Lucia and he wants to give it to me. Funny, Lucia never told me about it.'

Julia frowned as she pinned her hat into place. 'Perhaps there is no notebook,' she said. 'It could be a trap.'

'No, I believe him,' Evie said, folding the letter and putting it in her pocket.

'That's because you want to,' Julia said. 'Not because you are thinking sensibly.'

'Well, what do you suggest?' Evie cried, her frustration erupting despite her earlier apology. 'Do you really think I should ignore it? It could be important. This notebook could answer so many questions. And I still need that ruby. Like it or not, Julia, I am going to—'

'You're going to go back,' Julia said.

'I have to,' Evie said hotly. 'And there's something else I ought to tell you. When I—'

'Evie, you can do so much good with this gift, why do you want to take on so much more?' Julia asked.

'Because I must,' Evie said. 'Can't you see? It's my responsibility now. All of it. Mine alone. I must protect the harp and its magic, and to do that I have to know every threat from every source, even if it means mortal danger.'

'Are you sure you're not just being stubborn?' Julia asked. 'Perhaps *very* stubborn? It wouldn't be the first time!'

'No!' Evie cried.

'But you are!' Julia replied.

'I am not!' Evie cried defiantly. 'I just—'

'There you are!' Evie's father said, hurrying down the stairs, causing both Evie and Julia to gasp. 'I thought I'd walk to the town hall with you.' He stood smiling at them, though Evie guessed he had noticed they were both rather cross and hoped he hadn't heard their row. She should be more careful.

'Well? Isn't the rehearsal at three o'clock?' Evie's father asked. 'I'm just visiting the library, but you two don't want to be late. Come along!'

'Goodness! Look at the time!' Julia said.

Evie ran to get her flute, pulled on her overcoat and they walked quickly into the town together. It was a relief for Evie to leave such a prickly conversation behind, though she knew it wasn't over. Luckily, her father had lots to talk about, and babbled on about his friend Howard Carter and how he hoped to unearth an important tomb in Egypt soon.

Despite Mr Reid's absence, the rehearsal went very well under Julia's direction. Just as they were packing up, Mr Reid arrived into the hall with his son. All eyes turned to the eighteen-year-old boy they had heard so much about. He was taller than his father, with dark wavy hair and almond-shaped brown eyes. Little dimples appeared on his cheeks when he smiled at everyone.

Some of the girls moved forward, wanting to be the first to greet him, his handsome looks and pleasant demeanour instantly noted. Evie watched as Matthew responded politely to all the attention, while she waited with Grace until the throng of introductions was over. Then they went to say hello.

'Matthew, this is Evelyn Wells, our very talented flautist,' Mr Reid said proudly. Then he turned to Evie. 'Evie, this is my son, Matthew.'

Evie and Matthew shook hands. Evie tried to speak normally but found herself stuttering over a simple hello. What was wrong with her? Her heart was fluttering and her cheeks and hands were very warm. She wasn't actually blushing, was she?

'It's very nice to meet you, Evie,' Matthew said in a rich baritone voice. 'I look forward to hearing you play. My father praises you highly and often. Although I have been practising at school, I hope I don't make too many mistakes on my first day with the Hartville Ensemble.'

There were lots of oohs and aahs at the mention of a name.

'You heard correctly,' Mr Reid announced. 'We are now officially the Hartville Ensemble. I was asked to come up with a name by the mayor, and there you have it. Our next rehearsal will be at the same time tomorrow – three o'clock sharp – but two o'clock on Wednesday to give you time to rest before the concert that evening. And don't worry, Matthew will be practising at home to catch up.' He smiled warmly at his son, clearly delighted to have him home. Evie knew her tutor greatly missed him when he was away, especially since Mrs Reid had died. Matthew might be home for longer soon, as he would be graduating from boarding school in just a few months' time.

'Matthew, this is Grace Finch,' Mr Reid said. 'Grace, my son, Matthew.'

Grace smiled shyly and they shook hands. 'I play the piano too,' she said, 'but I think I was really only filling in for you.'

'Oh, I doubt it!' Matthew said politely.

'Nonsense, Grace. You play very well indeed,' Mr Reid said. 'It's splendid to have you both to accompany all the soloists. We are lucky to have two excellent pianists, and soon I hope you will both play solo too.'

'Oh my!' Grace said, swallowing hard. 'I, um, thank you, Mr Reid.'

Evie knew Grace was nervous about performing due to her poor eyesight, and unfortunately their first concert would be by candlelight.

'Well, it's time we were going,' Julia said. 'Would you like me to assist again at tomorrow's rehearsal, Mr Reid?'

'I would indeed, Miss Pippen, thank you,' Mr Reid said.

'Until tomorrow then,' Julia said.

But Mr Reid needed a little more of Julia's time, and Matthew was left with Evie and Grace for a few minutes. Evie found herself smiling but not managing to say very much. Luckily Matthew had plenty to say about his journey from school, how he was looking forward to the concert and having time at home with his father. Then he suggested they might plan an outing together.

Evie found it difficult not to stare at him.

'That would be lovely, wouldn't it Evie?' Grace said, nudging her.

Evie had no idea what she was talking about. 'Yes, lovely,' she said anyway.

Matthew smiled. 'Excellent! And I won't let you down at rehearsal or at the concert, I promise. I will practise very hard.'

'See you tomorrow, then,' Evie said.

The girls went to wait for Julia, who was gathering up her music sheets.

'Matthew likes you,' Grace whispered.

'How do you know?' Evie asked.

'He couldn't stop looking at you,' Grace said.

'But he was talking to you,' Evie said. 'I couldn't think of anything to say. I must be very tired or very dull.'

'Don't you mean preoccupied?' Grace said.

Evie looked at her nervously.

'No, I'm sure,' Grace said. 'Matthew was talking to you *and* looking at you, even if you couldn't speak.' She giggled. 'He definitely likes you. Definitely.' Grace coughed politely, then muttered under her breath. 'He's looking at you again.'

Evie turned and indeed Matthew was smiling at her and she found herself smiling back.

'Um, Grace, I have something to tell you,' Evie said, recovering. 'And something to ask you. I hope you won't mind.'

As they walked outside to wait for Grace's father and Julia, Evie told her friend about Charlie's letter.

'He has her notebook and he's going to give it to you?' Grace asked, her eyes looking enormous with surprise behind her new, even thicker lenses.

Evie nodded. 'He wants to give it to me in person. He doesn't want to risk it falling into the wrong hands. I may have to show him her personal diary as proof that I really knew her.'

'That's all very sensible, but he lives near Crompton village, doesn't he?' Grace said. 'Oh! Evie, you're not suggesting ...'

'Do you think he'd mind? Would he? Very much?' Evie asked. 'It's my only chance to go back there, and only to the Crompton Arms to meet Charlie, not to Dower Hall. We could go there, I'd collect the notebook and we'd be gone. No delays. I promise.'

'I couldn't ask Samuel again,' Grace said. 'I don't think I would dare after the last time.'

'Did he get into trouble?' Evie asked.

'No, we both blamed the horse and the farrier,' Grace said.

'Thank goodness for that,' Evie said. 'Perhaps this time we could ask Matthew to come too. Samuel might like another young man to talk to. I don't think he enjoyed Freddie's antics too much.'

'You mean, two couples out for a picnic?' Grace said. 'Oh, Evie, I don't think so. It wouldn't be right, and we've only just met Matthew. You can't use people like that.'

'I'm not using people!' Evie cried indignantly. Then she lowered her voice. 'I'm trying to do what's right for Lucia. I can't explain it right now.'

'I'm afraid it would be using people, Evie,' Grace said softly but pointedly. 'How can I understand what you mean when you say "what's right" if you won't tell me what this is really about? Look, there's my father. Think about it. I'll see you tomorrow at rehearsal.'

With that final remark, Grace walked over to her father's carriage. She looked a little glum, gazing out the window as they drove away.

Lying in bed, Evie expected to have another bad night. First, she had had a row with Julia that was mending only slowly, and now she had had her first row with Grace. Evie hated rows; they made her feel so uncomfortable, so not herself. She wanted to mend relations with both of them, but that would mean telling Julia how urgent things were now that Evie had found Nala's head, and that would only stress her governess even more. After a couple of hours of turmoil, Evie had made up her mind. She needed more support, and she didn't want to lose her closest friendships by lying or pretending. She was going to tell Grace the whole story.

But Julia counselled her strongly against such a move when Evie announced her intention the next morning.

'I think it will harm your friendship rather than save it, and it could put Grace in real danger,' Julia said. 'She is such a kind, sweet girl, she will want to help you. But she will worry and fret, just like I am. The more people who know your secret, the sooner someone will let it slip, even if they don't mean to.'

'We're trusting Freddie and he's only ten,' Evie reminded her. 'I feel I must explain myself to Grace. She must think I'm behaving very badly, and I don't want to lose her as a friend.'

'First of all, Freddie is an extraordinary boy who has had the most unusual start in life. It's a wonder he is normal at all,' Julia said, a little tetchily. 'But he was in on this from the start through no fault of his own, and we can't undo that. I agree you must be careful not to lose Grace as a friend, but that's not a reason to involve her in your secret life. Please reconsider, Evie. I really don't know what else I can say to convince you.'

Julia left the room, cutting their lesson short yet again. Evie sat for a long time with only her tangled thoughts and emotions for company, as she tried to figure out the right thing to do.

Chapter Fifteen

The first concert by the Hartville Ensemble would take place in their local town hall. The final rehearsal early on Wednesday afternoon went very well and everyone felt ready. Matthew was totally relaxed and played without the slightest hitch despite joining the group so late. Grace had a little wobble early on but recovered, and played very well after that. Evie breezed through two Mozart pieces, music she knew well and loved. With her nervousness now a thing of the past, she hoped she could help Grace overcome her jitters too.

'You were flawless, Evie,' Matthew said.

'Thank you. I love Mozart,' Evie said modestly.

'How are you finding your new spectacles, Grace?' Matthew asked. 'I thought you played very well today.'

'Thank you,' Grace said. 'They are an improvement, but I still find it difficult to play by candlelight. I hope the hall will be well lit this evening.'

'It's wonderful the town hall has electricity now,' Matthew said. 'Though I hear it can be a bit unpredictable at night. These high ceilings create a wonderful sound.' He gazed up at the wooden beams in the vaulted ceiling.

'We'll be using gas lamps as well as the electric light,'

Evie said. 'It was Julia's idea, just in case the electricity fails, and the electric lights aren't always that bright as the evening wears on. A few candelabras will be placed on the stage too, but mostly to look pretty.'

'Oh dear,' Grace said. 'Candles and gas lamps. They throw such awkward shadows over the music sheets.'

'Don't worry,' Evie said. 'You have such a good memory, you could play everything by heart.'

'Really?' Matthew said. 'Good for you, Grace. Problem solved!'

There was a tapping sound, Mr Reid had an announcement. The ensemble hushed their chattering and everyone turned towards their instructor.

'We meet here at seven o'clock for a light warm-up,' Mr Reid said. 'You all have the order of play, so each musician must be ready to play when called. Good luck everyone and I'll see you all on time please.'

Everyone arrived before seven, keen to tune their instruments. It was a cool, calm spring evening. All the townspeople filed in through the heavy, oak double doors, chattering merrily once the town hall opened shortly after seven-thirty. Everyone was eager to attend the concert by local students, the first in such a long time. Evie felt a flutter of excitement, peeping around the dark-green velvet stage curtain to see her parents among the throng. They were thrilled that Evie would be opening the concert with two pieces from Mozart's Flute Concerto.

After Mr Reid's introduction, Evie and Grace walked on stage to warm applause. Evie smiled at the audience as she walked to the front and centre of the stage, while Grace seated herself at the upright piano over to one side. Taking a few slow, even breaths, Evie turned to Grace and nodded. She raised the flute to her lips and began.

Evie excelled, the notes flowing smoothly from her flute, filling the hall with the most beautiful sound. Grace didn't falter in her accompaniment either, and the audience was enthralled. Evie beamed with delight, bowing low at the hearty applause before being escorted off stage by Mr Reid. Grace remained at the piano to accompany the next performer, a cellist.

'That was absolutely splendid,' Mr Reid whispered excitedly.

'Congratulations, Evie,' Matthew said, standing in the wings. 'Absolutely magical.'

'Thank you,' Evie said, blushing again, much to her annoyance. She stood beside Matthew to listen to the other performers. He would replace Grace as the accompanist halfway through the first hour, and again halfway through the second hour. There would be a short break in the middle of the concert for about twenty minutes when everyone could take some refreshment.

The second half of the concert was going just as well as the first. Evie was enjoying the violinist, who was finishing her piece with a great flourish, when Mr Reid tapped her on the shoulder. 'Evie, the young lad who plays the xylophone isn't feeling well,' he whispered. 'I think his nerves have overwhelmed him. Perhaps I expected too much from an eleven-year-old. Would you mind taking his place and playing again?'

'Of course, Mr Reid,' Evie said, a little surprised. 'What would you like me to play?'

'How about the Handel sonata we worked on a little while

ago?' he said. 'Would you know it well enough? I know Matthew knows it. It was one of his mother's favourites.'

'Matthew?' Evie murmured. 'Um, yes, I know the sonata quite well, I think.'

'Excellent!' Mr Reid said. 'You're on next.'

Evie felt a tiny tingle of nerves. She had to push them aside or she would make a right mess of Handel. She had never been accompanied by anyone but her music teachers and Julia, and more recently Grace. She didn't want to make a fool of herself in front of Matthew – and the whole town. He wouldn't be expecting this change to the order of play either. But it was too late to worry about it.

Evie watched from the wings as Matthew took a bow with the second violinist of the evening and escorted her off stage.

'Evie, Father, what is it?' Matthew said, as soon as he reached them. He was looking from one to the other.

'Matthew, I want you to go back on with Evie,' his father said. 'That young boy, Rupert, isn't it? He's not feeling well. Evie is going to fill in with the Handel sonata. You know, the one your mother loved.'

'Of course, delighted,' Matthew said. He turned to Evie. 'Are you happy to play it, Evie? You can't have rehearsed Handel as much as the Mozart pieces.'

'I think I'll manage it, with your help,' Evie said.

'You can trust me,' Matthew said. 'I'll follow your lead, and we'll just go with the music. You know how.'

Evie nodded and smiled, and they walked on stage together.

The concert was a resounding success, the town's people amazed by all the talent in their midst. Everyone was clamouring for another performance, as they chatted with the ensemble over refreshments afterwards.

'We would be delighted to return,' Mr Reid said to the well-wishers surging around him. 'And as soon as possible. But we have more engagements coming up. Miss Pippen has received some invitations, I believe.'

'Why, yes,' Julia said, turning to the gathering. 'I can now announce that our next performance will be in Millbury parish hall on Easter Saturday. I'm sure you all know Millbury, the town beside the village of Crompton. They are looking forward to hearing us play, and you are all very welcome to join us there at three o'clock sharp, this Saturday afternoon.'

'Notices of additional concerts will be posted on the noticeboard here in the town hall in the coming weeks,' Mr Reid added, beaming from ear to ear.

Everyone clapped.

Evie sidled up to her governess as soon as the crowds thinned out. 'Thank you, Julia,' she said. 'I don't know Millbury, but you said it's near Crompton – the village near Dower Hall?'

'The very same, and it wasn't difficult to arrange,' Julia said. 'I spoke to Mr Reid as I promised. He readily agreed to my checking out more venues – he hates the organisation side of things. So I wrote to a number of town clerks. Millbury's clerk was the first to reply and said the town would love to host a musical event. I received his letter only this morning.'

'What a stroke of luck!' Evie said, thinking of her reply to Charlie. She must write immediately, telling him she would be nearby and soon.

'Yes, let's hope so,' Julia muttered to herself.

CHAPTER SIXTEEN

E vie began plotting her next move as she strummed absent-mindedly on the harp. I perform first, she thought. Once I'm finished my pieces, I'll sneak out while the others are performing. I'll borrow a carriage and drive over to Dower Hall by myself. How hard can it be? I drove a cart once before. It should be much the same. And it's so close I won't even be away long. No one will miss me and no one needs to know. I should have time to meet Charlie too.

Evie was excited by her plan. She was so determined to find the Black Ruby she dismissed any thought of the risk she was taking. The concert would take two hours, she mused, continuing her train of thought, not including the short interval, but enough time to get to Dower Hall, see Charlie and be back before the encore.

Ideally she would borrow her parents' carriage, otherwise it might feel uncomfortably like stealing. If that wasn't possible because of stabling arrangements she would borrow Samuel's. Grace had confirmed he would be coming to their next concert. He was keen to hear her perform as an accompanist, a role she would be sharing again with Matthew. Evie smiled momentarily, thinking how Samuel must surely be sweet on Grace.

After going over her plan a few more times, Evie had to admit it was reckless but she convinced herself that she could pull it off and that it was worth it. Despite her defiant mood, Evie struggled to keep certain facts from invading her positive thoughts. Facts such as a forest of tall attacking trees, and that she had actually crashed a cart and never driven a proper carriage at all. But her determination did not fade. After all, danger was no reason to quit.

The Hartville Ensemble's second concert was arranged for the afternoon, making it a less formal event than an evening performance. Evie made sure to wear sensible shoes and a comfortable skirt rather than her best one, which she would normally prefer to wear for a concert. Knowing she would have to mount and dismount from the driver's seat of a carriage, she decided to wear her most flexible clothing. She bemoaned the fact that she could not wear trousers. Men and boys have it so much easier with clothes, she thought.

Evie's parents accompanied her to the concert, but Julia was in bed with another bad cold and wheezy cough. No wonder Julia had been so cross lately, Evie thought, she must have been feeling unwell. At least Evie hoped that was the reason. She made a mental note to wish for better health for her governess at the April full moon the following week, hoping there wouldn't be any more emergencies to change her intention. After that, she would definitely make a wish for Grace.

Everything went according to plan at first. The town hall in Millbury was more like a school hall, not nearly as spacious as the one in Hartville. And although a smaller town too, the narrow hall was packed with smiling concertgoers. Evie opened the concert and played very well, accompanied by Matthew this time. Mr Reid had rearranged the order of some performances, and Matthew would remain on stage for a full hour until the interval, when Grace would take his place as the accompanist for the entire second half. An excellent pianist, Matthew was quick to understand how Evie liked to play her pieces, helping her to relax into the music and show off her talent. Mr Reid couldn't have been happier.

Evie took her bows, enjoying the warm applause, then Matthew escorted her off stage. In the wings, he gave her a little mock bow, whispering, 'Well done, Evie! You really were marvellous! We'll talk later.' He grinned broadly, then returned to the stage with the next soloist, a trumpeter, leaving Evie momentarily delighted with herself. The loud and dramatic opening to the next piece of music brought her quickly back to her senses and her task. Slipping back stage to the cloakroom, she quickly donned her overcoat and hurried around to the stables.

There, Evie encountered her first problem: her parents' carriage was blocked in, and she couldn't spot Samuel's at all. The stable boy had made a mess of guiding the guests and their carriages into sensible rows. She looked around; there was no one about, no sign of the stable boy. He must have gone on a break while the concert was on. Perhaps it was just as well, now that she had to change her plan. Emboldened by her mission and with a rising sense of urgency, Evie mounted the nearest small carriage, took the reins, turned the horses and headed off down the road.

With a brisk wind in her hair and the sun on her face,

Evie felt exhilarated as the horses trotted obediently along, taking her back to Dower Hall. She slowed the carriage as they approached the towering, rusty gates, turning carefully under the stone arch and onto the long driveway. She marvelled at how the scariest parts of being a Harp Maiden seemed to disturb her less than some of the nuisances of daily life, like what to wear to the concert, and how not to embarrass herself in front of Matthew. Protecting the harp, searching for the Black Ruby, and even facing up to demons had become almost normal. How her life had changed in just a few short months!

Evie steered the horses towards the old stable block. She jumped down from the driver's seat and secured the horses, glad to see them start munching on some hay. Leaving them content, she began her search for the ruby.

Minutes ticked by as she carefully checked through rubble and debris, working through imaginary squares to try to put some order on her search. She stopped for a moment, stretching her stiff back. Gazing around, she groaned. It would take incredible luck and hours and hours of searching to find anything in all that mess. She thought of Olga. What was she doing in that cave all these months? Evie's curiosity fired in her brain. Olga might have found the ruby in the last day or two. She simply had to check that cave again to be sure. Evie convinced herself she would have time, but only if she were very quick. Without further hesitation, Evie abandoned her search of the rubble and headed off in the direction of the gorge.

Following the same trail as before, Evie had almost reached the spot when she got such a shock that for a few perilous seconds she forgot to try to hide. She stood staring. Somewhere nearby a raven cawed, startling Evie, and she ducked into the long grass. Still crouching, she moved slowly and steadily towards a few large rocks. Trying to control her breath as her heart thumped wildly, she dared to look. A big, hulking man in a dirty, ill-fitting overcoat was stomping towards Olga's cave. Could it be? Evie's eyes followed the man closely until she could no longer see him. Then she went after him.

Nearing the mouth of the cave, Evie could just make out three voices inside, one male and two females. She needed to get closer to hear what was being said. Slipping inside, but staying hidden by the rocks and boulders, she approached warily.

Olga was there, and so was the casket, the two little doors open. The large male in the dirty overcoat had his back to her. He was speaking a language Evie didn't recognise and Olga was replying with ease. Demon language, Evie thought. The other voice, a woman's, didn't speak much but when it did, it spoke in English but with an accent. It was the same voice Evie had heard before. Her eyes scanned the cave for anyone else. The thought that a voice was coming from a casket was both startling and intriguing.

The male stood up and tossed off his coat. He was very tall and muscular, his shirt pulled so tightly across his back and shoulders it had ripped in several places. His head was high and broad, his dark hair dirty and wild. When he turned and moved nearer to the casket, Evie knew for sure. It was Volok. How powerful he must be, she thought, to have regenerated so far after that botched ritual. He looked different, a little less green, but more whole, more fearsome.

Olga handed him a drink. Evie caught the scent of one of Olga's herbal brews. Volok took the bowl and slurped noisily, handing back the empty bowl without a glance or thanks. He bent down to the small, decorated casket and slapped the doors shut. Evie ducked out of sight just before Volok stood, turned and began moving around the cave unpredictably. He was agitated.

'How could you bargain with that foul head?' he roared.

'For you, my lord, everything I do is for you,' Olga said. 'How can you be angry with me after I have done so much? I promised the sorceress I would leave King Udil's descendants alone, but only so she would tell me how to re-awaken you. Yes, it was a bargain, and it took a long, long time, but it worked. It was the start of your recovery and your return.'

'I don't like doing anyone a favour,' Volok said.

'The favour was greater for you, my lord,' Olga said. 'And there was no other way to free you from your prison inside the harp's wooden frame. I had to do something. I was desperate.'

'You could have lied,' Volok roared, turning to Olga, his back to Evie again. 'You could have promised her anything to ensure my release, and then killed King Udil's people anyway!'

'That is long in the past, my lord,' Olga said, wearily. 'You know I must keep my promises. It is my tribal oath.'

'It is your tribe's weakness, and not your only one,' Volok roared back at her.

Olga looked deeply offended but continued to plead. 'I have never broken a promise to you, my lord, never. I never could.'

'Yet despite your promise, I still don't have the Black Ruby,' Volok said.

'I had it in my hands!' Olga cried. 'I told you!'

'But you don't have it now, do you?' Volok said. 'And more importantly, NEITHER DO I!'

Time was pressing and Evie sensed there was about to be a full-blown row. She had to leave, but how? Olga was following Volok as he moved around the cave. One sudden glance from either of them and Evie would be discovered. She remembered that demons have a powerful sense of smell and worried that they might pick up her scent. Even the horses' scent from her clothing might reach their nostrils and arouse their suspicion.

Evie closed her eyes for a second, trying to work out how long she had been there, and how late she would be getting back – if she got back. Then she heard a little creak and that voice again. Lowering herself to the ground as far as she could, she dared to peep around the side of the boulder this time. Volok stared angrily at the casket as Olga opened the doors wide. Evie could just make out the profile of the head inside.

'If you do not tell me what I want to know, this is what I will do,' Volok said, lowering his head to the casket. 'I will find and destroy your magical harp, your precious legacy, and each and every person who protects it and the Harp Maiden. I will hunt down and kill your entire tribe. And finally, I will ensure that you remain rotting slowly in that casket for all eternity with no hope and no relief.'

Evie needed both hands to stifle a scream. She struggled to control her breathing as it came in dry gulps, prone to making noise. Taking her hands slowly from her mouth she clenched them instead into tight fists, concentrating hard on staying calm and thinking clearly.

'I know who the Harp Maiden is,' Volok said. 'We found her. She calls herself Evie. She is young, naïve and weak. It will be easy to persuade her to play for me and release the rest of your magic for my own ends. But that will come later. First, I will find the Black Ruby and I will use its power as was always intended – the resurrection of a demon. Second, you will tell me its other secrets so I may make my wife supreme. Third, you will never be released from your tiny prison, Nala. But your tribe need not suffer if you cooperate with me. I know your ancient magic. Enchantments were your specialty, so you must have enchanted the ruby to respond to a call, a signal of some kind. I believe another enchantment will release the ruby's other powers. Now, sorceress, tell me what I want to know.'

Then the voice from the casket spoke. 'I am Nala, sorceress to the King of Yodor. The Black Ruby is as old as time, a powerful, ancient talisman. But it never belonged to me, and therefore it was never mine to enchant. I cannot call it, no more than you can.'

'You dare to defy me!' Volok roared. 'You are not in a position of strength anymore, Nala, sorceress of *nowhere*. I know your king banished you before he died. Your people shunned you. You are completely alone. You have been for centuries.'

'King Udil did not understand what I told him,' Nala said. 'He was bewitched by the ruby and consumed by his own hunger for power. You cannot harm me any more than you already have, so I would not help you or your servant again, even if I could. The Black Ruby is not controllable, that is why it is so dangerous. It is an unstable jewel, a cursed talisman.'

Volok snorted with anger, but the voice in the casket continued.

'As for the harp, you are too late,' the voice said. 'No matter what you think of her, the Harp Maiden now commands the harp's magic. It will *never* be yours, just as it is no longer mine. And there is no guarantee you will find the ruby. You have failed on all counts.'

'Enough!' Volok roared.

He picked up the casket and was about to fling it against the wall when Olga leapt up and took it from him. She put it down out of his immediate reach.

'We must not break it, my lord,' she said. 'Nala could still be of use to us.'

At that, Volok let out a terrible roar and walloped Olga on the cheek, knocking her several feet back. The veins in his neck bulged as his fury rose.

'The Black Ruby is my last hope,' he said. 'My other talismans will be useful once my wife is restored, but only the ruby can bring her back to life. I have already begun the long and tortuous ritual. I need that ruby NOW! That ugly sorceress must tell me how to find it!' Volok began sweating profusely, stomping his feet, clenching and unclenching his fists. His eyes blazed with rage as he turned to Olga again.

'You must find the ruby,' he said, pointing a large finger at the ogress. 'I will use every power I possess, every talisman I own, and every last drop of darkest magic to restore my wife to her former glory. We will rule this world together, just as we ruled all the other worlds, side by side until we grew tired of them. We will find a way to become immortal and reign together forever! But first – you must find that ruby!'

Volok stormed off to the back of the cave. Olga slumped onto a boulder, rocking back and forth, her cheek swelling black and green.

Evie had to speak to Nala. She had so many questions, but it was more than that. As Harp Maiden, she felt it was her duty to free the harp's maker from her prison. But how? If only Nala's head was inside the casket, where was the rest of her body? Evie shuddered at the thought and wondered if Nala could be put back together again or not.

Luckily, Evie didn't have long to wait until the coast became clear. Volok roared for Olga to join him at the back of the cave, giving Evie the chance to creep away. Her thoughts were whirling as she hurried back to the carriage and Millbury parish hall.

CHAPTER SEVENTEEN

Knowing she had been away much longer than planned, Evie didn't spare the horses on the way back. Forced to slow down as she entered the little town with its narrow, bustling main street, she headed impatiently towards the parish hall and the crowded stable yard beside it. At the easier pace, she realised just how sore her arms were. Her muscles had been working hard to control the horses at speed, and her hands looked red and sore from holding the reins so tightly.

She directed the carriage towards the spot where she had found it, pulled the horses to a halt, put on the wheel brake and jumped down from the driver's seat. She was in such a hurry, she tripped off the carriage step, and tumbled on to a pile of straw. Her fall unsettled one of the horses who began to whicker and stomp. She stood up and brushed herself down, but the horse remained jittery. If she didn't calm it quickly, it would surely draw attention. Steam was rising off both animals after the fast ride. Evie knew they needed water but she couldn't see a bucket nor a tap, and she had to get back inside. To add to her fluster, a door groaned; someone was coming out of the stable block.

Evie's brain rummaged for an excuse to explain what she

was doing there. She sighed loudly with relief on seeing a face she recognised.

'There, there, easy boy,' Charlie said, coming over and soothing the horse with an experienced hand. 'We should go,' he said, looking over his shoulder. 'The stable boy is out back but he'll have heard the horses. Follow me.'

They left the stable and walked around to the side of the parish hall. Hearing the applause inside, Evie knew the trombonist had just finished his solo performance. The encore would be next.

Evie was relieved to see Charlie even though he had caught her returning someone else's carriage. She was about to open their conversation with an excuse, but Charlie raised a hand.

'No need to explain,' he said. 'It was like that with Lucia too. I learned not to question. You have that same look about you that she did, a look that tells me what you do is for a greater cause than what normal folk do. Well, so be it.'

'Thank you,' Evie said softly.

'I saw the notice about the concert and came to hear you play,' Charlie said. 'As my note said, I also came to give you this. Save you the trouble of travelling to Crompton.'

'It will save me time and a lot of explaining,' Evie said. 'Thank you. It was thoughtful of you. I wasn't able to bring Lucia's diary to show you proof that I knew her. It was too big to fit in my skirt pocket and I didn't know how I would explain why I was bringing it to a concert.'

'No matter,' Charlie said. 'I gave it some thought and I'm happy this is the right thing to do. You're an excellent musician, Miss Evie, just like Lucia was. And that young lad with you in the inn, what he said convinced me that you really were Lucia's friends.'

'We were, and thank you, Charlie,' Evie whispered, relieved.

'I noticed you were missing from the stage, and thought to check outside,' Charlie said. 'Best to give this to you now before there are lots of people about.'

Evie looked down at Charlie's hand. He was holding a well-worn old notebook. Though small and neat, it had a leather cover and was tied with two thin, leather straps, each secured with a tarnished silver buckle. It looked like a miniature of Evie's satchel, and it was crammed with yellowed pages.

'The notebook,' Evie whispered. 'I'm so very grateful.'

'Lucia told me it must never fall into the wrong hands,' Charlie said. 'She said it belongs with that harp and should only be read by whoever plays it. You have that harp, don't you, Evie, the same one Lucia used to play? Though you didn't play it this afternoon.'

'Yes, I have the harp,' Evie said. 'I only play the flute at concerts.'

'And you play it so beautifully,' Charlie said. 'But that harp is special. Even I can see there's somethin' different about it, and not just its size.' He looked deep into Evie's eyes. 'Don't you worry, I can keep a secret, not that I'm entirely sure what the secret is. I'm giving you this notebook simply because Lucia asked me to.'

'She *asked* you to?' Evie said.

'She asked me to keep it safe and pass it on to the next Harp Maiden,' Charlie said, lowering his voice. 'That is you, isn't it?'

Evie stared, unsure whether to answer. Julia's words were echoing in her ears: 'How do you know you can trust him, Evie?'

'Well?' Charlie said, sounding a little impatient suddenly.

'Then you know,' Evie said. 'You know about the harp, about all of it.'

'I know a little, and I can guess some more,' Charlie said. 'But somethin' tells me I don't really want to know. I just can't think of anyone else who might be like her, except you, and I feel it's time to pass this notebook on.'

'I'm so very grateful,' Evie said.

'All right, Miss Evie,' Charlie said. 'If you need my help, you know where to find me.'

'I'll keep it safe,' Evie said. 'I promise.'

Charlie nodded, tipped his cap then quietly walked away. Evie watched him walk down the road then disappear around a bend. Nearby, cymbals crashed and trumpets blew as the ensemble finished the encore with a flourish.

Evie ran towards the stage door, stuffing the notebook into one of the deep pockets in her skirt. She was struggling to fit it in when she bumped straight into Matthew.

'Oh, hello!' Evie said.

'There you are!' Matthew said. 'You've missed the encore, we both have. I've been looking for you.'

'Oh!' Evie blurted out.

'Oh, again!' Matthew said, smiling.

'I'm sorry, I ... I ...'

Evie was still struggling to find an explanation for Matthew when her parents appeared.

'And you're sure you are feeling better, Evie?' Matthew asked, in a concerned voice.

'Oh, um, yes, thank you for your care, Matthew,' Evie said, realising he was trying to help her out. 'I'm perfectly well now.'

'What's this? Not feeling well?' Evie's father asked. 'We didn't see you on stage for the encore and wondered what had happened. Your performance was splendid, simply splendid!'

'Were you ill, Evie?' her mother asked. 'I was worried.'

'I'm perfectly fine,' Evie said.

'Evie went outside after her performance,' Matthew explained. 'I followed as soon as I was finished, to see if she was all right. I think Evie just needed a little air. The sun was shining through the windows all morning making the room very warm by the time the concert started.'

'Yes, very warm,' Evie said, blushing at her lies, hoping her parents would accept it as acute embarrassment.

'It was a big crowd in a rather small hall,' her father agreed. 'But I think everyone enjoyed it immensely. Are you sure you are fully recovered, dear?'

'Quite sure,' Evie said, attempting a smile, difficult though it was after the afternoon she had had.

Grace's father, Mr Finch, joined them, distracting Evie's parents by introducing them to some of his friends.

'Thank you, Matthew,' Evie whispered. 'Did you really follow me?'

'Twice,' Matthew said. 'First, I saw you borrow a carriage and gallop away. Impressive!'

Evie stared at him, wide-eyed and speechless.

'And just now,' Matthew continued, 'I saw a grey-haired old man hand you something rather furtively, it must be said.' He raised his eyebrows inquiringly.

'He wanted to give me a notebook,' Evie said quietly. 'It's in my pocket.' She patted the side of her skirt. 'It belonged to an old lady we both knew, a musician. She played the harp, which I am also learning. She was a special friend to me, the lady who died in the fire in Dower Hall.'

'Goodness, Evie! I am sorry. I didn't mean to pry,' Matthew said. 'Really, you don't have to explain anything private. I'm just glad you're all right. I didn't know who that man was, though he looked friendly enough, but I thought I should stay nearby. I was worried when I noticed you had left the hall. You looked very anxious, and very … determined. A woman on a mission.'

'I hope I am always determined, Matthew,' Evie said, perking up. 'Actually, Grace, Samuel and I had met that man before. His name is Charlie McGinn. We met when we stopped in Crompton to get one of the horse's shoes repaired. It was last weekend when we were out for a picnic. Charlie wanted me to have the notebook because I already have the lady's diary. She gave it to me before she died.'

'I see, quite a story,' Matthew said.

'I'm not sure my parents would understand, Matthew, so please keep this between us,' Evie said. 'I don't want to alarm them.'

'Alarm?' Matthew said. 'I hope there is no reason for alarm.'

'Oh, no, none at all,' Evie said. Then she remembered the demons and blushed again. 'But you know what parents are like.'

'Indeed I do,' Matthew said. 'My father has told me about some odd acquaintances he's had over the years. Musicians can be a strange lot, can't they?'

'I suppose so, sometimes,' Evie said, a little surprised.

Grace and Samuel joined them, then Mr Reid came over too. He was very animated.

'Well done, everyone!' he said. 'You'll be delighted to hear we have been invited to perform at Branston, just down the road from here.'

'That's great news,' Matthew said. 'When? I hope it's soon.'

'Next Saturday, 21 April,' Mr Reid said. 'Isn't that marvellous? News is spreading fast! Well done, everyone. Well done!' He moved off, shaking hands with more well-wishers.

'Will you still be here, Matthew?' Evie asked.

'Yes,' Matthew said. 'I was due to go back to boarding school that weekend but Father has arranged with the school principal that I can take an extra week off to help him with a particular project.'

'Then I assume you'll be performing with us again,' Evie said.

'I hope so,' Matthew said.

'I wonder how many more concerts there will be,' Grace said. 'It is rather fun, visiting different places like this.'

'The Hartville Ensemble will be famous yet,' Samuel said.

Evie was already thinking of how to organise another visit to Dower Hall, only this time from Branston. She'd never manage to borrow a carriage a second time, would she? Suddenly, Evie was aware that everyone was looking at her.

'Are you sure you're all right, Evie?' Matthew asked.

'Yes, I was just thinking,' Evie said. 'Why don't the four of us go for a walk after the concert next week, or the day after? I know just the place, quiet, out in the countryside and not far from here or from Branston.'

'Let me guess,' Samuel said. 'Dower Hall?'

'Why not?' Evie said, hoping her idea wouldn't be shot down. 'It would be nice to show Matthew what we've been talking so much about.'

'Sounds great,' Matthew said. 'I have to admit, I am rather curious to see the place.'

'I'm afraid I'm on duty next weekend,' Samuel said. 'How about the following weekend? You'll still be here, won't you Matthew?'

'I will, because of the extra week at home, but it will depend on what time my train leaves,' Matthew said. 'I'll see if I can borrow our carriage.'

'That would be most helpful,' Samuel said.

'Would that suit you, Evie?' Matthew asked.

'Um, yes, of course,' Evie said. 'Whatever suits everyone.'

Evie was momentarily frustrated: she really needed to go to Dower Hall much sooner. There was no guarantee she would be able to sneak away during the next performance. Waiting another week was bad enough; waiting two weeks was out of the question.

'It's settled then,' Matthew said. 'I'm looking forward to it.'

While Samuel explained to Matthew all about his first visit to Dower Hall back in January, Evie wasn't sure what Grace was thinking. The look on her friend's face wasn't one of absolute joy, that was certain. This will be another favour I owe her, Evie thought, and all the more reason I must confide in her soon. Evie hoped she hadn't missed the chance to bring her friend in on her secret, if she were to keep her as a friend at all. She was also deliberately misleading Samuel now, and Matthew too. She felt stung by the thought that perhaps she really was using people, just like Grace had said.

CHAPTER EIGHTEEN

While Julia remained in bed feeling poorly, Evie and Freddie were catching up on their studies together. Freddie decided that meant he could read any number of books, all of which he loved, while Evie remained preoccupied with her thoughts and her diaries. She now had three: Lucia's diary which she had found in Drake's overcoat pocket, recounting the old lady's time as a Harp Maiden; the notebook Charlie had given her that 'belonged with the harp', and a new diary she had begun in January that year, telling her own story. All three were kept locked in the bottom drawer of her dressing table.

Evie liked to write often in her personal diary, adding information, including anything of interest from the books in her father's study, as well as her recent discoveries, new experiences, thoughts and concerns. Writing down her worries helped to unclutter her mind and soothed her. She wondered how many diaries she would fill in her time as Harp Maiden – in her whole lifetime.

Early one morning, Evie was in her bedroom writing furiously. Her mind was spinning with the many complicated questions that arose from her visit to Olga's cave, as she now called it. Rescuing a head from a casket was a peculiar mission. It was certainly a crime to sever someone's head, but there was no way she could go to the police. They wouldn't believe her story and probably dismiss her as a child having some sort of hallucination. But if the head was talking, was the person really dead? And where was the rest of the body?

Pausing from her writing, Evie let out a long, frustrated groan. Julia and Freddie will believe me, she thought, when I eventually tell them about the casket. Julia will caution me vigorously again, but Freddie would willingly follow me into a fire! She wondered then if anyone else would believe such an incredible tale. Would Grace? Would Matthew?

Evie closed her diary and went over to her dressing table. Taking the tiny key from a chain around her neck, she unlocked the bottom drawer and took out the notebook Charlie had given her. It was unremarkable yet alluring, like everything to do with the harp. She hadn't had a chance to examine it properly yet; her parents had been fussing after the concert, and with Julia unwell again, Tilly and Evie's mother were coming and going to their two bedrooms like never before. Evie had forced herself to resist looking at it properly until it was quieter.

With nervous excitement, Evie unbuckled the leather straps that held the cover around the thick pad of old pages. Then she jumped at a knock on her door.

'Evie, are you in there?' her father called.

Evie stuffed the notebook back into the drawer, banging it shut in her hurry. Her father put his head around the door.

'Am I disturbing you?' he asked.

'No, ahem. No,' Evie mumbled. 'I was just … tidying some things, away, in the drawers.'

'Your mother is still worrying about you missing the encore, and now she has me worrying too,' her father said. 'Are you sure everything is all right?'

'Everything is fine. Please don't worry.'

'Hmm, all right, then.' He paused, studying her over his spectacles. 'You would tell me if something was troubling you, wouldn't you, dear?'

'Of course.'

'Good. I'd prefer if you came to me rather than your mother,' her father said. 'She tends to worry excessively about everything. But you can tell me anything, Evie, anything at all. I have seen and heard so many strange things in my colourful career that nothing could possibly surprise me.' He smiled warmly.

'Really,' Evie said, 'everything is just fine.'

'Very well. I'll leave you to your … tidying.'

Evie was reaching for the bottom drawer when her father popped his head around the door again.

'Matthew Reid is a very nice young man,' he said. 'Clearly musical talent runs in his family. You have a lot in common, you and Matthew, and it was thoughtful of him to look out for you.'

Evie smiled, cursing herself for the hot flush on her cheeks. What was wrong with her lately? Her father winked at her and closed the door softly behind him.

After she heard her father descend the stairs, Evie bent down to the bottom drawer and took out the notebook again. She sat down on her favourite chair and looked at it. The old brown leather was very wrinkled but surprisingly soft. Evie gently ran her fingers over the creases, then ran a fingertip along the sweeping silver letters, *HM*. The leather was unusually warm to the touch, yet the lettering cool, the silver ink unblemished despite the notebook's obvious age. She lifted it up and smelled it – a faint musky scent, a slight sweetness too. As she stared at the cover, she knew she was about to delve into an ancient, magical place.

Then she stopped. Her excitement was mixed with a nagging concern. Why hadn't Lucia mentioned it? Could this notebook be a fake or some sort of trap like Julia had suggested? Surely Charlie was being truthful. He seemed to be. And he knew things. He had been trusted with the notebook – or had he stolen it?

Thoughts bounced back and forth in her head, confusing and annoying her. Evie scowled. Was she really so foolish and naïve? Even Volok had described her so. And Julia was smart and very observant. Her brain agreed with Julia's logic, but her heart was leaning the other way: trusting Charlie, needing to. It was like that a lot lately – she felt one thing but thought another. The more she discovered, the more her feelings conflicted with her thoughts. I really am stuck in a web, she thought, a tangled web of secrets, lies and so many things I can't be sure of yet! And why had her father winked at her? He suspected something. She saw it in his face, but what? He didn't seem cross, nor overly concerned, not really. And the way he mentioned Matthew. Suddenly, Evie burst into a giggle, releasing some tension. Then she felt cross. 'Oh, for goodness' sake! Concentrate, Evie, concentrate!' She looked again at the cover. The notebook was incredibly old; how had it held together? It must have gone through generations of people, she thought. Who were all those Harp Maidens?

'Every Harp Maiden must have looked after you so carefully, and I will too. I promise,' she whispered to the notebook. Slowly, respectfully, and with bated breath and a quickening heartbeat, Evie opened it.

To her surprise, Evie immediately recognised the handwriting. 'Nala,' she whispered. She had found a letter from Nala in Thorn's study in Dower Hall, and now here was another letter.

Dearest Harp Maiden,

With luck, you will have met your predecessor and she will have passed on her personal diary to you. It will tell you the kind of life you must lead and the challenges you may face as Harp Maiden. You should keep a diary too, as it may help future Harp Maidens on their journey. If you are reading this letter, then you have taken possession of my notebook. Keep it safe, secure, and bequeath it to someone you would trust with your life, to pass on after your time is done.

That's why Lucia never mentioned it, Evie thought. It's another secret, only to be passed on to the next Harp Maiden *after* death. She read on:

My advice, secrets and instructions are hidden by magic, revealed only by playing a piece of music on the harp. Each piece is a magical, musical charm. If you succeed, the page will reveal its words, one secret at a time, each tied to its own unique musical charm. As you advance, you will be allowed to choose your own music. By then, you will have been endowed with your first inklings of magic, barely noticeable but very real.

On the first step on the Ladder of Charms, you will have one chance to play the charm perfectly on the harp, or you must wait until after the next full moon to try again. Be careful. Time is precious. Do not waste it. These secrets are meant only for a Harp Maiden — for you. The harp has chosen you for reasons that may never be revealed, but the harp always knows best. Trust it.

There are six steps on the Ladder, and within each step are several charms. The completion of every charm on every step will bring you closer to the harp's most powerful magic. The taking of vows is a choice I hope you will make, one that will deepen your commitment to your role and to magic. You alone must decide whether to begin this journey, as the benefits of magic often come at a price.

There is no going back once you go down this path. The complete Ladder of Charms is not for everyone, so consider carefully before you begin each new step. Good luck Harp Maiden, and may the magic go with you.

Nala of Yodor, First Harp Maiden

With her heart thumping wildly in her chest, Evie looked at the music on the next page and immediately began to hum the tune. It was short, with Middle Eastern or African nuances — she couldn't quite place it. She turned more pages but they were all blank. Of course, she thought, only one piece of music is revealed at a time. How clever! Every step, and each part of every step, must be passed in strict order. Suddenly, Evie was struck by the power of this ancient magic, and excited by the charms. She decided to begin the first one straight away.

The harp was downstairs in its usual place, on a small table in the bay window in the parlour. She would bring it to her bedroom after dinner, practise the tune on the flute till it was perfect, then play it on the harp. The piece was short, so hopefully it wouldn't take long to master it. She turned over the rest of the pages to check again – all empty. 'The words will be revealed if I can unlock the secrets with magical charms,' Evie whispered to herself. 'Unbelievable, yet here it is in my hands.'

Evie knew she couldn't resist the temptation of reaching 'the top of the Ladder of Charms', whatever it would mean and whatever would be revealed. She was not a quitter; she would have to finish it once she started. After locking the notebook safely away, Evie slipped the key onto the chain around her neck and tucked it inside her blouse. Walking downstairs to dinner, she felt a new energy. At last she would know more. And she would know magic too. She felt emboldened, certain, and above all, ready. Or was she?

CHAPTER NINETEEN

Evie had read Lucia's diary from cover to cover several times. Although it was useful, it was a simple account of her activities with the harp, her hopes and dreams to do the best she could. Evie marvelled at the former Harp Maiden's devotion to keep, use and protect the harp to the best of her ability and at any cost.

Lucia's plans to become a concert pianist had ended when she inherited the harp from her grandmother, a Harp Keeper. In her diary, Lucia explained more about the Keeper's role, which sounded very much like that of a protector or guardian. Charlie might be a Keeper, Evie thought. He had protected both the harp and Lucia without really knowing about its true purpose. Hadn't he? A doubt still lingered, but she brushed it aside for the moment.

'I wonder how long Lucia's grandmother was keeping the harp safe for her,' Evie muttered to herself. 'But during that time, no one was making any wishes. Well, perhaps she had her reasons. At least she was protecting it from falling into the wrong hands.'

Freddie knocked at the door, then rushed straight in.

'Freddie, I could have been dressing!' Evie cried.

'Sorry,' Freddie said, a trifle embarrassed. 'I heard you

talking and I thought it would be all right.' He plonked down on Evie's bed, disturbing the perfectly smooth quilt.

'I have a lot to think about,' Evie said. 'Sometimes talking out loud can help, though writing things down is often better.'

'Can I look at the diary again?' Freddie asked.

Evie handed it to him. She knew Freddie missed Lucia and liked to read her diary.

'I have a new piece to learn on the harp,' Evie said.

'More magical music?' Freddie asked.

'It certainly is,' Evie said.

'I knew there had to be more,' Freddie said.

'I'm going to learn it first on the flute,' Evie said, 'then I'll try it on the harp and we'll see what happens.'

Evie opened Nala's notebook and looked at the notes. They were written in a very old style, beautifully done, intricately decorated. She lifted the flute and tentatively played the first few notes, taking it slowly. She soon got the hang of it and played it without stopping. It was a soft, winding tune.

'I like it,' Freddie said. 'What will it do?'

'Each charm will unlock a secret hidden in this ancient notebook,' Evie said.

'You mean Nala's notebook?' Freddie asked. He looked at her, like it was just an ordinary question.

'How did you know that?' Evie asked, surprised.

'It looks so old, who else could it belong to?' Freddie said. 'Except maybe the demons because they live such a long time.'

'You are very clever,' Evie said. 'But please, we should be careful talking about this. It's another big secret, understood?'

'I understand,' Freddie said. 'What's this in here?'

Evie put down the flute. 'Let me see.'

Freddie was tugging at the back of Lucia's diary. 'There's a piece of paper in here. I can feel it.'

'Be careful, don't tear it,' Evie said, taking the diary from him. She looked at the inside of the back cover and saw a tightly concealed pouch, smooth and flat, with a cleverly disguised flap. It was so carefully stitched, Evie was surprised Freddie had found it at all.

'What is it?' Freddie asked.

'Another secret,' Evie said, glancing at the bedroom door. She went quickly to her dressing table and picked out one of her new hairpins. She slipped it under the flap to loosen it. There was a two-inch slit running down the crease that was barely visible. Evie slid the hairpin along the crease, then pushed it gently under the flap to feel around.

'There is something here!' she said, excited now.

'Come on, Evie, let's see,' Freddie said.

Slowly, steadily, Evie pulled out something small and square. But it wasn't paper, it was a delicate piece of folded silk. Evie opened it very carefully.

'Aww, nothing!' Freddie said.

'Nothing,' Evie said. 'So why was it hidden like this?' Then she thought of the charms and the invisible messages in Nala's notebook, and wondered.

'There has to be a reason,' Freddie insisted.

'I agree,' Evie said, turning it over gently, afraid it might dissolve in her hands. She stood up and crossed to the window and held it up to the sunlight. Still nothing.

'Try candlelight,' Freddie suggested.

'Good idea,' Evie said. She pulled the curtains, lit one of

the candles on her bedside table and held the silk in front of the flame. Slowly, a word appeared.

'Is that a name?' Freddie whispered, while Evie read and reread the word on the silk. 'And what's that other one? It's all twisted.'

Sure enough, a thread had pulled through the delicate silk, gnarling the weave. It was hard to make out the second word – and there were only two. Then Evie thought she knew what it was.

'It's too hard to make out,' she said, a lump in her throat. In that moment, she decided not to tell Freddie, and she wouldn't tell Julia either. Not yet.

'It could be a puzzle,' Freddie said. 'I love puzzles. I'm going to work it out.'

Before Evie could blink, Freddie was running down the stairs to get his puzzle book. Holding the silk close to the candle again, Evie was certain of the message. It wasn't a puzzle at all, it was crystal clear. But who had written a warning that said, 'Beware Madruga'?

CHAPTER TWENTY

Over the next few days, Evie struggled to keep a clear head. In between all the rehearsals for the next concert, she had to practise the strange charms on the flute without drawing attention to herself. The Black Ruby had to be found, and Olga and Volok were still out there – up to something. There was also the matter of Nala's head. She took a few deep breaths, just like she used to when she needed to soothe her nerves before her music lessons. When she felt calm, Evie played the first charm one last time on the flute. She played it perfectly. 'I'm ready,' she announced to herself. 'Ready for the first charm.' She left her bedroom and went downstairs to get the harp.

Evie had decided to play the first charm upstairs to avoid any interruptions. After returning to her bedroom, she placed the harp on a footstool and knelt beside it. She opened Nala's notebook on the page that she assumed would reveal the first secret. Looking at the blank page, she hoped it would be something good, something special. After placing the notebook on the floor, she turned the page back to the musical charm and began to play.

Evie finished the piece and waited for something to happen. It happened so quickly she shrieked, having forgotten to turn over the next page to where the secret would appear. Turning it in a flurry, she saw that it had almost vanished. Nala's handwriting was fading away to nothing. Did she catch it in time, all of it? Then it was gone. Evie's heart was thumping fast and loud. In her eagerness she had almost missed it. 'Stupid! Stupid!' Evie hissed through her teeth, staring at the now blank page. But she had seen it, and fortunately it wasn't a surprise, so it was easy to remember. She had been lucky.

> *1/*
> *Whatever the weather, a Harp Maiden must always prepare a wish for the ritual. However, if the moon does not appear clearly, full and bright, the magic will not be complete and the wish will not be granted.*

Well then, Evie thought, I was lucky with my first three wishes. There were clear skies and a bright full moon each time. Then it hit her. 'Oh!' she cried. 'If it's cloudy and some wishes have to wait a whole month to be granted, that may be too late. And it could be more than a month, two, even three.' She turned the page to see if anything else appeared. She watched in awe, as the next musical charm materialised, gradually forming lines, bars and notes in the same decorative hand.

Despite feeling a little flustered, Evie began practising right away.

A few minutes later there was a knock on the door.

'Come in,' Evie said.

It was Julia. She stood in the doorway but didn't enter.

'I thought I heard you playing,' she said, her voice croaky.

'Is everything all right? You don't usually play the harp up here.'

'I brought it up so I could concentrate,' Evie said. 'It's a new piece I'm trying out.'

'I thought it sounded rather strange,' Julia said.

'It is,' Evie said. 'Are you feeling any better?'

'A little,' Julia said. 'I don't know how I caught such an awful dose, and in April too. It's so annoying.'

'It will pass,' Evie said. 'Get plenty of rest. You still look pale.'

'I will,' Julia said. 'I hope you're finding time for your other studies.'

'We both are, so don't worry,' Evie said. 'Freddie is working very hard, and so am I, come to think of it.'

'I'm lucky to have two dedicated students,' Julia said.

'You know I have to rehearse for the concert as well,' Evie said.

'Of course. How are the rehearsals going?' Julia asked.

'Mr Reid is very particular, but everyone is doing fine,' Evie said. 'I think he misses your help organising everything.'

'I'm glad to hear it!' Julia said. 'I should let you continue.' Then Julia paused in the doorway. 'Evie, I know we've had some harsh words lately, but you know I will help you if I can … without giving you this cold.' She sneezed into her handkerchief. 'Oh, dear, I'd better get back to bed. Goodnight.'

'Goodnight, Julia.'

It was quite late when Evie returned the harp to the parlour. Pausing in the hall, she decided to see if she could find anything about ancient charms among her father's collection of books. She noticed a light under the study door. Her father was working late again.

Professor Wells looked up from the huge book he was reading, letting his spectacles slide down his nose and fall off into his waiting hand. 'Looking for something to read before bed?' he asked.

'Your library has always amazed me,' Evie said, looking up at all the books. 'You were such a good storyteller when I was little.'

'I hope I still am!' her father said. 'Lots of what I told you was true, or rumoured to be, though I might have exaggerated just a little bit on occasion.'

'I remember,' Evie said.

'And now?' her father asked.

'I'm curious,' Evie said.

'About what?' her father asked.

'Well, how much was true, and how much was fiction?' Evie said.

'Give me an example,' her father said.

Evie tried to choose her words carefully. 'Take the wars and the power struggles, for example. Were those fantastic characters real, based on fact, or mostly made up by historians trying to tell a good story? And things like talismans and charms, and even monsters and demons ... was any of it based on reality?'

'Oh my! What a list!' her father said. 'Every story from ancient times is based on at least a few facts. It is my job as an historian to weed out the facts from the fiction. Over the centuries, storytellers tend to add their own details to show off or to make it more interesting for their audiences, and not just for children, I might add. Where would you like to start?'

'Charms, I think,' Evie said. 'Magical charms, with music, preferably a harp or a flute.'

'I see,' her father said. 'Your favourite things.'

'Exactly,' Evie said.

'I'll bet you're hoping your two favourite instruments were endowed with magic once upon a time,' her father said. 'What a marvellous thought! Come over here.'

Evie tried not to show her surprise at his response and followed him to a particular shelf that was so high up even her father needed the ladder. He climbed up a few steps, checked a few books and brought one down.

'I think you might find this one interesting,' he said. 'It's from somewhere in ancient Egypt I think, though many historians have argued the point, and no one has been able to figure it out. Nor is it dated. It's a sort of mystery book.'

'Sounds perfect,' Evie said.

Evie's father descended the ladder and placed the book carefully on the desk. Puffs of ancient dust and a rich musky scent spurted out of its deeply yellowed pages.

'Let's dive into history, shall we?' he said.

Professor Wells adjusted his glasses and sat down in his grand leather chair. Excited, Evie pulled up a cushioned stool beside him. Her father took a magnifying glass out of a drawer in his desk and carefully opened the book.

'What are you looking for?' Evie asked.

'Evidence,' her father said, examining the title on the second page.

'Of what?'

'Its origins, and therefore its purpose,' her father said. 'I had forgotten how intriguing this book is.'

'Really?' Evie said.

'Oh yes,' her father said. 'We can try to tell a book's age by examining the paper, the ink and the binding that was used to put it together. All sorts of information can be gleaned before you even read it. But it's not an easy task, and painstakingly slow.'

He perused the book closely, concentrating. Evie knew she wouldn't be able to search for what she wanted while her father was so engrossed.

'It's late, I'll leave you to it,' Evie said. 'I can take another look tomorrow.'

'What? Oh, yes, goodnight, dear. I'll let you know if I find anything exciting!'

CHAPTER TWENTY-ONE

Evie didn't find out much from her father the next morning. In fact, he hadn't gone to bed at all, such was his interest in the book he had selected for Evie to read! He ended up going to bed for a nap just when everyone else was coming down to breakfast.

'I hope you don't mind if I study it a little longer,' he said to Evie later. 'It could be helpful to my research into those pieces that came from Dower Hall. You remember, the antiques that were in that upturned cart. The museum wanted me to report on all the items as soon as possible, and there are two that are still confounding me.'

'Not at all,' Evie said, trying not to let her disappointment show. 'Let me know when you're finished.'

'Thank you, dear,' he said. 'This is work for me – work that I love, but work all the same, and work must come before pleasure.'

While waiting for her father to finish with the book, Evie concentrated on the next musical charm, only the second of step one. The new piece was more difficult than the first but still had that ancient Eastern/African quality which she was beginning to like. Playing it on the flute reminded her of a snake charmer playing his pipe to call a snake out of its basket – something her father had mentioned seeing on his travels.

Harp Maiden

Evie mastered the second charm without too much trouble, and when the parlour was free that evening she felt confident enough to try it on the harp. This time she was ready to watch the secret appear as soon as she completed the piece. It was short.

2/

A Harp Maiden cannot wish for herself —
Her duty is to grant wishes, not receive them.

Understandable, Evie thought. Turning the page, she watched the new notes appear and she moved on to the third charm of step one. It was a little trickier than the first two but nothing Evie couldn't manage. She pressed ahead, still impatient to finish them all but happy with her progress so far.

But when Evie was in too much of a hurry, she could be reckless. She decided to risk playing the third charm before going to bed. Stumbling over a couple of notes, her heart fluttered as she cried out at the notebook, 'No! No! I'm sorry, no!' The page curled up as if lit by fire, wrinkling, curling then turning blank. Suddenly, the old notebook shut by itself with a 'whump!'

Evie nearly choked on her own breath. 'What have I done?' she croaked. Terrified she had made a monumental mistake, she gingerly opened the notebook and tried to smooth out the wrinkled page. To her horror, a new message appeared.

You have been careless! Because of your error, the
third charm cannot be completed until after the next
full moon. Respect this magic and take greater care.
Heed this warning.

Once the shock eased, Evie felt furious. She had been over-confident and her carelessness had led to a foolish mistake. Magic was not to be taken lightly. She must take better care in future, but there was nothing more to be done now. Fortunately it wasn't long until the next full moon, though after that fright it would feel like an age.

Evie took out the flute to practise for the concert. As she placed the instrument to her lips, she noticed that her hands were trembling. She was lucky her mistake – and the consequences – had not been worse.

Evie was quieter than usual at the next rehearsal, her mind full of recent revelations and the warning from Nala's notebook. The rehearsal itself brought some welcome relief from all her concerns, and Evie hoped to have time to chat to Grace and Matthew. But everyone seemed to be in a hurry that day. Matthew had to race away once rehearsals were over, his father's project keeping them both occupied, though he said he was looking forward to their day out. Evie wondered what the mysterious 'project' was all about. Grace wasn't particularly talkative either, leaving quickly as her father was waiting for her. Grace must still be cross with me, Evie thought. I'll have to do something about that soon.

Saturday, 21 April, arrived, and the Hartville Ensemble gathered outside the town hall. The concert in Branston was scheduled to begin at eleven o'clock, so it was an early start. A light lunch would take place after the concert. All the musicians would travel together in four carriages. Matthew had arranged for their driver to take himself, his father, Evie and Grace together.

'It's just like the day of the auditions, isn't it?' Grace said, standing beside Evie. Evie barely nodded, feeling a little tense. Her plan to sneak off after her solo had worked before, but something was telling her that she might not get away with it so easily again. At least her parents weren't coming this time. Her father had asked if she didn't mind – she didn't – as he was 'on to something important' in his research, and her mother thought she was coming down with Julia's cold.

'Yes, it's strange to be standing here again,' Evie said after a minute. 'Thank goodness it's a completely different occasion.'

Grace nodded.

'I hope you're not still cross with me, Grace,' Evie said quietly. 'I know you know something is going on, and I will tell you. I promise I will, but not now. It's … it's too … too strange. You believe me, don't you?'

Grace smiled and squeezed Evie's hand. 'Of course. But tell me soon, Evie. I want to help if I can.'

Evie felt so relieved, and she had made up her mind: she would tell Grace everything, perhaps this very weekend. She hoped the conversation would go well.

All the carriages arrived promptly at nine-thirty, reaching Branston just before ten-thirty. The musicians went straight to the town hall to prepare.

Everything went according to Evie's plan. She played her pieces beautifully to loud applause, then she sneaked out of the hall and ran around to the stables. There, she stopped abruptly. A stable boy was brushing down one of the horses, another was forking hay. Evie didn't like the look of them.

'I need to borrow a carriage,' she said with a confidence she didn't feel. 'It's urgent. Please, which one can I take? I won't be long, it's very important.'

The two stable boys looked at each other. One of them spoke.

'And which one would be your carriage, Miss?' he asked cheekily.

'Um, that one,' Evie said, pointing to the smallest one, parked near the way out.

The stable boy looked at his mate, who shrugged his shoulders and returned to his chores.

The first boy said, 'Maybe you have a few shillings, so we could look after your horses when you get back. They'll be sore tired after another run, and they have to take you home again too, don't they?'

'Yes, all right,' Evie said, rummaging in her pocket. She pulled out her red velvet purse, took out all the coins and handed them over.

'That should keep your secret safe,' the stable boy said, grinning roguishly. 'For now.'

Evie glared at him, climbed up onto the carriage and took the reins.

It took almost twenty minutes to reach Dower Hall. Evie left the horses and carriage at the side of the ruined manor and ran around to the back of the house. She scoured the ground. 'Where are you?' she cried after half an hour of searching. She glared around the vast area of rubble. 'If only I knew exactly where to look!' she cried, sweeping her arms wide in frustration. A sudden roar made Evie stumble then crouch to the ground, despite the lack of cover. At the second roar, she scurried over to a piece of crumbling wall, then peeped out from behind the broken blocks.

Now and again a branch rose out of the distance and disappeared with a whack. It had to be Olga, repeatedly thrashing the ground as she walked back towards the cave. Without the slightest hesitation, Evie followed.

Suddenly Olga stopped, and Evie ducked. Had the ogress heard her? Had she smelled her? Evie peered out of the long grass, trying to stay hidden, wondering what had startled such a scary demon. Olga was staring at a different part of the gorge. She looked anxious, disturbed. It was so unlike her. Evie followed with her eyes, then she saw the reason for Olga's nervousness. She was watching Volok but she didn't seem to want him to see her. Strange. Olga moved on, treading carefully to avoid detection. Evie did likewise.

It was a different path and a dangerous climb down around the edge of the gorge. Easy enough for demons, Evie, thought, as she watched Olga scramble and claw her way along on all fours, even with her big, awkward form. Evie on the other hand, had to tread with care, hoisting the hem of her skirt above her dainty boots, watching every tentative step, clinging on to small jutting rocks and thick winding vines for support as she shimmied and slid along. Looking up just in time, Evie saw Olga cautiously approach a wide slit in the rock – another cave. She hurried on.

Despite her eagerness to find out what was happening inside, Evie held back near the opening until she heard movement. With a shock, she saw Olga wasn't far from her, about twenty feet away, and the ogress was doing the same thing as Evie: watching, waiting. She's spying on Volok! Evie thought with a jolt. What could he be doing that Olga is not meant to know? The wind whipped at Evie's back, cold and sharp as it raced through the gorge and bounced off the rockface. It whistled eerily at the mouth of the cave, as if to warn of the danger within.

Then Evie heard shuffling and muffled words. Volok was speaking to someone, but his voice was strangely soft, concerned. Through the long, weedy grass that was shrouding her, Evie saw the ogress stare into the cave, a look of absolute fury on her monstrous face.

Suddenly, there was an almighty roar and Evie almost screamed herself with fright. She managed to choke it off, though Olga must have heard her even if her attention was focused elsewhere. Evie held her breath, cringing, just waiting to be discovered. Olga stood up straight and tall, but to Evie's surprise the ogress charged not at her but towards the cave. Volok emerged looking utterly hideous. The green hues on his brutish face were turning purple, his nostrils were stretched wide and began to puff, then snort. His huge hands were clenched into tight fists. They stood face to face, Volok standing aggressively, Olga screeching hysterically at him. An almighty row broke out, though Evie couldn't understand why. Then Volok grabbed the ogress with both his hands and flung her against the rock face.

Silence followed. Evie sank as low to the ground as she possibly could, not wanting to see any more. But after a minute her curiosity won out. She dared to peep and this time it was Evie who screamed. Volok grabbed her by the hair, dragged her up to the cave and tossed her inside.

CHAPTER TWENTY-TWO

I t was a damp and slimy place, worse than the first cave. The smell was revolting, the air heavy with demon sweat, huge quantities of bat droppings and somewhere further in, a few rotting carcasses. Volok began roaring, saliva dripping from the corners of his mouth. He flashed his eyes at Evie, a bright orange flash, and she hoped he wouldn't transfix her with his demon stare. His nostrils flared and snorted as he stomped over to her.

'You dared to follow me here?' he bellowed.

Evie didn't reply.

'You and the ogress both?' Volok roared.

He turned to watch Olga stagger to her feet, one huge hand holding her head while her other hand steadied her bulk against the cave wall. At first, she looked dazed and deflated. Then, with a marked effort, she let both hands drop down by her side and she stood up straight.

'I was worried about you,' Olga said. 'You are not long released from the curse. I thought you were hiding here because you were ill.'

'You were spying on me,' Volok said with a snarl.

'Everything I do is to serve you,' Olga said. 'Everything.'

'But not everything I do is for you, ogress,' Volok said. 'I have big plans, bigger than you.'

'Why are you here? What is this place?' Olga asked.

'You already know,' Volok said. 'You can smell the pool.'

Olga looked utterly horrified. 'So it's true?' she cried. 'Why didn't you tell me?'

Evie looked from one to the other, confused.

'I would have told you when you brought me the Black Ruby,' Volok said.

'You will have the ruby,' Olga said. 'Soon. I promise.'

'No!' Evie cried, unable to stop herself.

'Ha! See how she fears it,' Olga said, back to her usual sneering.

'Do you know what the ruby can do, Harp Maiden?' Volok asked, his eyes still blazing.

'Um, I ... I ...'

'She knows,' Olga said. 'That's why she's here, looking for it. She thinks it will bring her brother back from the dead. Ha!'

Evie gulped. How did they know about Ben? Drake must have told them last year. As their researcher, he must have found out all about her family and told the demons everything. She began to tremble with a mix of anger as well as fear.

Olga limped towards Evie, stopping directly in front of her. Dipping into her pocket, she took out her hand and blew something into Evie's face. Evie caught the sharp whiff of something dead and rotting, then passed out.

Evie woke lying on her side. She tried to move, but her arms were tightly bound behind her back. Her ankles were bound too, and there was a rag tied around her mouth. For a moment, Evie felt panicked. She blinked her eyes open, squinting then at the slit of bright light coming in through the cave opening. It was still daytime; that was a relief. She felt groggy and shook her head to wake herself. With painful effort, Evie managed to sit up and lean against a large boulder. Somewhere towards the back of the cave, she heard Volok grunt and snort. But there was no sign of Olga. Evie wondered where she had gone.

The answer came soon enough. Light in the cave dimmed as the ogress entered, momentarily blocking most of the daylight. She was carrying the casket.

'Put it over there,' Volok said, pointing to a spot as he emerged out of the dark.

The ogress placed the casket on the ground as instructed. Evie could see it clearly from where she was and wondered if they were going to open it. Olga was covered in bruises on her face, neck and hands. There must have been quite a fight while Evie was unconscious.

'Now, you will see what my plans are,' Volok said. 'Both of you.'

Olga's face turned to thunder at Volok's words. This isn't just about the casket, Evie thought. Volok has been keeping a big secret. Olga won't like being kept in the dark like that. After all she has done for him, he treats her like a slave.

But Evie had more immediate concerns. Volok stomped over to where she was sitting on the ground, picked up a boulder and threw it towards the back of the cave with a terrible crash. He did it again, releasing his frustration.

'Pay close attention,' he said. 'I am about to show you something very special.'

Evie watched as Volok turned and reached down to a pool of slimy green water. The boulders had hidden it from view, but it explained the bad smell which grew stronger now the pool was exposed. He reached into the water and lifted out an oil sack, about the same size as his hand. Thick green goo dripped slowly from the package, which was tightly secured with vines. Evie glanced at Olga to see if this was a surprise to her too. It wasn't, but her expression had turned to one of pure hatred. Evie nervously wondered why.

'This is my next goal,' Volok said. 'Without this, nothing else matters.'

He untied the slime-covered sack and peered inside. As he did so, his eyes glowed a deep red rather than the usual yellow or bright orange. Evie noticed how the sack was moving slightly, a steady throb. A terrifying thought came to her, and she thought she would throw up. If she did, she could choke with a rag tied around her mouth. Evie struggled to control herself, as her breathing came in sniffy bursts through her nose. She whimpered, unable to cry out, revolted by what she hoped wasn't true.

'This is all I have left of my love,' Volok said, gazing adoringly at the dripping bundle. 'This is what the Black Ruby is for – to bring my beloved wife back from the dead. All I need is her heart and that ruby.' He turned his head and glared at Olga.

'It may not be enough, my lord,' Olga said. 'We need to know more about the ruby's other powers. We can't be certain how—'

'Yes, we can,' Volok said. 'Let me show you.'

Evie looked sharply at Olga on hearing her gulp very

loudly. The ogress was staring at Volok; he looked elated, even a little mad. Switching her gaze from one to the other, back and forth, Evie was puzzled by their starkly different reactions.

Volok held the oil sack just above the pool, almost but not quite touching it. With his other hand, he scooped up a fist full of herbs, leaves, dead insects and other stuff Evie couldn't make out.

'No!' Olga cried, her protest echoing around the cave.

'Yes!' Volok roared back, louder, angry. He threw the concoction over the sack and lowered it gently into the pool until it was just covered by the green gloop. 'Now watch,' he said.

Volok slowly dipped the oil sack in and out of the pool. The gooey water thickened with each dip, eventually covering the sack before he raised it up high, his arm at full reach. Something told Evie this was very bad news. Olga, meanwhile, looked fit to explode.

'She is more than just a shimmer now,' Volok said. 'My preparations and care have brought her to a level of some substance already.' Sure enough, Evie could see the gloop become a shape. A wobbly, blurry body was forming from the gloop that stretched from the oil sack all the way down to the pool. The gooey substance waxed and waned, almost but never quite becoming solid. Then Evie spotted a gap in the chest – a space for the missing heart.

'You see? We can be sure that the ruby will revive her,' Volok said. 'She is almost ready to receive her heart. Once she is whole, I will use my five primary talismans to smooth her path back to a full life, and make her the queen she used to be. Then I will use the ruby's other powers as a special treat – enhanced powers to welcome her home.'

The green gloop began to break apart and Volok reluctantly lowered the oil sack back into the pool.

Olga looked decidedly uncomfortable. 'You have made much progress, my lord,' she said reluctantly.

'Indeed,' Volok said. 'If only I had the ruby, I would be very happy.'

'I had it in my hands,' Olga said, a little frantically, 'but this girl and her stupid friends messed up my plan.' She glared at Evie, her eyes burning with hatred. But Evie saw something else too. Was it panic? Desperation? She couldn't believe that Olga was only angry with her. It was more complicated than that. It had to be.

'You weren't careful enough!' Volok roared, his rage returning. 'You should have kept it safe. Time is running out. I cannot keep her heart in that pool forever. I need that ruby now!'

'It was safe, my lord. I told you,' Olga said. 'The safest place was on my person.'

'Obviously not!' Volok roared back.

Evie watched Olga struggle to keep her temper in check. Suddenly it dawned on her that the ogress might not want to bring Madruga back. Then she remembered the piece of silk. 'Beware Madruga,' it said. It didn't matter who had written it, the warning was enough. Evie began to perspire profusely.

'What are you waiting for?' Volok roared.

With a snarl, Olga turned to leave.

'GO!' Volok roared. 'Have the ruby back here by the time I return from feeding.'

HARP MAIDEN

Olga ran out of the cave. Shortly after, Volok left too.

Evie was left alone, with the heart of a demon lying nearby in a disgusting green pool of slime, and the head of an ancient sorceress in a casket on the ground just a few feet away. It was all she could do to stay sane. Think, Evie, think, she told herself. But her mind was in a spin. She tried to hum one of her favourite tunes to straighten out her thoughts, but couldn't manage it with streaming eyes, a sniffy nose, and a soggy rag over her mouth. Looking around, she tried to spot a rock with a rough edge. Then she saw just the one – no, there were several. She didn't care how much it hurt, this might be her only chance to escape.

Evie shuffled on her bottom over to the green pool where there were several sharp shards that had broken off the boulders. Up close, the slime gave off a mighty stink. Evie tried hard not to think what it was made of or what lay beneath, swallowing repeatedly to keep her stomach in check, difficult though that was with her mouth tightly stretched by the rag. She shuffled into position then leaned back against a sharp piece of stone. The jagged edge should cut through the binds, but it was much more difficult than Evie expected. Oh, come on, she thought, rubbing her bound wrists up and down against the stone. I have to be quick! Come on!

Evie wriggled about, frustrated, increasingly cross and desperate. She was almost crying and close to choking. Bang! Evie froze mid-wriggle. What was that? Through her teary eyes she could barely focus. Was it a face? No, a box. A box and a face. Oh, no! Evie realised with a fright what it was she had heard, and what she had done. The casket! she thought. I've knocked it over!

CHAPTER TWENTY-THREE

fter the initial shock, Evie continued her efforts to cut the binds around her wrists. At the same time, she tried to bite and chew her way through the rag tied around her mouth. Finally, she felt some movement at her wrists – she was almost through. She doubled her efforts, though her shoulders burned, and her wrists started to bleed, the blood trickling down her hands making them sticky.

Evie tried to get angry instead of weak, tired and scared. But she was in pain and horrible thoughts were invading her mind again – and she had just kicked over a casket with a talking head inside it! A nagging voice in her own head told her she had failed; she should give up, give in, beg for mercy, do whatever the demons wanted. NO! NO! NO! I won't! she argued with herself, kicking the heels of her shoes into the ground, sending out muffled cries of, 'Agh!' through the rag and out into the cave. The sides of her mouth were raw from all the chafing and chewing, but still she gnawed at the piece of cloth, and rubbed her bound wrists up and down, up and down, wearing the rope slowly away.

Finally, her arms burst free. Evie fell onto her back from the force of her effort, her long hair narrowly missing the smelly, green pool. She ripped the rag away from her face, gasping and coughing. In her continuing distress and frustration, Evie struggled to cut through the rope around her ankles. Giving up on the task for the moment, she wiped her bloodied mouth on her sleeve, and shuffled and crawled back to the casket.

It lay on its side. One of its two doors had fallen open. Evie righted the casket and stared into Nala's face. The sorceress looked asleep, almost dead.

'No! No! I can't have killed her!' Evie croaked. 'Please, no!'

The dark eyes flickered open. Evie gasped and fell back onto her rear end with a bump.

'I'm so sorry,' she whispered, lunging forward awkwardly, her ankles still bound. 'So very sorry. I didn't mean to, to—'

'Quiet, child,' the head said. 'I am Nala of Yodor, imprisoned in this casket by trickery and black magic. The ogress Olga is cleverer than she appears, cleverer than her lord and master knows.'

'Yes, I know,' Evie whispered.

'Untie yourself,' Nala said.

'What? Oh!' Evie grabbed a sharp piece of flint that was lying right beside the casket and finished cutting through the rope around her ankles.

'You are bleeding,' Nala said. 'Tend to your wounds, quickly now.'

Evie used the same implement to cut into the hem of her skirt. After making strips of the cloth, she bandaged her wrists, then took a handkerchief from her pocket and dabbed at the cuts around her mouth.

'How can I help you?' Evie whispered.

'We have more pressing concerns than me,' Nala said.

'Which one first?' Evie asked. 'I mean, they'll be back soon, and I can't just leave you here.'

'They have gone to feed, then Olga will resume her search,' Nala said. 'But we should not delay. How much do you know about the ruby?'

'A little,' Evie said. 'But I'm not sure what to do with it if I find it. Volok wants it desperately, so Olga is bound to keep looking until she finds it, and then ...'

'Then she will give it to Volok,' Nala said. 'He will resurrect Madruga and that will be the end of this world.'

Evie stared back.

'It won't be that easy to find, from what I've heard,' Nala said. 'Which means you have a chance to find it before Olga. A demon's eyes are not as sharp as their ears and nose. Dark colours are difficult for them to make out.'

'Good,' Evie muttered. 'Can the ruby really bring someone back from the dead?'

'Only a demon, and only if used correctly. Black magic is complicated,' Nala said. 'Madruga was a very powerful demon. I am not certain the ruby will be enough for her – not for completeness. Olga seems to agree with me on that point, though she has other reasons for not wanting Madruga back.'

Evie moved closer to the casket. 'How did this happen to you?' she whispered.

'More black magic,' Nala said. 'When I discovered what the Black Ruby truly was, I was very afraid. They came after me even after I had hidden it and fled.'

'How do we stop them?' Evie asked.

'You are Evie, the Harp Maiden?' Nala asked.

Evie swallowed hard. 'Yes.'

'Volok mentioned you,' Nala said. 'Are you willing to do whatever it takes to stop them? Think before you answer. I was willing to do anything and look at me now. Stopping Volok's plan to revive his wife, and destroying both him and the ruby, are tasks fraught with danger and sacrifice. You will be a changed person if you succeed, something you must be willing to accept. All these secrets will be a great burden too, and you must take them to your grave.'

'I will do whatever I can, whatever you tell me,' Evie said, brushing aside all her gathering doubts.

'A Harp Maiden can do many things you have yet to discover, *if* she is prepared to stay the course,' Nala said. 'Shortly, you must leave here and find the ruby. But first, listen carefully and remember what I tell you. We may not get another chance to talk like this.'

Nala began her story. Volok blamed the House of Yodor for the death of his wife, though the sorceress denied their involvement.

'We had nothing to do with it,' she said. 'The king's army was aware of a strange and dark force roaming the wastelands, but they never encountered it directly. I believe it was the demons at war with each other, using black magic and engaging in monstrous acts of violence.'

She paused, thoughtful, then continued.

'Madruga was Volok's wife, the powerful demon-queen of his tribe. You wouldn't think it possible, but it was Olga who lured Madruga into a trap and she also arranged my imprisonment in this casket. Though she planned those events, she was shrewd enough to engage others to commit the murder and perform the enchantment. This ancient head-curse is one I had only heard of but never dared to try.' Her eyes rolled around, looking at each side of her prison. 'But what Olga did to Madruga was even worse. Being so in love with Volok, Olga naturally hated his wife. It sickened her to have to serve Madruga while watching Volok's devotion to her. So she patiently planned her attack, before carrying it out so carefully and at such great personal risk.'

'You mean Olga did it?' Evie said. '*She* killed Madruga?'

'Olga arranged the murder, but she wasn't foolish enough to actually kill the queen,' Nala said. 'She hired others to deliver the fatal blows so she could deny it. Coming from the serving order of demons, Olga cannot directly lie to her superiors.'

'Then who else was involved?' Evie asked.

'Unknown assassins, they said,' Nala continued. 'Volok searched for and found Madruga's broken body, knowing he could restore her with the Black Ruby. All it would take was her heart, if it were properly preserved.'

'Who had the Black Ruby back then?' Evie asked.

'I did,' Nala said. 'King Udil's army found it on one of their campaigns. I knew it was special right away, but not how dangerous it was. I studied it and over time I discovered some of its history. But it was shrouded in evil. I could sense it. I told the king it should be secretly buried, hidden for all time. No one should use such power or even keep it.'

'But he wanted to keep it, didn't he?' Evie said.

'He was bewitched by its power,' Nala said. 'We argued and I lost his favour and my position. I left the House of Yodor to find a new direction for my talents. Sometime after that, Volok stole the ruby from the king's palace. He was caught by the royal guards. They used powerful potions to weaken him before he was imprisoned with the tree curse. The magic to capture him was all mine – my potions, and a curse I had created and entrusted to only one other sorcerer, one who would later betray me to Olga.'

'How did Olga find you after you had fled?' Evie asked.

'Demon trickery and my own foolishness,' Nala said. 'It was years later, Volok was still imprisoned in the tree and Olga had sworn to find and free him. But she needed my help to undo the curse. One day a note appeared under my door. Someone claimed to have information about the Black Ruby's whereabouts. I should have known it was a trick. I had moved far away and befriended no one. Olga must have sent hunters to find me. You see, they believed that I knew a lot more about the ruby as well as the tree curse.'

'Do you?' Evie asked.

'A little, but I doubt if anyone knows everything,' Nala said. 'I assumed Olga wanted it to gain favour with Volok, but I don't think she realised why he really wanted it. He kept that part a secret.

'But I was curious about the note and the ruby, and so I fell into a trap laid by Olga and a traitor from the palace, the same sorcerer who had been my trusted friend. Olga beheaded me and then the sorcerer used black magic to keep my head alive in this enchanted casket. It nearly cost him his own life to perform that ritual. But he kept his promise to Olga by doing it, and she kept her promise to him by letting him return to the palace alive.'

'What a story!' Evie whispered.

'Later, Olga forced me to tell her how to wake and release Volok from the harp's wooden frame. My beautiful magical harp was corrupted by a terrible twist of fate. It sounds foolish now, but I believed all her threats to murder my king and wipe out my tribe. She would have killed so many innocent people if I did not do as she instructed.'

'I read that the tree in which Volok was imprisoned was cut down,' Evie said, 'and a carpenter unknowingly took the wood with Volok still trapped inside it. Then he made the frame for the harp.'

'Good, you know some of the story,' Nala said. 'It revolted me to help Olga, but in return, she promised that future Kings of Yodor and their people would be left alone. It was a terrible bargain, but I had two reasons to believe that Olga would keep her word. First, because of her absolute devotion to Volok and her need to please him. The second reason was the strange code of honour among Olga's tribe to always keep their promises, and I knew she had already kept her promise to the sorcerer. So, you see, Olga needed my knowledge to free Volok, but Volok still needs the Black Ruby to bring Madruga back.'

'If Volok knew about Olga's involvement, her utter betrayal,' Evie said, 'he would be beside himself with rage. He would want revenge.'

'Oh, yes,' Nala said. 'He would kill her.'

'But there's no proof, it was so long ago,' Evie said.

'If Volok succeeds in bringing Madruga back,' Nala said, 'she will confirm the tale herself.'

'No wonder Olga didn't want to give him the ruby when she had it,' Evie said. 'But then why did she promise it to him? She *has* to give it to him now.'

'There is a time limit for keeping a heart preserved for a ritual,' Nala said. 'Volok must be getting anxious, whereas Olga must be hoping time will run out.'

'How long?' Evie asked.

'I don't know exactly, but I suspect they know,' Nala said. 'Olga will try to delay long enough to ensure Madruga cannot return. Volok, on the other hand, will be in a hurry.'

'She wants to take Madruga's place as his queen,' Evie said, the realisation dawning on her.

'It would appear so,' Nala said.

'But that's crazy,' Evie said. 'Volok doesn't care about her at all, and—'

'And he may kill her whether she finds the ruby for him or not,' Nala said. 'Yes, Olga is walking on dangerous ground. But so are we.'

Evie sank back and leaned against the boulder again. 'How on earth do we stop all this?' she asked.

'Find the ruby, and bring it to me,' Nala said. 'Go now while they are busy.'

'What about you?' Evie asked. 'Can't I take you away from all this?'

'No, I don't want them to know we are allies just yet,' Nala said. 'Nothing and no one can restore me now. This is how it will end for me, but I would like to set in train a plan to defeat those demons first. Go now, Evie. Once you find the Black Ruby, I will explain more.'

CHAPTER TWENTY-FOUR

A s Evie began her trek back to the waiting horses and carriage, she remained on her guard as Volok could be anywhere, and Olga would be at the ruins searching for the ruby. She suddenly wondered what it was that demons ate. Surely not horses! With that awful thought clawing at her brain, Evie chose a different route, more challenging but more direct. Keeping low, she scrambled through long grass and bushes, over rocks and rough terrain, as quickly as she dared. With every minute she was more keenly aware of how late she must be. Finally, she emerged scratched and dusty beside the carriage.

Evie had left it hidden behind a small copse of trees and wild bushes, a little distance from her usual spot. Her decision had been fortunate. Peeping through the trees Evie spotted Olga digging vigorously through the rubble in search of the ruby. There was no way Evie could search now, no matter what the urgency. She climbed up onto the driver's seat and drove away without looking back.

When she alighted from the carriage back in Branston, still feeling rather rattled, she got another fright when she looked down at her clothes.

'Oh, no!' she cried. 'How on earth do I explain this?'

'Evie, there you are!'

'What! Oh!' she muttered, startled.

Matthew ran over to her. 'Evie, what happened?'

'Evie!' Grace called. 'Thank goodness you're back! Oh my!'

'Where have you been?' Matthew asked, his face full of concern.

'I'll tell you later, but please, not now,' Evie said. 'Have I missed the encore?'

'I'm afraid it's long over,' Matthew said. 'We've been worried sick.'

'Evie, your clothes,' Grace said. 'And your wrists. Are you all right?'

'I'm fine, I'm so sorry,' Evie said. 'I had an urgent errand. Please don't ask me to explain. I'll tell you as soon as I can, really I will … I … oh.'

Evie almost swooned and had to grab onto Matthew's arm.

'We'll help you inside,' Matthew said, putting his arm around Evie's waist to support her. 'Best not to let my father see you or he will have a lot of questions. And he'll want answers too.'

'Oh dear,' Evie muttered.

'I'll help you tidy up inside,' Grace said. 'Perhaps Matthew could organise some tea with lots of sugar.'

'Lovely, thank you,' Evie said, feeling a little woozy.

'Good idea,' Matthew said. 'I'll bring it round to the dressing rooms behind the stage. There's no one there now. Everyone is at the lunch, which is almost over too. I'll see if I can find a few sandwiches for you.'

Once inside, Matthew hurried off and Grace led Evie into the ladies' dressing rooms. Grace began to wash Evie's face after soaking her handkerchief.

'You must have a very big secret, Evie, but it's looking serious now,' Grace said. 'Can't you tell me anything?'

'I will, Grace, I promise, but not now,' Evie said wearily. 'It would take too long and it's quite a story.'

'Just tell me, are you in danger?' Grace asked.

Evie looked at her friend, unable to keep the truth from her eyes.

'Oh, no! Oh, Evie!'

'I'm all right, just a bit shaken,' Evie said. 'I'll tell you soon, in private. But you cannot tell anyone else no matter what you think of me or my secret. No one. Not your father, not Samuel, no one. You have to promise me.'

'I understand,' Grace said, handing Evie a face towel. 'We should wash your wrists and redo the bandages. Those strips of cloth are dirty and unravelling.'

'Thank you, Grace. I seem to be always apologising to you and telling you what a good friend you are,' Evie said. 'I hope you don't think me completely awful.'

'Nonsense,' Grace said. 'Here, I have another handkerchief that will do the job nicely. I'll tear it in half, and each strip should be just long enough to wrap and tie around each wrist. Now, your lovely hair! Goodness me! There are all sorts of leaves in it, and bits of – I don't know – are those cobwebs?'

'Probably,' Evie said, picking at her hair. 'I had to crawl through bushes.'

'Where were you, Evie? Oh, no, don't tell me. Was it ...?'

'Yes, Dower Hall,' Evie said, guiltily. 'I wanted to look for the ruby while we were here. I was suddenly snatched by the, um, the housekeeper.'

'She's alive? She's still here?' Grace was almost shrieking. 'You must tell my father immediately! He will send the constables after her.'

'No, it's too dangerous even for the police,' Evie said.

'Too dangerous for the police but not for you?' Grace was searching Evie's face for answers. 'You must tell him. Or I could, if you prefer.'

'NO!' Evie shouted. 'I'm sorry, Grace. That's another thing I'll have to explain ... another day. I'm sorry, this is just awful, I—'

'Evie, Grace, I have the tea and some cake, but no sandwiches, I'm afraid,' Matthew called to them from outside the door. 'Is everything all right in there?'

Grace looked anxiously at Evie.

'Yes, we're coming now,' Evie called back. 'There's nothing to be done about my skirt,' she said quietly to Grace, as she tried to smooth it down. 'Hopefully, no one will notice the tears at the bottom.'

'We must be heading back to Hartville soon,' Grace said. 'Have your tea, and I'll go and see what's happening.'

Grace left Evie with Matthew. They sat down on a couple of wooden chairs that had been left in the corridor, and Evie tucked hungrily into the cake, gulping down her tea.

'My, you certainly needed that,' Matthew said. 'Evie, I must ask, are you hurt? Those look like bandages on your wrists. New ones. And, well, you looked a little upset and dishevelled when we found you. Are you sure you're all right?'

'Yes, Matthew, thank you,' Evie said. 'There were, um, robbers, when I was looking for my necklace, the one I lost in Dower Hall.'

'You went to that place to search alone?' Matthew said incredulously. 'You really are brave!'

'More like foolish,' Evie muttered. 'Anyway, I managed to get away.'

'How many were there?' Matthew asked.

'What?'

'Robbers.'

'Um, two, I think,' Evie said. 'I must have slipped and bumped my head. I was dazed for a bit. I don't remember much, but I have quite a headache now.'

'You mean you went out for air again, and some ruffians tried to rob you,' Matthew said, filling in a few details for her.

'Um, something like that,' Evie said, grateful that Matthew was helping her with her story again. 'I needed air … again.'

'These stuffy halls will have that effect,' Matthew said. He looked at her in half-jest, but inquiringly too.

Evie looked away, then said quietly, 'Please don't mention this to anyone. I hate a fuss, and I'm fine, really.'

'Your wish is my command,' Matthew said. 'But Evie …'

'Yes?'

'Please let me know if I can help, any way at all,' Matthew said. 'I hate to see you upset like this. I would be your friend and you can trust me, truly. Grace too. But you know that already.'

'Thank you, Matthew,' Evie said. Without thinking, Evie squeezed Matthew's hand and immediately felt herself blushing. 'Actually, there is s—'

'Quick!' Grace shrieked, running down the corridor in a flurry. 'We're leaving. We have to board the carriages right away.'

'My flute,' Evie said.

'And my music folder,' Matthew said.

They met at the door with all their belongings, the last to board. Two carriages had just left and the third was about to pull out. Theirs was the fourth, but Mr Reid was absent. They boarded the carriage and waited.

Suddenly, Evie felt a big wave of relief. It was unlikely Grace or Matthew would ask any more questions in front of Matthew's father, and right now all she wanted to do was sleep. Fortunately Mr Reid appeared quickly, carrying heaps of music sheets which he always brought with him, though everyone had their own. He stopped at the open carriage door.

'There you are, Evie!' he said, sounding a little perplexed. 'What happened earlier? I was calling you to play again and you didn't reappear! The audience loved you, you know, and then you missed the encore as well.'

'Oh, Mr Reid, I am dreadfully sorry,' Evie said, mortified.

'Evie needed a little fresh air, Father,' Matthew said. 'It's very stuffy in these small parish halls. It was stifling with the morning sun beating in through the windows all through the performance, wasn't it, Grace?'

'Yes, very warm,' Grace said. 'Just like the last time.'

'We should have opened the windows before we started,' Matthew continued. 'But Evie's fine now, aren't you, Evie?'

Evie managed a nod and a smile.

'Dear me, yes, you're probably right,' Mr Reid said. 'Well, never mind. So long as you are all right, Evie. But next time, you must remind me to make sure the hall has more air so you can all play comfortably and perhaps for longer too. And not miss any more encores. Yes, such a pity. Matthew, make a note to remind me. Good idea, yes, yes, indeed.' He got in, closed the door and called to the driver. 'We're ready to go now, Winston, thank you!'

Mr Reid kept muttering to himself as they pulled out of the stable yard, fussing over his sheet music and then spilling half of it on the floor. Evie and Matthew bent down to pick up the music. As Evie handed Mr Reid the last sheet, she stared in shock. There was no mistaking it: Lionel Thorn's name and address, written on the back of a sheet of music.

A shiver ran down her spine, then another. Evie's distress went unnoticed as the carriage jolted into motion. The driver whipped up the horses and they sped off.

CHAPTER TWENTY-FIVE

Evie could barely remember arriving home and going to bed. Waking up the next morning, she felt much better after a deep sleep. That is, until her list of worries hit her. She would have to add Mr Reid to the list now too. She almost cried out with frustration when there was a knock on her door. Evie opened it to see Freddie looking very excited. He bounded into the room.

'What happened?' he asked. 'I know something did. You were late home and then you had dinner in your bedroom and didn't come down again. You were lucky Uncle Henry spent the whole day in the study and Aunt Clara was busy packing. Miss Julia peeped into your room last night, but she said you were sound asleep. Did you find the ruby?'

'Shh,' Evie said. 'No one must hear us.'

'They won't,' Freddie said confidently. 'Uncle Henry has gone to meet someone important, something to do with his research. He won't be back till late. Aunt Clara left very early to catch the train. She's gone to visit her very, very old Aunt Maud, who is ill. Mr and Mrs Hudson have gone to church. Tilly is on her day off, and Miss Julia is still in bed. Mrs

Hudson brought her up some breakfast before she went out. She said Miss Julia is still poorly and not to disturb her.'

'Right,' Evie said. 'I think you have covered everything. I'll check on Julia, anyway. Oh! The walk!'

'What walk?' Freddie asked. 'Do you mean another picnic?'

'Maybe, I'm not sure,' Evie said, frowning. 'I mean, we planned to go for a walk, Grace, Matthew, Samuel and I. Maybe it's next week. Or was it cancelled?'

'You didn't find the ruby, did you?' Freddie said.

'No, not yet,' Evie said. 'I might try again today while everyone is busy. It could be my last chance to look for it before I upset absolutely everyone – permanently.'

'You won't like the weather,' Freddie said. He pulled back one of the curtains. It was raining with no sign of any break in the clouds.

'Oh, dear,' Evie said. 'I'll get up and have a quick breakfast, then decide.'

Freddie ran downstairs to wait for Evie. When she came down, there were two letters on the hall table for her. She read them as she munched on her toast and marmalade. The first one was from Matthew.

Dear Evie,

I hope you are feeling better today. My father has unexpectedly decided to host a little party in our house, a sort of "welcome home" and "sending off" for me, though the latter is a little early. As you know, I will be staying on another week. I've invited some old friends and Father has asked a few of our relations. I would still like to go for that walk next week before I leave. With a bit of luck, the good weather will return in time. I do hope you'll be able to come today, and Grace too, around three o'clock.

Your friend,

Matthew

Evie felt her heart flutter as she closed the note. She would love to go to the party to see Matthew and Grace, but also to ask Matthew about his father's connection to Mr Thorn. Hopefully, there wasn't one, but it was a disturbing coincidence, seeing his name like that. With her own house virtually empty, however, she had an unexpected opportunity to go to Dower Hall. She wrote a quick reply to Matthew, thanking him and accepting the invitation but adding that she might be a little late. Then Evie opened the second envelope.

Dear Miss Wells,

I called to your house early this morning, but your butler wouldn't let me see you. I have found what you were looking for. Please come to the Crompton Arms as soon as you get this note.

Charlie

'Do you know when these letters arrived?' Evie asked.
'That one during breakfast, my *first* breakfast,' Freddie

said, pointing to Matthew's letter, 'and that one just before the Hudsons went out.'

'Not long then,' Evie said. 'Did you see the man leave?'

'I saw him leaving,' Freddie said. 'He was driving a cart like the one Wilf used around Dower Hall, an old rickety thing.'

'Good, then he can't have gone far,' Evie said. 'I have to go after him, Freddie. Will you be all right on your own until the Hudsons return? Julia is upstairs. You could sit with her and read if you like.'

'No way!' Freddie cried. 'I'm coming with you!'

Evie and Freddie grabbed their hats and coats and ran around to the stable yard. To Evie's surprise, Freddie quickly and expertly led the two horses out of their stalls, hitched them up to the carriage and climbed up.

'You are good at this!' Evie said, impressed.

'Jimmy showed me,' Freddie said. 'It's easy once you take lessons.'

The stable boy appeared.

'He's a quick learner, Miss Evie,' Jimmy said. 'He's got a real way with the horses too.'

'Jimmy, would you do me a favour?' Evie asked. 'I have to catch someone on the road. Would you deliver this note to Mr Reid's house? You know where he lives, don't you?'

'Your music teacher? Yes, Miss,' Jimmy said. 'I'll run over there now. You won't be long, Miss, will you? Mr Hudson will be cross with me for letting you take the carriage out on your own.'

'No, don't worry, we won't be long,' Evie said.

'All right, then,' Jimmy said, not sounding at all convinced.

Evie smiled the most reassuring smile she could muster, took hold of the reins, and they set off.

Evie felt sure that Charlie's old cart couldn't travel that fast, so there was every chance they would catch up with him. The rain was keeping most people indoors and the roads through the town were quieter than usual. Good, Evie thought. Fewer people to spot us dashing about in our family's carriage.

After rounding the final bend near the end of the town, however, they sped past the Hudsons walking back from church. Freddie ducked so as not to be seen, but Evie was concentrating on the horses as they picked up speed.

'Did they see us?' Freddie asked.

'Who?' Evie asked.

'The Hudsons,' Freddie said.

Evie groaned. 'Oh no, and let's hope they don't go home yet and find us both gone.'

'They won't,' Freddie said, sitting up again. 'They always go for a long walk in the park after church.'

'Even in this rain?' Evie asked.

'I think so,' Freddie said. 'Mr Hudson took two umbrellas with him.'

'Oh, good,' Evie said, surprised at how much Freddie noticed about everyone. She wondered then if she were mad racing off like this, getting both of them in trouble and putting Freddie in unnecessary danger. 'No, I can't. I just can't!' she cried suddenly.

'Can't what?' Freddie asked.

'I can't put you in danger,' Evie said. She pulled the horses to a stop at the side of the road. 'You have to go home, Freddie. Once I catch up with Charlie, I have to do something else, and it might be terribly dangerous. It really would be better if we both don't get into serious trouble – with everyone.'

'What do you mean?' Freddie asked. 'What are you going to do? Tell me, Evie.'

'Charlie has the Black Ruby,' Evie said. 'He left me a note when he called this morning, telling me he had it. I must get it from him now. Then, I have to bring it to someone else, someone who might help us defeat the demons. Olga and Volok are out there, Freddie. I've seen them.'

'But maybe I can help,' Freddie said. 'Where are they?'

'They're hiding out in a cave beyond Dower Hall,' Evie said.

'Can't I go with you, please?'

'I'm sorry,' Evie said. 'I'd never forgive myself. You'll have to make some excuse to the Hudsons for me, and to Father too, if I'm not home before him. Doing that for me will be just as important as what I'm doing now. Go, please. I must catch Charlie.'

'Who are you giving the ruby to?' Freddie asked crossly. 'Tell me, then I'll go.'

'It's ... it's Nala,' she said.

'But she's dead!' Freddie said.

'It's all to do with magic,' Evie said. 'Her head is kept alive inside an enchanted casket. She can talk, Freddie. She asked me to bring her the ruby right away.'

'Whoa!' Freddie said. 'That's a lot of magic!'

'You must tell no one, no one at all,' Evie said. 'If you are asked, just say I took the carriage to go to Matthew's house.

The Reids are having a party this afternoon. I'll try to get there later.'

'But you could walk there, it's not far,' Freddie said. 'They won't believe me.'

'They might because of this rain, so say it anyway unless you can think of something better,' Evie said. 'I must hurry now. Please, go home.'

Reluctantly, Freddie climbed down from the driver's seat, the rain dripping steadily off his cap. 'If it's so dangerous,' he said, 'you'll need someone to help you.'

'You are helping me,' Evie said more gently. She flicked the reins. 'I'll be back as soon as I can,' she cried, as she spurred the horses to a gallop, leaving Freddie gazing after her in the rain.

CHAPTER TWENTY-SIX

Evie's cut wrists ached as she held the reins tightly.
She was quickly soaked in the pouring rain despite
her heaviest coat and hat. Once or twice Evie thought
the horses were going too fast, and she had to hold her nerve
as the wheels lifted slightly off the ground on a couple of
bends. It would be difficult to keep up this pace as the rain
turned the country roads to mud. But time was short and her
task most urgent. There was no sign of Charlie yet, and she
wondered where on earth he could be. Surely, he couldn't be
much further ahead.

The rain was still sheeting down as Evie arrived at the
outskirts of Crompton. She spotted a blur in the distance.
'Charlie, at last,' she muttered. He had made remarkably
good time despite his old cart and the weather.

'Charlie! Charlie!' Evie called, but he couldn't hear her in
the downpour, wrapped up tightly in his cloak and cap.

Evie spurred the horses to close the gap between them and
called out again. 'Charlie, wait, pull up!'

Finally, Charlie looked over his shoulder and brought his
horse and cart to a halt. Evie pulled on the reins too sharply
and the horses skidded then bucked, almost throwing her out
of the driver's seat and onto the road. Charlie reached over

and grabbed the harness to steady them.

'You are a very determined young lady,' he said.

'Thank you,' Evie said. 'I got your note. Is it true? You found it?'

'Yes, I have it,' Charlie said. 'I spotted that big housekeeper roamin' around, but I made sure to avoid her. Was she lookin' for it too?'

'Yes, she was, she still is,' Evie said. 'It's really important that she never gets her hands on it again.'

Charlie reached into his pocket. 'What is it?' he asked.

'An ancient ruby,' Evie said.

'Never thought to see one that size or colour,' Charlie said. 'Looks more like a lump o' coal to me.'

He turned the ruby over in his hands. For a moment, Evie felt the hairs stand up on the back of her neck. Was Charlie going to hand it over? If not, how would she take it off him? Evie watched him very closely. What was he thinking?

'Charlie,' Evie said as calmly as she could, 'I'm very grateful to you for finding my ruby but I really need to take it now. Please give it to me.' She held out her hand.

Charlie looked at her strangely and still he said nothing, just kept turning the ruby over and over in his hand.

'Charlie, please,' Evie said, her voice anxious. 'It's urgent.' Anxiety was quickly turning to panic. She couldn't let the ruby out of her sight, even if it meant walking into a trap. Suddenly Evie felt completely at Charlie's mercy.

'Lucia never mentioned this,' he said. 'What makes it so important? Is it worth a lot?'

'No, not at all,' Evie said, though she didn't know. 'Look at it, it's an ugly lump.'

'Another one of Lucia's mysteries, eh?' Charlie said. He paused yet again. Evie was growing impatient as well as fearful.

'But like I said before,' Charlie said, 'it's probably best if I don't know. Here, take it. I hope it brings you all you hoped for.'

Evie nodded, greatly relieved but still a little wary. 'I hope so too. Thank you, Charlie. You take care.'

'You too, Miss Evie,' Charlie said. 'Those horses aren't used to being out in a deluge like this. They could stumble on the muddy ruts in the road. Another cart must have come through here recently. You can see how it's very cut up on this stretch and it'll be even bumpier further on.'

'I'll be careful,' Evie said. 'Goodbye, Charlie.'

'Goodbye, Miss Evie.'

With the precious ruby in her coat pocket, Evie left the carriage in the little copse and hurried on past the ruins of Dower Hall. Once out of the forest, she stopped abruptly. She couldn't be sure where Nala's casket would be. Olga might have taken it back to the first cave, or it might still be with Volok in the second cave, further down the gorge. Evie decided to go to the nearer cave first.

She had chosen wisely. The casket was under Olga's watchful eye, but there was also a man present. Evie was surprised and curious. Staring at the man for a moment, she tried to place him. Yes, she had seen him in the Crompton Arms. He was particularly odd looking, skinny, unkempt, with one small, deep-set, darting eye – a black eyepatch over his other eye made him hard to forget.

Annoyingly, Evie would have to wait to talk to Nala now, and she hoped that Olga and this man would leave soon. Evie could not allow herself to be snatched again, not with the ruby in her pocket. She moved as close as possible to the mouth of the cave. Settling down, hidden behind boulders and a huge clump of wild thorny brambles, Evie strained to hear the conversation taking place inside.

'I followed him all the way to Hartville,' the man said, grovelling pathetically. 'He had the black stone you told me about. I saw him look at it. Then he travelled a long way to a townhouse, but he wasn't let in. He looked very disappointed. Then he headed back home.'

'You failed,' Olga said.

'No, no, mistress, I did what you asked. I followed him and came back to tell you what I saw,' the man said. 'It was a hard drive, there and back, tiring and difficult for a poor man like me. A wheel came off my cart, so I had to stop and fix it. That's what took me so long. And in the terrible rain too. But after my efforts, we now know who has that black stone, don't we?'

Olga snorted loudly. 'Do you know where this man lives?'

'Oh, yes, I do,' the man said, sounding very pleased with himself. 'I also know the inn he frequents.'

'You will show me the way to his house, not the inn,' Olga said. 'Now.'

'Perhaps I might have something to eat first?'

Foolish man, Evie thought. Who does he think he's dealing with?

'No, we go now,' Olga said.

'Well, if it's that urgent, I suppose I could show you the way now,' he muttered.

'It is and you will,' Olga said. She grabbed him roughly by the arm and marched him out of the cave.

Evie didn't have time to move. She scrunched her body into as tight and small a ball as she could, holding her breath while they passed unnervingly close to where she was hiding. Olga looked like thunder, the skinny man perturbed. He should be very worried, Evie thought; no – absolutely terrified. It was very likely Olga would dispose of him once she got what she wanted. They must be heading to Charlie's house, but he didn't have the ruby anymore. Evie wasn't sure if that meant Charlie would be safe or not, and she wondered whether she should have told him more. But his behaviour on the road had unnerved her, and Julia's warnings were still ringing in her ears. Perhaps she would never know the truth about him.

Looking towards the mouth of the cave, Evie was desperate to locate Nala. She waited patiently, not moving an inch until Olga and her helper were well out of earshot and out of sight. Once the coast was clear she hurried into the cave, eager to show Nala the ruby and hear the rest of her plan.

Evie saw the casket and rushed over. She gently opened the two little doors. Nala blinked repeatedly, adjusting her eyes to the light.

'I have it!' Evie whispered excitedly, taking the ruby out of her pocket. 'I have it! Look!'

'You did well,' Nala said. 'Now, you must finish the charms. All of them, as quickly as you can.'

'What?' Evie cried. 'There isn't time for that!'

'You must reach the highest step on the Ladder of Charms,

sealing your commitment to the harp in order to release its most powerful magic. Only then can you reduce the Black Ruby to nothing. Only then will you be able to stop those demons. There is no other way to finish this.'

Evie felt suddenly ashamed.

'What is it?' Nala said, irritation creeping into her voice.

'I can't do it,' Evie said. 'Not yet.'

'What do you mean? You must!' Nala snapped. 'No. NO! You failed one of them, didn't you?'

Evie felt her whole body sag.

'Yes, I failed. I'm so sorry,' she said. 'I thought I was ready. I made one tiny mistake, and then a message appeared saying I have to wait until after the next full moon to try again.'

'Foolish, foolish girl!' Nala cried.

'Can't we just hide the ruby until I finish step one?' Evie asked.

'Step one is only the beginning, the easy part,' Nala said crossly. 'There are six steps on the Ladder, and each step has several charms. You must reach the very top before the harp will endow you with enough magic to do … what you must.'

'I'm so sorry,' Evie whispered, choking back tears. 'I've been trying so hard to do everything right. How can I fix this?'

'Stop whining!' Nala said crossly. 'Hiding the ruby is only a temporary fix until you are ready. It is not the answer to the problem. Volok will never stop looking for it, and even if he did, there will always be someone else. The ruby must be destroyed.'

'And Volok?' Evie asked.

'Let me think for a moment,' Nala said, frowning horribly.

Evie waited nervously for Nala to speak again. Minutes passed.

'Nothing can be done about this delay,' Nala said, more calmly. 'You must finish the charms after the full moon without incident.'

Evie nodded.

'I knew one day that powerful magic would be required to deal with this sort of threat, demon magic and their insatiable ambition,' Nala said. 'And so, at great risk, I enchanted the harp with both light and dark magic. Such power cannot be trifled with, but it is our only chance of success.'

'Chance?' Evie whimpered.

'Yes. Chance,' Nala said. 'If only you had advanced further by now.'

'I have only been the Harp Maiden since January,' Evie said. 'I've tried to find out all I can. I've read Lucia's diary. Then I found your notebook – I only have that a couple of weeks – and I have to keep what I'm doing a secret. And there are so many secrets, I feel like I'm drowning in them!'

Tears began to pour down Evie's face again.

'Stop feeling sorry for yourself,' Nala said. 'Look at me! My head has been trapped in this casket for centuries! Kept hidden by that ogress for all that time, I have been forced to do her bidding to protect my country of birth, my king – who banished me because the allure of the ruby twisted his mind – and his successors, my kinfolk. And I was betrayed by someone I trusted!' Nala took a moment to calm herself. 'Now, stop snivelling and listen.'

Evie wiped her eyes with her handkerchief, clenched her

jaws and her fists and sat up straight. She looked directly at Nala.

'Because of your carelessness, we have no choice but to hide the ruby until after the next full moon,' Nala said.

'That's tomorrow,' Evie said.

'Fortunate,' Nala said sharply. 'But at least we have the ruby in our possession, and they don't. A critical difference.'

'I'll do whatever it takes to stop them,' Evie said, with a burst of passion. 'I won't let you down. I'll finish the charms immediately, all of them.'

'Good,' Nala said. 'That's the spirit of a true Harp Maiden. But you will be doing it alone, for I will no longer be here.'

'What?' Evie cried. 'I can't do this alone!'

'You can, you must, and you will,' Nala said. 'The only safe place for that ruby is in this casket. Once you place it in here, you alone will be able to retrieve it. I will see to that. It will be the last magic I cast before I die.'

'Die? What? No!' Evie cried.

'It is time,' Nala said. 'I cannot allow myself to be used anymore, and I have spent long enough in this casket prison.'

'But …' Evie clasped one hand over her mouth in case she started to cry again.

'There can only be one magical object in this casket at any time,' Nala explained. 'You must remove me from the casket and in so doing the magic keeping me alive in here will end, and so will I. Then you must place the ruby inside and take it to a safe place. Hide it carefully. Tell no one you don't absolutely trust. The rest of your instructions will come once you complete all six steps.'

'But you can't leave now!' Evie pleaded.

'I must, as I have just explained,' Nala said. 'Leave all other cares behind you and concentrate on being the Harp Maiden. Finish the charms and you will command the magic of the harp. All of its magic. No Harp Maiden has ever succeeded in doing that. I would know if they had, and I would like if someone did.'

Evie only managed a nod.

'I have told you more than any Harp Maiden would have discovered in a lifetime,' Nala said. 'You must use this knowledge and the magic when you receive it, to rid the world of the demon that you and I helped bring back into it. It is our duty, our responsibility.'

'I'll do it,' Evie said.

'Good, and do not be sad for me,' Nala said. 'I will finally be free. My part in this terrible quest is over. Finish it for me, Evie. My magic will live on in you. It will come slowly with each charm, but once you finish the Ladder, you will feel it and see it. Moon magic is powerful, and it will be with you always.'

Evie stared at Nala, searching for something to say.

'Now, Evelyn Wells, Harp Maiden,' Nala said. 'Remove my head from this wretched casket.'

CHAPTER TWENTY-SEVEN

Evie quickly composed herself. Reaching out to Nala's head, she saw that her hands were remarkably steady. Perhaps she had found that new resolve she craved, and just at the right time. A rush of wind came from nowhere, encircling Evie and the casket as Evie's fingers moved steadily towards Nala's head. Nala looked remarkably serene, her eyes closed, her lips curled into a soft, expectant smile. But before Evie took a hold of her head, a shadow darkened the space, and a thunderous bellow made her jump.

'What is this?' Olga roared.

Evie withdrew her hands instantly and looked up at the ogress standing over her. Out of the corner of her eye, Evie caught a tiny movement. Nala was moving her head a tiny bit left and right, indicating, Evie thought, that she should say nothing about what had been about to take place.

'Thought you'd take another look?' Olga said. 'Your annoying curiosity was bound to get you into trouble – and here you are, right where I want you!'

Olga took one big stride towards Evie and grabbed her roughly by the hair. Evie screamed as she was dragged along the stony ground, then dumped in a heap away from the casket.

'I will not make the same mistake with you again,' Olga said. 'Leaving you too near sharp stones was careless. Maybe I will break your legs to stop you moving this time.' The ogress smiled evilly, as she flexed a long green vine between her fists. 'Unfortunately Volok wants you alive for the moment, though I do not. But he will be pleased that I caught you again.' The long length of vine looked ominously like the green tendrils that had once attached Volok to the harp. The thought made Evie gulp.

Olga bound Evie's wrists tighter than before, the vines pinching and cutting her. Evie looked over to the casket, wondering if the sorceress could do something, anything. Nala had mentioned some last bit of magic she would use to make the ruby untouchable inside the casket, untouchable except for Evie. Had she enough magic left to do something now as well?

The doors of the casket were still open. Shifting her position slightly, Evie could see Nala's face. To her surprise and annoyance Nala still looked calm, almost uninterested. Why isn't she doing something? Evie thought, her rising irritation making her perspire. She looked anxiously towards the mouth of the cave.

'Don't worry,' Olga said. 'Volok will be back soon.' The ogress grinned. 'He takes longer to feed now that he's back to full strength.'

Evie didn't respond.

'What were you talking about?' Olga asked. 'Are you good friends now, you and the former sorceress? Bah! I think not.'

'Why are you helping Volok?' Evie asked, throwing

caution to the wind. 'He loves his wife. Bringing her back is all he cares about.'

Olga grabbed Evie, this time by the face. For a moment Evie thought her cheekbones would be crushed.

'You don't know anything,' Olga hissed into her face. 'I will regain his respect, then I will win his love. When I have that ruby, I will use it for other purposes only I know of, but Madruga is never coming back. I will make sure of that.'

'How?' Evie shouted at her, as soon as Olga removed her hand. 'How will you do that? Why would he switch his affection to you? You heard what he said. Madruga means more to him than anything. He won't need *you* anymore once she is back.'

'No! You are wrong! She is not coming back!' Olga roared. 'I have been his most loyal servant for centuries. Finally, he will love me, and I will take my place by his side as his queen.'

'He would never make a servant his queen,' Evie said.

The silence that followed was nerve-wracking. Steam rose from Olga's sweating body. Evie felt her own pulse accelerate, fearing she might have gone too far.

Olga's face turned purple, her eyes reduced to angry slits as she raised a fist and took aim at Evie's head.

'You can't hurt me,' Evie said, bracing herself for the blow. 'Volok wants me alive, remember? He'll be angry if you kill me just because you lost your temper. He might even kill you this time.'

Olga paused, snorting loudly. Evie recoiled at her foul breath.

'I have to keep you alive – for now,' Olga said, dropping her arm. 'But let me tell you how it really was, then you will understand how it will be, especially when Volok no longer needs *you*. You will not be so brave then.'

Olga sat down on a boulder that groaned under her weight. To Evie's surprise, the demon-ogress began to tell her story.

'Madruga was Volok's wife, powerful and feared. But not loved. Even by demon standards, she was brutal and vindictive. It was easy to find those who hated her enough to want to kill her and remove her from power. I chose the team well and we took our time, planning carefully. I believe every creature has a weakness and eventually we discovered Madruga's – in the small of her back. Another weakness was her ambition. It blinded her to enemies who were so close to her. We waited patiently for the right opportunity to come along. And it did.

'We ambushed her when she was full of food and drink, celebrating after another slaughter. My assassins made a hundred cuts to the small of her back, ensuring she was dead. But they hated her so much, I had to promise they could carve her up into little pieces. They buried each bit of her in as many places. Volok managed to find the drunken fool who had buried her heart and forced the location from him. Volok dug it up himself but refused to tell anyone where he later hid it, not even me.

'It was here,' Evie muttered. 'All that time?' She stared at the ogress.

'Yes, preserved in that green pool,' Olga said.

Then it struck Evie: despite Olga's physical strength and cunning, one of her weaknesses was surely her pride, another her devotion to Volok. She should never have revealed the truth to Evie, but she just couldn't resist because of her pride.

Evie wondered how she could tell Volok this story and make him believe her. She didn't have to think about it for long.

'You? You did it? A mere ogress killed my wife, my queen?'

Volok's roar was so loud the boulders in the cave rumbled and shook. Dust fell from new cracks that appeared in the ceiling. He stomped into the cave. Evie gasped at the look of utter rage on his face. His eyes flashed bright yellow, his nostrils heaved and his mouth oozed saliva. Volok was literally shaking with fury, growling, baring jagged teeth. Evie turned her head slowly to look at Olga. What would she do now?

Evie had never seen the ogress look petrified before, and it was quite pathetic at first. She watched the ogress rise slowly to her feet then turn to face her master.

'My lord, I believe that Madruga planned to betray you,' Olga mumbled. She was a poor liar. 'I had to act quickly. It was my sworn oath to protect you.'

'STOP!' Volok roared. 'My wife would never have betrayed me. *You* betrayed me when you betrayed my wife to those assassins! It was *you* who planned this monstrous act, and *you* who carried it out! All this time, it was YOU!'

In a startlingly quick move, Volok lifted a boulder from the ground, raised it over his head and flung it at Olga. Evie felt the air whip over her head as the boulder hit its target, sending Olga smashing into the wall beside her, the boulder splitting into pieces. Volok bounded into the cave and stood over her, breathing hard. He picked up two large pieces of broken rock, one in each of his enormous hands, and pummelled the ogress hard, over and over, all the time roaring.

'It was you! You betrayed us! Aaaaaaaghh!'

Black blood spattered all over the nearest wall, on the

ground and on several rocks and boulders around the site of the assault. But still Volok punched and thrashed, releasing his great rage.

Evie felt utterly revolted and turned her eyes from the horrifying attack. Glancing at the casket, she saw that Nala had closed her eyes, not wanting to see it either. Evie sat on the floor of the cave, helpless, terrified at the thought of what Volok might do once he was finished punishing his servant.

CHAPTER TWENTY-EIGHT

Volok's rage wasn't over once he stopped punching. After that, the demon lord took his temper out on his surroundings, causing a partial cave-in as he repeatedly threw boulders into the darkness at the back of the cave. He seemed to have forgotten that Evie was still there, tied up, a witness to it all.

Evie tried to catch Nala's eye. They couldn't risk speaking – even a whisper might direct Volok's rage at both of them – but perhaps they could understand each other's signals. After a couple of attempts, Evie caught Nala's attention.

Nala looked around until her gaze drifted to a spot near Evie's feet, then back to Evie's eyes. And again. Evie looked down. Then she saw it too: a pointy shard of rock that had flown off one of the smashed boulders lay within reach. With Volok kicking and smashing through the debris of the cave, he mightn't notice Evie manoeuvring to get it. She had to try. Though risky and awkward, after a few attempts she reached it. Holding it firmly in her hands behind her back, she began to saw at the vines.

But it wasn't working. These vines were sappy, making them difficult to cut, unlike the dry rope before. Even the razor-sharp edge on the stone wasn't enough to cut through.

Evie looked at Nala, trying to convey the problem with an anxious look. Nala made a tiny nod and closed her eyes. Evie was puzzled. She watched the sorceress concentrating, then she thought she heard a faint humming. What was she doing?

Volok followed his smashed boulders to the back of the cave where he continued to roar, bellow and bash about. Evie thought Nala might be going into a trance. She looked different; her face was moving strangely, quivering and wobbling, and the humming was growing louder too. Evie kept looking around to see if Volok had heard it. Luckily he was too busy making his own noise. But something was happening, Evie could feel it.

To her dismay, Volok let out an almighty roar, making the rocks judder again, and then sheets of dust fell from the ceiling. Evie feared the cave might completely collapse on them before they could escape.

Evie turned to Nala in desperation.

'You're a sorceress! Do something, please!' she cried.

Nala seemed to be ignoring her. Her eyes were closed again but her humming was growing louder still, a peculiar, squeaky sound. Evie watched the sorceress's face move through a range of expressions. She didn't know what Nala was doing but hoped it would be helpful. The humming ended abruptly in a choking gasp. Nala's face was still and pale, her eyes stared out blankly, and beads of sweat began to trickle off her brow.

CRACK!

The vines around Evie's wrists and ankles suddenly broke and flew off. Evie rushed over to Nala. Her eyes closed slowly, and her head slumped to one side. She looked drained of energy and so much older.

'Nala! Wake up! Please, talk to me!' Evie whispered, as loudly as she dared.

There was no response.

Evie made a quick and daring decision. She closed the two little doors on the casket, then checked her coat pocket. To her great relief, the Black Ruby was still there, it hadn't fallen out. She lifted the casket, then she froze, horrified to see Olga rising to her feet, black demon blood streaming from her many wounds.

'Impossible!' Evie whispered.

'You,' Olga hissed, glaring at Evie. 'This is all your fault. My plans were perfect until you came along! I am going to kill you, if it's the last thing I do!'

Olga tried to charge, but her injuries were so great, she staggered and fell.

Evie's own legs suddenly felt like lead. She couldn't believe that Olga had survived such a brutal attack. She watched Olga struggle to stand without falling over. Turning her gaze towards the back of the cave, she knew Volok could re-emerge at any moment. She was caught between the two of them. How would she get out alive?

'Evie,' Nala said. 'Take out the Black Ruby. Now! Do it!'

'Wh-what?' Evie said, looking down at the head in the casket. 'Are you crazy?'

'Trust me,' Nala said. 'Just do it!'

Holding the casket under one arm, Evie fumbled in her pocket and pulled out the ruby with her other hand.

'Hold it up high,' Nala said. 'Make sure Olga sees it.'

Evie was deeply confused. What sort of a plan was this? Had she been completely fooled by all of them?

'Aha!' Olga cried. 'You have it. Look, my lord, she has it! The Black Ruby is here! I'll bring it to you now, after I kill her.'

'Don't move, Evie,' Nala said, defiantly. 'Stand your ground and hold the ruby as high as you can.'

'I don't understand,' Evie said. 'This is sheer madness!'

'No,' Nala said. 'This is magic. Believe it.'

Olga approached only slowly, limping awkwardly, stumbling frequently, and unable to get Volok's attention as he continued to thrash and bash his way around the back of the cave. The walls and ceiling juddered with every crash, and even his roars were causing new cracks and more rockfalls.

'At last,' Olga cried, her eyes locked on the ruby. 'After all this time, all this effort and sacrifice, I will finally reach my goal.'

Evie was standing with one arm raised, the ruby in her hand, as instructed. Tucked under her other arm was the casket. She risked a quick glance down.

'Nala, do something, please,' Evie pleaded.

But Nala wasn't listening anymore. She was chanting now, her voice strangely deep, her words unfamiliar. Evie's arm began to ache as she watched Olga inch her way across the space between them.

Then the moment came. With a wolf-like howl from Nala, black lightning shot from the ruby in Evie's hand, blasting Olga back against the far wall. Her injuries had been bad before, but this time they were horrific. This time she really was dead.

Stunned, Evie let her raised arm drop to her side and she stared at the weapon in her hand.

The shockwaves from the lightning strike reverberated around the cave, causing so much damage, a complete cave-in was inevitable now.

'Evie! We must go,' Nala said. 'Evie! Now!'

Shaking herself back to reality, Evie thrust the ruby into her pocket, held the casket tight and turned to run. But her way was blocked by huge lumps of rock and earth crashing down all around her. She huddled against one wall, bracing herself for an avalanche. But before it came, Volok's howling grew louder, then he thundered past Evie and ran right out of the cave. Evie followed close behind him, but Volok was so enraged he didn't stop. Somewhere outside, a tree crashed to the ground, then another. The demon lord was on a rampage.

Standing at a safe distance, Evie watched the cave collapse in a huge cloud of dust, rock and earth – on top of Olga's remains. She felt strangely calm and without a trace of remorse.

Volok had left a trail of destruction behind him. Trees were uprooted, bushes flattened, rocks had been moved violently. Whether he had seen her use the Black Ruby or not, Evie knew he could return at any moment. She broke into a run.

Once again, Evie hoped and prayed that her horses and carriage would be waiting where she had left them. Hurrying along, her concern turned to Nala. Was she still alive? Was the running movement making Nala's head bump around inside the casket? Would that be the final mortal blow? Would her death be Evie's fault after all that had happened, and what then would she do with the head?

'No, please no!' Evie cried. Suddenly, tears filled her eyes, blurring her vision. The impact of having killed someone, albeit a demon, finally hit her. Several times she stumbled, making her fear even more for Nala's safety as well as her own. She could feel herself weakening as the distance she ran never seemed to end. When the carriage finally came into view, Evie blurted out a few cries of joy and relief. The horses whinnied softly in recognition as she climbed up. She tucked the casket under the driver's seat and took hold of the reins.

Evie left the horses and carriage with their stable boy. She had no time to explain herself and hurried inside – straight into the housekeeper.

'Oh! Mrs Hudson.'

'Hello, Miss Evie. I hope you enjoyed the party at the Reids' residence. Goodness me! Were you out in that awful rain earlier?'

'What? Yes. Um, it's stopped now,' Evie said. 'The party, yes, I was. I mean, I am. I'm going now.'

'Now? But it must be nearly over,' Mrs Hudson said. 'It's almost six o'clock. Your father will be home soon. He works so hard, and on a Sunday too.'

'Yes, he does,' Evie said. 'Where is Mother?'

'Mrs Wells?' Mrs Hudson said, frowning at Evie like she was a naughty little girl. 'You got up late this morning, Miss Evie. Mrs Wells left very early to go to your Great-aunt Maud for a few days. Your Aunt Agatha and your mother have decided to take turns looking after her after her recent fall.'

'Oh, yes, of course,' Evie said. Freddie had mentioned something about that.

'And Miss Julia would like to see you. She's still too weak to get out of bed.'

'I'll go and check on her,' Evie said.

'I spent a lot of time with Miss Julia today with no one else available,' Mrs Hudson added. 'Mrs Wells is worried about her. That cold is lingering too long. And everyone thought you were at a party.'

'I um, I had an errand to do,' Evie mumbled, annoyed at Mrs Hudson's prying. The housekeeper had a way of behaving like she was in charge whenever Evie's parents weren't around. 'You must excuse me, Mrs Hudson. I have to take this—'

'Evie, you got it!' Freddie cried, as he tore down the hall, sliding expertly on the polished parquet floor. 'I knew you'd find it! I knew it!'

'What? Oh, yes, here you are,' Evie said, handing him the casket.

'I'll take it up to my room,' Freddie said, taking the casket and running straight upstairs.

'Careful! Don't open it till I come up,' Evie called after him, as Mrs Hudson eyed her suspiciously. 'Just something I promised to pick up for Freddie while I was out. He's very excited.'

'So I see,' Mrs Hudson said. 'I'm surprised you could collect anything on a Sunday. What a strange day this has been.' She turned and went back to the kitchen.

Evie bolted upstairs, holding her skirt so she could take two steps at a time.

'Freddie! Don't open it!' she whispered fiercely.

'Don't worry, I was waiting for you,' Freddie said. 'Is this something special, something magical?'

Evie looked at him. Freddie stared back.

'It is, and how do you always know so much?' Evie asked him.

'Look at it!' Freddie said. 'It's obvious!'

'I suppose,' Evie said, taking the casket from him. 'That was very smart, by the way, when Mrs Hudson bumped into me. Thank you for covering for me, and yes, this is another big secret.'

'Can you tell me what's in it?' Freddie asked.

'Not yet,' Evie said, wincing.

'Aw, but you said, "don't open it", so there must be something important inside.'

'All right, yes, you're right – again,' Evie said. 'There is something inside, but it's rather frightening.'

'I'm never frightened,' Freddie said. 'Show me and tell me everything.'

Before dinner, Evie went to see Julia in her bedroom.

'How are you feeling?' Evie asked.

'Plagued by this dreadful cold,' Julia said. 'Mrs Hudson has been fussing. Apparently, your mother has said that a physician will be called if I don't improve by the time she returns. Where have you been, Evie? I kept everyone as distracted as I could, which wasn't easy from here. So did Freddie. He was a great help.'

'Thank you,' Evie said.

'So what happened?' Julia asked. 'You seem to have been very busy.'

Evie told her governess the whole story. It was almost too much for Julia in her weakened state. Freddie joined them, offering Julia some chocolate he had opened, though she didn't feel much like it.

'Now you both know everything,' Evie said.

'Where is the casket now?' Julia asked.

'In Freddie's room,' Evie said.

'Under my bed, beside my box of soldiers,' Freddie added.

'Tilly would certainly spot it in my room,' Evie explained.

'If she finds it in my room, she'll just think it's another toy,' Freddie said.

Evie nodded. 'But we can't leave it there for long.'

'Certainly not,' Julia said.

'Nala is insisting that I remove her h– remove her from the casket while she is still alive,' Evie said. 'If she were to die in the casket, the enchantment will be broken and it won't be able to contain the Black Ruby or anything, for that matter.'

'What happens once you remove her head?' Freddie asked.

'I don't know,' Evie said.

'Uh oh!' Freddie said.

'I was hoping the enchantment will take care of that,' Evie said.

'When are you going to do this?' Julia asked.

'When she wakes up,' Evie said. 'I want to talk to her first. She only woke for a brief moment when I was telling Freddie the story. She said she needed to sleep, something about preparing for her last magical moment. I thought Nala was going to die after using magic to untie me, and then again with the black lightning.'

'It's remarkable she could do anything in that state,' Julia said.

'I don't think she can use magic often in the casket,' Evie said.

'She's probably been saving it for something really important,' Freddie said. 'And at least Olga is gone now.'

'Yes, it is a relief,' Evie said. 'One demon down, one to go, and one to prevent coming back. I don't feel at all sorry about it. Should I? Olga is dead after all.'

'Absolutely not!' Julia said. 'You were lucky to get out alive.'

'I suppose so,' Evie said. 'If there hadn't been that cave-in, Volok would have turned his wrath on us.'

'Hopefully now, he'll just run away and never come back,' Julia said.

'If only,' Evie muttered.

Suddenly, the whole household was interrupted. Opening the bedroom door, Evie listened to the kerfuffle downstairs. The police were at the hall door looking for her. She hurried downstairs. Matthew and Grace were standing in the hall beside a very bewildered Mr Hudson.

'Evie, you're all right!' Matthew cried.

'Thank goodness,' Grace said. 'We were so worried.'

'What has happened?' Evie asked. For a split second Evie almost burst out laughing at the question, thinking of all that she had just been through.

'When you didn't turn up this afternoon, we thought you might have gone to – Dower Hall,' Grace whispered.

'Why don't we talk in the parlour?' Evie said. 'Mr Hudson, would you please ask Mrs Hudson to bring us some tea?'

'Thank you, but we don't have time for tea, Evie,' Matthew said.

'Oh?'

'Samuel, I mean, Constable Banks wants us to go down to the police station right away.'

'The police station?' Evie said.

'That's right,' Samuel said. As he stepped into the hall Evie caught a glimpse of two more constables waiting outside. 'I am the bearer of bad news, I'm afraid,' he said. 'There has been a murder.'

CHAPTER TWENTY-NINE

E vie turned to see her father walk quickly up the driveway towards the hall door. He was wearing his overcoat and carrying his briefcase. He looked tired.

'What on earth is going on?' he asked brusquely.

'I'm sorry to interrupt your evening with unpleasant business, sir,' Samuel said, stepping aside to allow the professor to enter his house. 'There's been a murder in Crompton village.'

'How dreadful!' Evie's father said. 'Anyone we know?'

'A local man, a Mr Charles McGinn,' Samuel said. 'Miss Wells was acquainted with Mr McGinn, so I must ask her to accompany me to the station.'

'I beg your pardon!' Evie's father cried. Looking absolutely horrified, he turned to Evie. 'Do you know this Charles McGinn?'

'Only a little,' Evie said. 'We all do, except Matthew. We met him on our way back from the picnic a few weeks ago. You remember, I told you we had to stop to have a horse reshod. Mr McGinn was in the Crompton Arms where we waited and sheltered from the rain. We only spoke briefly. He told us he knew Lucia, the woman who died in the fire in Dower Hall.'

'Well, Constable?' Evie's father said. 'What else do you need to know from my daughter?'

'I was instructed to bring everyone who met Mr McGinn over the last few weeks to the station for questioning, sir,' Samuel said uncomfortably. 'My sergeant would expect me to include Miss Wells as I have already questioned Grace ... I mean Miss Finch. I understand that Miss Pippen is unwell, and therefore unavailable.'

'I see,' Evie's father said.

There was a pause. Samuel began tapping his pencil against his police notebook, waiting.

'I think it's just routine, Professor,' Matthew said quietly. 'Best to get it over with.'

'Yes, very well,' Evie's father said. 'But why are all of you here? What else is the matter?'

'Nothing, Father,' Evie said quickly. 'You heard Constable Banks and Matthew. The police just want to get a sense of what happened before—'

'Precisely,' Samuel said. 'It won't take long, sir. I will escort Miss Wells back here myself.'

'You're too busy, Samuel,' Matthew said. 'I can do that.'

'Thank you both, but I will take my daughter to the station and I will bring her home again,' Evie's father said. 'Give me a moment please, Constable. I just want to leave these papers in my study. Get your coat, Evie, dear. Hudson, ask Jimmy to prepare the carriage please.'

'Certainly, Professor,' Hudson said, immediately hurrying away.

Satisfied that he had taken charge of the situation, Professor Wells returned to his study for a moment. When he came back out, he spoke briefly to Mrs Hudson, then ushered everyone outside.

Evie was shocked, wondering whether Charlie's death might have somehow been her fault. Even if it wasn't, not directly, she should have tried to warn him of the danger.

'Evie, dear, are you listening to me?' her father asked.

'Sorry, Father. Yes?'

'You are not to be alarmed, this is just routine,' he said. 'I would prefer if you didn't have to see the inside of a police station at all, ever. They are always full of rough types, as well as the constables and the sergeant, of course. But Constable Banks said it won't take long and Grace seems to have found the questioning all right. I'm sure you'll be fine.'

'I'm not worried about the questions,' Evie said.

'What then? You look most upset,' her father said.

'Mr McGinn was murdered,' Evie said.

'Yes, of course, dear,' her father said. 'A frightful crime, frightful. But you didn't know him *well*, did you? Did any of you?'

'No, we didn't,' Evie said. 'But he was kind to Lucia, and no one deserves to be murdered.' Evie squirmed, reminded of how she was responsible for Olga's death, even though magic had also been involved.

'Certainly not,' her father said. After a pause, he asked, 'Is this bringing back unpleasant thoughts? It would be quite understandable, you know. I'll make sure this interview doesn't take long, leave it to me. I'll telephone Mr Finch when we get to the station, just to be sure.'

Evie tuned out of her father's chatter. It really wasn't the interview that bothered her, but Charlie's death certainly did.

She was also concerned about Nala lasting long enough for Evie to return and do what she must: remove Nala's head and place the ruby inside the casket *before* Nala passed away. She wanted to talk to Nala too. She fidgeted impatiently, knowing it would all have to wait.

Fortunately the questioning at the station was swift, and there were no difficult questions or awkward moments for Evie to explain. It struck her that Samuel was trying to show off in front of his sergeant, and he wasn't a very experienced interviewer. When she came out of the interview room, Matthew and Grace were waiting with her father, and Grace's father was just walking in the door, looking frazzled.

'I'm sorry I took so long,' he said. 'I was dining early with Judge Forbes. He really does prattle on. Thank you for telephoning me, Henry.'

'It's a good thing all the stations have a telephone installed now,' Evie's father said.

'We were just waiting for Evie,' Grace said to her father. 'But her interview is over now, so I think we can leave.'

Professor Wells and Mr Finch began to chat, as they always did whenever they met. Evie, Matthew and Grace stood outside to talk.

'Samuel said he would be "buried under all the paperwork he had to do",' Evie said. 'He won't be joining us.'

'I think he's very excited about the investigation,' Grace said. 'He's going to be involved right from the start, unusual for a new recruit, but he was the first constable at the crime scene.'

'It's a good opportunity for him,' Matthew said. He turned to Evie. 'Your note said you were coming to the party, Evie, but when you didn't arrive Grace was convinced something dreadful had happened. I was worried too.'

'We decided to look for you,' Grace said, looking keenly at Evie as if she knew every secret she was keeping.

'There were lots of people in the house,' Matthew said. 'We didn't think anyone would notice we were missing, at least not straight away.'

'I suggested we call to the station and ask Samuel for help,' Grace said.

'Oh, dear, what a mess,' Evie said. 'That was so kind of you, though the police will be suspicious now.'

'Suspicious?' Matthew said. 'Of what?'

Evie said nothing.

'Evie, tell us what happened,' Grace said gently.

'All right,' Evie said, 'but you have to promise me you will never tell anyone.'

They promised.

Evie kept it short. 'Charlie called to our house early this morning, but our butler didn't know him and wouldn't let him in. Charlie left a note, telling me he had found the ruby from my necklace. So, I took our carriage and went after him.'

'My word! In that awful rain? You are brave!' Matthew said.

'Did you find him?' Grace asked.

'It took longer than I expected but yes, I caught up with him and he gave me the ruby,' Evie said. 'It's safe in my house now. But why were you in Crompton?'

'Grace thought you might have gone to Dower Hall,' Matthew said. 'I thought you might have gone to Crompton to find Charlie.'

Evie looked surprised.

'Remember, the notebook?' Matthew said.

'Of course,' Evie said, remembering that Matthew had spotted her talking to Charlie outside the parish hall in Millbury, near Crompton.

'Crompton was on the way, so we headed there first,' Matthew continued. 'Samuel and those two constables who were at your house just now came with us. When we arrived, however, the village was up in arms. Charlie had been found dead in his barn. The police confirmed he had been murdered.'

'They had to change their plan to look for you, and investigate the murder instead,' Grace said.

'One of the constables went for more help,' Matthew said. 'Meanwhile Samuel and the other constable started the investigation. The villagers were understandably upset. I'm sure they don't have many murders, and they didn't like strangers nosing around either.'

'We were stuck there for over an hour,' Grace said. 'Once the coroner and his team arrived, Samuel said we could take his carriage back, but we still hadn't found you, Evie. For a while, we thought you might be dead too!'

'Oh, Grace, Matthew, what an ordeal!' Evie said. 'What can I do to make it up to you?'

'We'll think of something,' Matthew said, smiling at her. 'More importantly, thank goodness nothing happened to you.' He paused. 'Is there anything else you want to tell us?'

'No, nothing at all,' Evie said. 'I'm sorry you had your whole afternoon and evening messed up because of me. And I'm sorry I have to say sorry so often! You don't deserve that.'

'As Matthew said, we're just glad you're all right,' Grace said.

Professor Wells and Mr Finch emerged from the station house.

'We must meet up soon,' Matthew said quickly. 'Let's go for afternoon tea, or perhaps that walk. Or both, and somewhere local. No driving madly in carriages! What do you say?'

'That would be lovely,' Evie said.

'Good idea,' Grace said.

'And we should ask Samuel too, if he's free,' Matthew said. 'I think he felt a little uncomfortable having to question the two of you. Was he any good, by the way?'

'I don't know,' Evie said politely. 'I haven't been questioned in a police station before.'

'Me neither,' Grace said.

Evie and Matthew smiled, but Grace still looked uneasy.

'Are you sure you're all right, Grace?' Evie asked gently. 'Arriving in the middle of a murder scene must have been awful.'

'I'm fine, thank you,' Grace said. 'We can talk about it again, but right now, I'd just like to go home.'

'Let's arrange that outing as soon as we can,' Matthew said.

This time Evie felt Grace wasn't just suspicious, her friend *knew* something was afoot, something big. Evie really couldn't put off telling her much longer. But there was that nagging doubt again – *should* she tell her?

Evie felt certain that it was Olga who had killed Charlie because he hadn't got the ruby when she went to confront him. Hopefully the ogress hadn't forced him to tell her where it now was, and then killed him anyway. The one-eyed man must have been spying on Charlie ever since they met at the inn. That meant he must also be spying on Evie, her family, her friends. In that case, everyone Evie cared about was in grave danger.

CHAPTER THIRTY

It was a relief to Evie that her shortened version of events had satisfied both her father and the police. Her father suggested that they wouldn't tell Evie's mother so as not to worry her, and Evie readily agreed.

After a late supper, Evie crept back to Freddie's room and took the casket back to her own bedroom. She desperately wanted to talk to Nala but had to wait patiently until she woke.

Shortly after midnight, Evie cleared her bedside table and placed the casket on top. She simply couldn't wait any longer. Sitting down on her bed, she gently opened the two little doors. Nala's sallow skin had a deathly pall about it now and the lines around her eyes had deepened. She looked drained, near death, Evie thought with a shiver.

'Nala, please wake up,' Evie whispered. 'We really need to talk.'

Evie watched Nala's eyeballs roll around under her eyelids for a moment. Then the sorceress opened her eyes wide and gasped for breath.

'I am still here, but only just,' Nala said in a croaky whisper. 'Performing the magic to free you, and then a second time to fire the black lightning, has weakened me.'

'I'm so sorry,' Evie whispered.

'I was glad to do it,' Nala said, trying to smile. 'Think of it as my parting gift.'

'But I have so many questions,' Evie said. 'Can't you stay with me a little longer? You would be safe here. I would take care of you, somehow...'

'I have run out of time,' Nala said. 'You must release me, even though it will kill me. That way, the magic will remain within the casket, keeping the ruby safe.'

'How does it protect the ruby?' Evie asked.

'It doesn't,' Nala said. 'It protects the world *from* the ruby.'

'Oh, I see,' Evie said, though she wasn't sure she did.

'No one must find it,' Nala said. 'No one. Ever. Remember, you *must* finish the Ladder of Charms to be endowed with the harp's magic. Destroy the ruby with the power it gives you, then you won't have to spend your whole life hiding it, fearing it, never to be free of it.'

'I honestly don't know if I can do it,' Evie said. 'But I will try my hardest.'

'No Harp Maiden knows what she can do until she tries,' Nala said. 'The harp chose you and that tells me you can succeed. But you must believe it.'

'I will, I promise,' Evie whispered.

'Always be on your guard, Evie,' Nala said. 'Volok is alone now and desperate, beyond furious. He may need more than the ruby to revive his wife fully because of the way she was killed and because she was such a powerful and complicated demon. That means he may come after you for the harp as well as the ruby, or for revenge – or both. Finding out it was Olga who betrayed him will send him into a blind rage.

He will see it as his fault, because he never even suspected her. That's what made it possible for her to carry out such an audacious task. Preparing Madruga's heart for the ritual should keep him occupied now, giving you the opportunity to complete the Ladder of Charms.'

'I understand,' Evie whispered, her voice barely audible.

'And lastly,' Nala said. 'Many powerful talismans are cursed. I don't know if it is true of the Black Ruby, but better to know just in case.'

'What kind of curse?' Evie asked.

'It could be anything,' Nala said. 'Always respect magic, good and evil alike. Take pride in what you do and who you are – a Harp Maiden. Given the tasks that lie ahead of you, Evie, you may be the most important Harp Maiden of all time.'

Evie took a deep breath, trying to control her racing heart, her whirring mind and her hands which were trembling again.

'My final moment will not be unpleasant,' Nala said gently.

Evie looked at her. 'Good. I mean, I'm glad for you. This is so … so weird.'

Nala smiled. 'Ask the boy to join us,' she said. 'I sense exceptional instincts in him. Keep him close, Evie. He will be helpful to you.'

Evie immediately went to find Freddie. He was sitting on the floor in Julia's bedroom doing a jigsaw puzzle, waiting for her.

'What's happening?' Freddie asked immediately.

'Nala wants you to be with me when she goes,' Evie said.

'Really?' Freddie said, getting quickly to his feet. 'I'm ready!'

Julia looked shocked.

'She said it will be all right,' Evie said.

'Are you sure?' Julia asked.

Evie gave Julia a firm look, hoping the governess wouldn't start arguing with her.

'All right, then. I'm coming too,' Julia said, getting out of bed. She paused. 'Do you think Nala will mind?'

'Er, no,' Evie said. 'Do you feel well enough?'

'I think so,' Julia said. 'This is an extraordinary moment. A moment I don't want you or Freddie to deal with on your own, and one I don't want to miss.'

Julia wrapped herself up in her dressing gown and followed Evie and Freddie along the landing to Evie's bedroom.

They sat beside each other on the bed – Evie, Freddie and Julia. The casket was still on the bedside table, Evie closest to it.

'Ready?' Evie asked softly.

'Yes,' Julia whispered.

Freddie nodded, his eyes locked on the casket.

Evie opened one door at a time. Her hands were steady again, her mind focused. Julia took in a sharp breath, Freddie a deep but silent one. Nala's eyes were already open; she was ready too.

'Just reach in with both hands, take hold of my head and lift me out,' Nala said softly. 'The magic will do the rest.'

'Goodbye, Nala, and thank you,' Evie said.

'Goodbye, Evie. Good luck.'

Their eyes met as Evie slowly reached in and gently lifted the head out of the casket. Evie held Nala's face level with her own, eye to eye, thought to thought, then it happened. A wind came from nowhere, whipped lightly around Evie and the casket, then Evie's hands and Nala's head as Evie held it for just a moment. Then Nala simply faded away, dissolving into moon dust which in turn disappeared, leaving only a tiny sprinkling falling through Evie's fingers and onto the wooden floor. Evie sat, watching the moon dust fall, her arms still raised, her hands at shoulder height as if stuck in position, empty. She wouldn't have believed it if she hadn't seen it for herself.

'She's gone,' Freddie whispered.

'Yes,' Evie said.

Julia took a few whooping breaths, and Freddie ran to the dresser to pour her a glass of water.

'It's, it's, I mean, it's so, so incredible!' Julia said, between gulps.

'Extraordinary,' Evie said.

'I think you mean dangerous,' Julia said, gulping more water.

'So much magic,' Freddie said. 'I always knew magic was real.'

'Now, for the next part,' Evie said. She went to her closet and took out her sewing box. A beautiful antique, it had belonged to her grandmother. Moving slowly and reverently, Evie took out the Black Ruby. 'I removed it from your room earlier,' Evie said to Freddie. 'I'll be glad to finally put it somewhere where no one can touch it.' She lifted a black shawl from her bed and sat down again. 'I'm going to wrap the ruby in this, so it won't rattle around inside the casket.'

'Good idea,' Julia said.

Evie wound the shawl several times around the ruby. 'Once I put it inside,' she said, 'it can never come out, unless I take it out. Only me.'

'What happens if someone else tries?' Freddie asked.

'I don't know,' Evie said, 'but you're not to try it.'

'I would never do that,' Freddie said. 'I told you. I believe in magic.'

'Where will you keep the casket now that it has contents again?' Julia asked.

'For now, inside Freddie's toy chest,' Evie said. 'It'll be surrounded by all his toys, so no one will notice, and only Freddie goes to his toy chest anyway. Right, Freddie?'

'Right,' Freddie said. 'I won't let anyone near that casket.'

'The Black Ruby is very powerful,' Evie said, looking at both of them in turn. 'I saw that with my own eyes when the black lightning shot out of it and killed Olga. We must never forget, never say anything by accident that might let anyone know the Black Ruby is here in this house.' Evie paused, letting the enormity of what she said sink in. 'Once I finish all the charms, I will have enough magic within me to destroy the ruby. But until then, I have a lot more to learn, and we have to keep the ruby safe. This is a huge and dangerous secret.'

'It most certainly is,' Julia said. 'I'm not sure I like it at all.'

'I promise to keep it a secret,' Freddie said. 'But I think Uncle Henry would love to know about it. He has told me great stories about magic, and he said today that he wants to talk to you about something he found.'

'Oh? Good,' Evie said, wondering what on earth that was about. 'I'd like to keep the casket in my bedroom tonight, but I'll bring it to your room early in the morning, Freddie. I don't want to risk making noise doing that right now. We have to be very careful. Always.'

'Well done, Evie,' Julia said, patting her shoulder. 'That can't have been easy, and it was definitely the strangest thing I have ever seen.'

'Thank you, Julia,' Evie said. 'I feel a bit strange myself, a bit numb.'

'I'm not surprised,' Julia said. 'Try to get some sleep. Goodnight.'

'Goodnight, Julia,' Evie said. 'Goodnight, Freddie, and remember, quietly back to your room.'

'I know,' Freddie whispered, then closed the door behind him without a sound.

Evie blew out the candle beside her bed and snuggled under the covers. She thought long into the night about whether the Black Ruby was really cursed, and, if so, how much trouble might lay ahead because of it.

CHAPTER THIRTY-ONE

Next morning Evie's father called her to his study. He sounded unusually tired, even a little cranky. She thought he might want to ask her about Charlie again, then with relief, she remembered.

'Freddie said you had something to tell me,' Evie said, closing the door behind her.

'That's right,' her father said, eyeing her over his spectacles. His expression softened a little. 'Let's sit on the sofa and we can look at the books together. But first I wanted to talk to you about some other, though I think related, matters.'

Evie's mind went into another spin. She sat down gingerly beside her father. There was a pile of books on the coffee table in front of them. Evie recognised the books; she had read them, each one important to her own research. She dreaded the thought of having to lie to her father if he came too close to the truth.

'As you know, I've been doing a lot of research on the artefacts, antiques and paintings that were either stolen from Dower Hall or destroyed in the fire,' her father began.

'You said some of them were very special,' Evie said.

'Quite so,' her father said. 'I'm almost finished figuring

out the last two: the decorated chest and a very, very old candelabra. I know they sound ordinary but believe me they are not. My research journey led me down many diverse avenues. Eventually, I found an amazing story that ties in almost perfectly with many historical facts I am already aware of, but also some of the artefacts from Dower Hall. I thought you'd like to hear it.'

'I'd love to,' Evie said, excitement quickly replacing anxiety.

'It's about the Harp Maiden, a girl born under a full moon on the first of January,' her father said. 'Just like you, my dear!'

'Oh! Um, really?' Evie stuttered, as her stomach did a flip.

'But first, Evie, help me to understand why you are so interested in these things.' He tapped the books on the table. 'I have been asking myself if they have something to do with your recent, uncharacteristic behaviour.' He raised a hand to stop any protest. 'I know there is something going on, so don't deny it. I just want to make sure you are safe and well, and not doing anything you shouldn't.'

'Um, what do you mean?' Evie asked.

'I think you know,' her father said, his tone serious. 'All these investigations of yours, and mine, keep leading us both back not only to Dower Hall and that awful incident last New Year, but to the study of dark magic and demons.'

Evie stared at her father and swallowed hard.

'I see I've struck a chord,' her father said.

Evie's thoughts and emotions were so stirred up she couldn't think what to say. No excuse would come to mind, and her father would be difficult to convince even if she thought of one. He was so clever, and this was his area of expertise. She didn't know how to get him off the subject. Then she was thrown a lifeline.

'It's all right, dear, don't fret,' her father said, taking her hand in his. 'I understand that you need to find some reason behind all the horror you endured, to understand your kidnappers' motivations. But these people are not the demons of the past, Evie, they are the demons of today, dangerous criminals, like the sort who murdered Mr McGinn. We must leave it to the authorities to hunt them down and deal with them appropriately. And no more borrowing carriages and racing off to Dower Hall to look for goodness knows what. More artefacts? Or the trail of the missing housekeeper? And making friends with strangers in remote villages! That's not like you at all, Evie.'

Evie was completely baffled. How did her father know so much?

'I know all about it,' her father said, almost reading her mind. This is impossible, Evie thought, feeling herself wilt, but her father continued. 'Jimmy felt he had to tell Hudson that you took the carriage, and Hudson told me. And Jimmy's cousin is a stable boy in Branston. Yes, I know about that one too.'

Evie groaned.

'It was reckless, Evie,' her father said. 'Both times!'

Finally, Evie spoke. 'I'm sorry for taking the carriage without permission, though I did find it rather thrilling.'

'Thrilling? It was dangerous!' her father said. 'You haven't driven a carriage before.'

'But I have!' Evie protested. 'That's how we escaped from Dower Hall.'

'That was a cart, not a carriage,' her father said.

Evie had a sudden thought. 'Actually, I think I'd like to learn how to drive a carriage, properly, and ride a horse too,' she said. 'Freddie would love it. We could learn together.'

'All right, we can talk about that again,' her father said. 'But that's not really what we're talking about now, is it?'

'No. And you're right, I do feel I have to understand what happened,' Evie said, truthfully. 'Despite being held a prisoner there, I need to go back … to try to finish it somehow.'

'But it's not safe,' her father said.

'What isn't?' Evie asked.

Her father sighed. 'A burnt-out, deserted manor house will attract robbers and vagrants,' he said. 'It's not a safe place to be. And this McGinn fellow, how did he know Lucia was in Dower Hall?'

'Well, Crompton isn't too far away,' Evie said. 'All the locals probably know the manor house.'

'And what about this notebook he gave you. May I see it?'

Evie was taken aback. 'It's just a notebook,' she said. 'He told me it belonged to Lucia, so he thought I should have it. She gave me other personal things too.'

'I'd like to see this notebook, Evie,' her father said, in a tone that wouldn't accept any argument.

'Now?'

'Yes, please.'

Evie left the room greatly disturbed. Her father would instantly date the diary to the mid-fifteenth century when Nala had written it. She ran up to her room. Her father mustn't hold onto it, she thought. She had to finish the charms immediately after the full moon and learn all the secrets. Oh! The moon! With all that had happened, Evie had nearly forgotten.

With a sinking heart, Evie took the notebook out of her drawer. She left her bedroom and walked reluctantly downstairs.

'Thank you,' her father said. 'My, my, this is very old indeed.' He stood up and went over to his desk, picked up his magnifying glass and studied the notebook carefully. Evie could only watch and hope as her father gently turned the pages.

'This is remarkable!' he said, finally looking up. 'It has to be at least four hundred years old, probably more. It must have had several owners, yet all the pages are blank except the first one. What an interesting letter, "Dear Harp Maiden". That phrase again. I must check into it some more. Evie, what is it?'

Evie had been staring at the notebook, appalled by just how close her father was to unveiling her secret life. She looked up to find him gazing at her very intently.

'Is there anything else you wish to tell me?' he asked.

'No, nothing,' Evie said, rather quickly. 'May I have the notebook back? I like to keep all Lucia's things together. I feel responsible for them.'

'Of course,' her father said, never taking his eyes off her. 'You won't mind if I take another look sometime, will you? Some of my colleagues at the museum might like to see it too.'

Evie nodded as he handed it back. 'Is that everything?'

'Yes, that's all, Evie,' her father said. 'And please, no more escapades. I just want you to be safe and well. You do understand?'

Evie nodded. 'Perhaps you could tell me that story another

time,' she said, 'when you're less busy.'

'Yes, I think you'll find it interesting,' her father said. 'I hope to know a little more when we next talk.'

Evie tried to smile as she left the room, but only managed a sort of half-twitch of her mouth. Her father was bound to uncover more, perhaps everything, about the Harp Maidens, the harp, Nala, Volok, all in his professional capacity. He would soon know as much as she did, perhaps even more. What would he say if he learned that she was the Harp Maiden? Evie wasn't sure but it worried her.

CHAPTER THIRTY-TWO

The day of the next full moon dawned overcast and Evie wondered if she would be able to make a wish at all. But by evening the clouds had broken and she was feeling more optimistic. The conversation with her father had been strange and she wondered if he knew more than he was saying, perhaps hoping Evie would reveal more.

At breakfast, the professor was reading the newspaper.

'Dreadful business, this Boer War in South Africa,' he said. 'Here at home there are reports of vandalism in the woods around Dower Hall.' He looked at Evie over the top of his paper.

'That's terrible,' Evie said, and continued munching on her toast.

'It says here that trees have been uprooted,' her father said. 'Good grief! That would take some effort. And a cave-in! Good heavens!'

Evie made no comment about the cave. She was glad Olga was gone, buried forever under all the rock and rubble till she rotted away to nothing. Volok might come after her when he was finished taking his rage out on the forest, or whatever else he could lay his hands on. Thank goodness it was a sparsely populated area, she thought. Hopefully, Volok wouldn't go into any of the villages. But as Nala had said, it was unlikely he would stray too far from where he was keeping Madruga's heart, not when time was running out to resurrect her. She sneezed, her nose irritated by the memory of the awful stink coming from the green pool.

'You're not catching Julia's cold, are you, dear?' her father asked. 'Perhaps you should stay indoors for a few days.'

'No, no, I'm fine,' Evie said. 'It was just a sneeze. Julia is feeling a little better at last. She's hoping to get up for a few hours today.'

'That's good news,' her father said. 'I hope you and Freddie are keeping up with your schoolwork without her.'

'Yes, we are,' Freddie said, entering the room. 'I'm starving.'

'You're late this morning, young man,' Evie's father said.

'Sorry, Uncle Henry,' Freddie said. 'I took ages to fall asleep last night.'

'Eat up now and off to your studies,' Evie's father said. He folded the newspaper and stood up. 'And I am off to my studies. I haven't forgotten about that story, Evie. Perhaps later.' He smiled and left the room.

The rest of the day passed normally enough. Evie and Freddie studied in the parlour. Evie kept a close eye on the weather through the window, wondering about the ritual.

'Full moon tonight,' Freddie whispered across the table. 'What are you going to wish for?'

'Better health for Julia,' Evie whispered. 'Her lungs have been troubling her for years. It's time she got some relief.'

'They're getting worse, aren't they?' Freddie said.

'I think so,' Evie said. 'She still looks ill, though she says she's feeling a little better. She's probably just making a big effort. Well, I will make things better for her tonight.'

'That's good,' Freddie said. 'But staring out the window won't make it happen any sooner.'

'No, but the moon must be out, and shining brightly,' Evie said. 'I hope those clouds blow away in time.' She put her book down. 'I've had enough of this French poetry. Do you mind if I practise the next charm? I can't concentrate on regular schoolwork right now.'

'I always like when you play the harp and the flute,' Freddie said. 'You know, we should study more history and learn all about magic and where it came from.'

'I'm trying to,' Evie said. 'But Father is already doing that. He's suspicious. He knows about the carriage rides too, and he wanted to see what Charlie had given me.'

'Nala's notebook? Whoa!' Freddie said, dropping his pencil.

'He knew immediately that it was really old, much older than Lucia was,' Evie said. 'He's a brilliant historian. How could he not know?' Evie sank bank in her chair. 'And he wants to look at it again. But I can't let him. I need it for the charms.' She got up from the table and walked to the bay window. 'If Father brings it to the museum to show to other people, who knows when I'll get it back?'

'Who told him about it?' Freddie asked. 'It wasn't me.'

Evie didn't know but she felt uneasy about it.

Evie was pleased with her charm practice before she moved on to some harp pieces, including the melodies that she liked to play during a full moon. Freddie enjoyed listening while he tackled his arithmetic.

'Oh, no!' Evie said, suddenly stopping her strokes. She ran from the room, Freddie hot on her heels. The two of them raced up the stairs and into Evie's bedroom.

'What's wrong?' Freddie asked.

'I don't think I have enough parchment for tonight,' Evie said, pulling out a drawer.

'But you said you have lots,' Freddie said.

'Yes, but it's in Father's study, and he'll be even more suspicious if I ask for it now! Again!' Evie rummaged through the drawer. 'I thought I had some spare sheets in here, somewhere. Where is it?'

'You sound like Uncle Henry now, always misplacing things,' Freddie said.

'Evie!' A voice came around the door.

Evie jumped back from the chest she was searching, pulling the drawer right out onto the floor with a bang, upsetting the contents.

'Sorry,' Julia said. 'I meant to give you this, but I've been cooped up in my bedroom so long, I forgot.'

'Oh, thank heavens!' Evie said. 'I completely forgot we decided to keep it in your room instead. What a relief!'

'Goodness me,' Julia said. 'You are tense.' The governess came in and closed the door. 'What has happened now?'

'Father is suspicious,' Evie said, then she related their conversation.

'I see,' Julia said. 'If he's working late again tonight, he may hear you leave the house. That will be difficult to explain.'

'We could cause a distraction,' Freddie said. 'Like he told me in our war games.'

'You mean a diversion,' Julia said.

'Exactly, yes,' Evie said. 'But what?'

'I could have a bad dream and keep him in my bedroom reading to me for ages,' Freddie said.

'Not bad,' Evie said.

'Or I could say I was hungry, and I could wake Uncle Henry instead of Tilly.'

'Perhaps not,' Julia said.

'You could give him one of Aunt Clara's sleeping draughts,' Freddie said. 'It always puts her to sleep, but she left it behind when she went to Great-aunt Maud's.'

Evie looked at Julia.

'I'm not sure,' Julia said.

'But it's perfect!' Freddie said.

'She keeps the sleeping draught beside her bed,' Evie said. 'I've mixed some for her before.'

'It's still there,' Freddie said. 'I saw it when I woke Uncle Henry a few times.'

'I'll take a look,' Evie said. She got up, hesitating. 'It is safe, isn't it?'

'Oh, many people take a sleeping draught,' Julia said.

'I might just use a tiny bit,' Evie said, 'and I'll ask Mrs Hudson to prepare a big, heavy dinner. That should definitely make him sleepy.'

'I'll stay awake and distract him if he hears anything,' Julia said. 'That has been my task at each full moon since January.'

'Thank you,' Evie said. 'I really can't afford to miss any full moon. And the sleeping draught?'

'It would be harder to explain that you're making a magical wish, if Uncle Henry finds you going outside in the middle of the night,' Freddie said. 'But it can't be as bad to just send him to sleep. He needs a rest anyway.'

And so it was decided.

Before going down to dinner, Evie placed the handkerchief in her pocket, the one that now held the pinch of sleeping powder. After much dithering, she decided to only use a tiny bit, hoping Mrs Hudson's generous dinner would help her father sleep soundly too. Evie had requested his favourite roast beef with all the trimmings as a special treat – she didn't say why.

Evie was all set, though she had a gnawing twinge in her stomach. She hated deceiving her father by playing a trick on him. But because he was up at all hours lately, she convinced herself that she had to take this precaution.

'Thank you, Mrs Hudson,' Evie said, taking her father's night-time tray of tea. 'I'll bring that into the study.'

'Very well, Miss Evie.'

'Thank you, dear,' her father said, looking up briefly. He had copious notes on the desk around a pile of books, all of them open.

Evie poured the tea, stirred in the two lumps of sugar he liked, then she added the powder and left it on his desk.

'Don't work too late,' Evie said.

'I won't, dear, I won't,' her father muttered, deeply engrossed.

Evie left the study, wondering if her father would drink the tea at all, let alone enough of it to make him sleep. Still, there was nothing more she could do, and he had eaten a very big dinner, though he had worked through lunch. She went up to her room still feeling a little uneasy.

As always on the night of a full moon, Evie went to her bedroom a little earlier than usual. She packed the satchel and laid out sensible clothes, then she lay down on the bed to rest. Having left the curtains open, she watched the clouds break up then gather again. Whatever the weather would be, would be; she would have to go out anyway.

Evie woke with a start having dozed off. That had never happened before. She looked at the clock. 'Phew!' she said out loud. It was only one o'clock in the morning; there was still plenty of time. But was there a moon? She looked out and to the right. Almost, yes, no. It was less cloudy but not completely clear either. Nonetheless, she gathered up her things and crept downstairs.

The light was still on in the study, but she didn't hear the usual mutterings that her father was inclined to make while he worked, nor the scratchings of his pen. The door wasn't fully closed so Evie peeped through the crack. Was her father in there or had he left the study, having forgotten to turn out the light? She needed to open the door just another tiny bit to be sure. Pushing it gingerly, it creaked. She winced, closing her eyes, trying to think of some excuse to explain why she was there at such a late hour. None came to her. She really needed to get better at finding excuses quickly. Opening her eyes and then the door, she saw that her father was sprawled over his books, fast asleep.

Evie donned her coat and hat, collected the harp and headed outside. By the time she reached her usual spot, the moon was shining brightly. But it wouldn't be for long. Large clouds were scudding towards it. Evie had to hurry and she was glad of her preparation: the wish was already written, the tiny bundle of firewood was ready and the matches were in her hand. She lit the fire and began to play. When it was done, she quickly quenched the fire, gathered her things and hurried home.

Professor Wells was still asleep slumped over his desk. It was just as well, Evie thought, that she had already made a wish for his arthritis to be cured, otherwise he wouldn't be able to move when he woke in the morning. She glanced at the door to the kitchen and the Hudsons' quarters. There were no concerns there; the Hudsons always slept soundly. All was well.

Evie yawned, suddenly feeling tired herself. Hopefully she would see a transformation in Julia's health as soon as tomorrow – no more bad colds, bouts of flu, wheezing coughs or anything else to bother her delicate lungs. Evie felt satisfied. Now she could concentrate on finishing the charms. Tomorrow, Evie thought. Tomorrow I will finish the next one and then sprint through all six steps, without delay. Then I will know exactly how to destroy the Black Ruby and that will put a stop to Volok's plans, and an end to Madruga forever.

But it wouldn't be the end of Volok. Once the ruby and Madruga were out of the way, Evie had to deal with the demon lord himself. Hopefully, there would be something in Nala's notebook to guide her through that horrifying task too.

CHAPTER THIRTY-THREE

Alone in her bedroom, Evie was ready. She had prepared well and played the next charm flawlessly. Watching the words emerge on the page as the secret was revealed, Evie got a shock.

Only one wish may be granted for any one person in their lifetime.

Evie smacked a hand against her forehead. 'Julia!' she cried, realising that she had already used a wish for both Julia and Freddie the night of her first wish on New Year's Day. 'That's why I didn't see her this morning. She isn't fully well. And I thought she would bounce into the breakfast room, right as rain.' She groaned. 'I've wasted a most precious wish!' Evie was almost in tears. 'Another mistake, and all because I didn't take enough care. I was in too much of a rush, then I was too slow! How foolish, how stupid! What an idiot I am!'

She looked around to find Freddie standing in the doorway.

'It's a mean rule,' he said. 'Maybe you should just wish for all the demons to die.'

'I never thought of that,' Evie said, calming down. 'I'm not sure I can. Maybe I'll find out when I finish more charms. Either way, I shouldn't say such things out loud. You must remind me, Freddie, make sure I don't do that again.'

'If you can make wishes come true, I think you should be allowed to choose whatever you like, good or bad,' Freddie said.

'I should have known it wouldn't be straightforward,' Evie said, bitterly disappointed. If she had known that she couldn't wish for Julia, she could have wished for Grace, after several postponements.

Evie was still cross with herself when she visited Julia later and explained what had happened.

'If I had known you were going to wish for me, I would have told you to pick a more worthy cause,' Julia said. 'Don't fret over it, Evie. It's another good lesson learned. And I'll be fine.'

'That's because you are completely unselfish,' Evie said. 'I just wanted to help you, to repay you for everything.'

'There's no need to repay me at all,' Julia said. 'And you did help me, enormously, when you saved me and Freddie in that snowstorm.' Julia took Evie's hands in hers. 'I am feeling better, but it will take another few days for my energy to come back. I've lived with this problem for most of my life. I can manage. Start thinking about next month's full moon, and the month after. Perhaps you could do something to help Charlie's family.'

'I already thought of that,' Evie said. 'I will wish for them, but I'll be more careful now. It's too easy to make a mistake.'

But Evie remained frustrated for the rest of the day. Just when she thought she was making good progress while facing up to so much danger, she was making errors like a novice. Well, never again, she thought, as she sat in her room staring into the mirror. I will work carefully through those charms and reveal all their secrets. I cannot afford to make any more silly mistakes, and who knows what the consequences might be?

Evie decided to avoid her father as much as possible for the next few days, not wanting to give him another chance to ask for Nala's notebook. But she was worried. Passing him briefly in the hall, she noticed that he didn't look at all well, and hoped it had nothing to do with the sleeping draught.

'He works long hours,' Julia said, after Evie mentioned it. 'I'm sure that's all it is.'

'Perhaps it was a risk using it,' Evie said. 'Another stupid thing I've done!'

'Now don't be silly,' Julia said. 'I was just fussing when I asked you to think about it. I get cranky when I'm not feeling well, as I'm sure you've noticed. And I've checked my first aid book. Sleeping draughts are harmless in small doses. In fact, they often don't work at all, and your father is a big, strong man. Don't worry, he'll be fine. We all will.'

Evie needn't have worried too much about avoiding her father, because he hardly left the study. But eventually, the professor was forced to leave his work when he went to collect Evie's mother from the train station. Her mother wrote saying that Aunt Agatha was taking over Great-aunt Maud's care for the following week, allowing Evie's mother to return home. Hudson was out on errands, so Evie's father went to collect Mrs Wells.

'All the trains have been held up,' Tilly said, when she returned from the town with some groceries. 'There was a fault on the line. Professor and Mrs Wells are likely to be delayed.'

'Father won't be pleased,' Evie said.

'Indeed no,' Tilly said. 'Perhaps Mr Hudson should have gone to collect the mistress after all, seeing as she'll be late.'

Then Evie had an idea. She grabbed her coat and headed off to the local library.

Miss Grimes was a most knowledgeable librarian, very polite though very strict and rather nosey too. She was a thin, wiry woman of about fifty, with grey hair wound tightly into a neat bun and piercing blue eyes behind small round spectacles. Her efficiency was widely known, and she had a curiosity to match Evie's. But Evie liked and respected her, agreeing with her father that she was an absolute 'fountain of knowledge'.

Evie approached Miss Grimes at the counter, observing the rule of silence, a rule the dedicated librarian took very seriously. They nodded in greeting, the fewer words spoken in the silent library the better. But before Evie could ask for anything, Miss Grimes put up a hand for Evie to wait. She bent down and lifted a pile of books up to the counter.

'The books your father ordered arrived sooner than expected,' she whispered. She smiled her tight little smile, proud of her high standards of service. 'I assume you are here to collect them?'

'Oh, yes! Thank you,' Evie whispered, trying to hide her surprise.

Miss Grimes nodded. 'Take a look,' she whispered. 'Make sure they are all there.'

Evie separated the books, checking the titles. She didn't know what books her father had requested, but they were all of interest to Evie: books on demons, talismans, ancient curses, and most startlingly of all, The House of Yodor.

Evie checked herself quickly, knowing Miss Grimes noticed everything.

'All in order?' she asked pointedly.

'Perfect, thank you,' Evie whispered back.

Miss Grimes date-stamped the books and handed them back to Evie. With another nod in acknowledgement Evie was dismissed, and Miss Grimes greeted the next customer with the same brief nod of her head and tight little smile.

The books were very heavy and by the time Evie arrived home, her arms were aching. She plonked the books down on the highly-polished hall table to ease her muscles for a moment, carefully avoiding the expensive Venetian vase – her mother's favourite birthday present from her father. It had been filled with a bouquet of fresh flowers from the garden by Mrs Hudson that morning. After removing her coat, Evie took the books to her father's study. Grabbing some paper and a pen, she sat at her father's wide mahogany desk. Today would be a day for study of a different kind, she thought. Evie opened the first book and knew immediately that she would not be disappointed.

She spent most of the morning reading and taking notes, now and again wondering where her parents could be. It must have been a dreadful delay, she thought, but it meant she had time to read without having to explain. At one point, Hudson popped his head around the door after returning from his errands. He was surprised to find Evie at her father's desk.

'I collected these books from the library,' Evie said. 'I'm helping with some research.' She smiled at Hudson. He was a very particular butler and undoubtedly worried that Evie might disturb her father's things.

'Very good, Miss Evie,' he said, but he didn't look pleased. 'I hope Professor and Mrs Wells will be back soon. I know he will not like long interruptions to his important work.'

Evie noted how the butler stressed 'important work'. How he doesn't like change, she thought, not even the tiniest alteration to his routine, or anyone else's. He's quite like Miss Grimes, really.

Evie looked down at her notes; she had written a couple of pages already. Perhaps she should leave the books and look at the notes in the privacy of her bedroom. Hudson was bound to find excuses to check up on her until her father returned. She gathered up the pages, closed all the books, leaving them in a neat pile on the desk and went upstairs.

In her bedroom, Evie reread her notes, written in no particular order.

> *Madruga and Volok embarked on many quests for talismans – magical artefacts, which they intended to use to increase their power and extend their realm. Their goal was to become all-powerful, perhaps even immortal, with the help of their powerful black magic. Together they led massive armies, slaughtered and conquered rulers and lands at will, anyone that stood in their way.*
>
> *Demons can hibernate for decades, regenerate their strength, then re-emerge and live for hundreds of years.*
>
> *Demons have extraordinary powers of healing, hearing and smell.*
>
> *Wick's End was once known as Witches' End.*

The legend tells how an army of demons defeated the witches who had lived there for centuries. They were the only group who finally stood up to the demons' endless aggression. Volok was the leader of the demons who defeated the witches of Witches' End, the last known coven of witches in the land. The placename was later changed to Wick's End.

The witches had been forest dwellers, rumoured to have enchanted the trees in the forests where they lived. Those trees would remain forever susceptible to magical influence or control, but only by someone who could command dark magic.

Demons were suspected of taking over the bodies of humans, using their new 'positions' to further their aims. Many grew bored or impatient with such practices and returned to their violent ways. The search for the five primary talismans by many demonic tribes caused endless death and destruction.

'I knew it!' Evie whispered into her notes. 'I knew there was something about those trees. And it wasn't Wick's End, it was *Witches'* End, where witches lived and enchanted those weird trees!'

Her mind was buzzing as she moved on to her notes about the Black Ruby.

It was rumoured that Nala of Yodor returned to the kingdom to hide the Black Ruby once King Udil was dead, placing it in the king's coffin so it would remain hidden forever. But a demon-ogress was later seen digging up graves. Eventually it was assumed that the ogress must have found it, for the king's grave was not only opened but destroyed. Some claimed it was merely robbers looking for treasure. Many feared that the ruby, believed to be powerful as well as cursed, had finally fallen into demon hands.

Evie was already aware that the Black Ruby could restore a demon's life, but here was more confirmation.

It was written: 'If the heart of a dead demon is preserved using demon magic, the Black Ruby has the power to bring the demon back to life.' There is no record of such a ritual being successful, but the rumours struck terror into the people of every neighbouring land.

Evie thought about the oil sack dripping over the murky green pool, and how the strange thing throbbing inside it had to be Madruga's heart – there was no doubt at all. She stood up and walked over to her mirror. 'You must finish this, Evie,' she whispered to her reflection. 'It is your quest now. There is no one left to stop them. Only you ... only me.'

She put away her notes and picked up her flute, deciding to practise the remaining charms of step one, and finish them on the harp that very afternoon. She was already curious, and a little nervous, about what steps two to six would reveal and how they would undoubtedly become harder as she edged closer to her goal. Evie's mind kept wandering and she put down her flute. She had made the mistake of rushing before and must not make it again, no matter how keen she was to finish. She looked at the harp beside her. Nala had told her that Volok might want the harp's magic as well as the ruby. All that was left of Nala's magic was inside the harp. That harp was in Evie's house, along with all the people she loved. So was the Black Ruby. She shuddered to think how Volok's desperate search might lead him right into her home.

CHAPTER THIRTY-FOUR

B y early evening Evie's parents had not returned. Julia made an effort to join Evie and Freddie at the table, but it was a quiet meal. Everyone was worried that there might have been an accident. Hudson had gone to the train station to see what was happening but there was no word yet.

Dinner came and went. Julia went back to bed. Evie and Freddie went to the parlour where Freddie read *Little Lord Fauntleroy* again and Evie prepared to play the next charm. She opened Nala's notebook and practised it one final time on the flute. There would only be one chance to get it right, or she would have to wait until after the next full moon – weeks away. She could not allow that to happen.

Evie had prepared well and played it without error. She quickly turned the page to see the secret of the fourth charm reveal itself.

> *No wish may be made that would cause injury, harm or death.*

'That's understandable, I suppose,' Evie whispered, after reading it out loud.

'Does that include Volok?' Freddie asked, looking up from his book.

'I suppose so,' Evie said. 'Violence and death are always terrible. Now, for the fifth and final charm of step one.'

'Step one?' Freddie said. 'How many steps are there?'

'Six,' Evie said. 'Each step is like a rung on a ladder, the Ladder of Charms,' she mused.

'Sounds like it will lead you somewhere,' Freddie said.

'To magic, Nala's magic, the magic that can destroy the ruby and then the demons,' Evie said. 'I don't know how many charms are on each of the next steps, but I hope it won't take too long.'

'You're doing really well,' Freddie said.

'I've only just started,' Evie said, sounding a bit deflated.

'You'll finish them quickly,' Freddie said. 'I know you will.'

Evie smiled at his optimism and hoped he was right. She picked up her flute and tried the next one. It sounded awful, a whining jangle of notes.

'That's a charm that would scare a snake!' Freddie said.

'Yes,' Evie said, unable to hold back a giggle. 'This one might take me a bit longer.' She tried it again. It was very awkward, but at least it was short, and she would work at it all evening. Hopefully, she would be ready to play it on the harp in her bedroom later, and then move on to the start of step two in the morning. She wondered if each step would be similar or completely different. Different, she decided. And probably increasingly difficult too.

Later, Evie was in her bedroom, warming up her fingers on the harp before playing the fifth charm of step one, when the sound of several voices in the hall disturbed her. Hurrying downstairs, she saw her mother standing in the hall with Hudson and a strange man. Her mother was being assisted, and she looked distraught.

'What has happened?' Evie cried. 'Where's Father?'

'Evie, dear, this gentleman accompanied me home from the hospital,' her mother said.

'What hospital?' Evie cried.

'Your father has had a stroke,' her mother said. 'The doctors are taking care of him.'

'What!' Evie shrieked. 'Will he be all right?'

'He's comfortable now,' her mother said. 'Dr Elliott is still with him, but he insisted I go home. Hudson met us on the way back.'

'Will he recover?' Evie pressed, her voice breaking as tears filled her eyes.

'The good doctor is very hopeful,' her mother said, then she swooned. The strange man, a hospital attendant judging by his uniform, rushed to her aid. Hudson swiftly opened the door to the parlour and the attendant helped Evie's mother to an armchair. He whipped out a small bottle of smelling salts from his pocket and waved it under her nose. It quickly revived her. Evie listened in shock as Hudson explained how he had picked up the Wells' carriage at the station, and quite by chance, caught up with Evie's mother and the attendant coming back to the house in another carriage. Quietly Hudson asked the attendant a few questions, receiving only brief answers. Evie couldn't hear what was said. She looked on, stunned. Nala's words hit her like a tornado: 'The Black Ruby is rumoured to be cursed,' she had said. The library book had mentioned it too.

'Evie, where is Evie?' her mother called, as she came to.

Evie went to her mother's side, held her hand and tried to comfort her. Mrs Hudson stood by waiting to assist, and Tilly appeared with a tray of tea for everyone. Thankfully, a little rest on the settle, together with some sweet tea and reassurance helped to calm Evie's mother. Then Evie, Tilly and Mrs Hudson fussed over getting the mistress of the house up to her bedroom. Julia and Freddie had come down from their rooms to see what all the kerfuffle was about.

'Will Uncle Henry get better?' Freddie asked tearfully.

'Of course he will,' Evie said. 'You know how strong he is. We mustn't worry.'

'But you can't wish for him again, can you?' Freddie mumbled.

'Shush now, we all wish him a speedy recovery,' Julia said. 'And Dr Elliott is an excellent physician. He will take care of him.'

Julia and Freddie followed everyone else up the crowded stairs.

When calm finally returned to the house, Evie found it impossible to sleep. She sat up and lit a candle. Despite her wakefulness, she couldn't risk playing the charm. With her head and her heart in such a spin, she was bound to mess it up. It could wait till morning, when they would hear more about her father's condition. But the thought of an ancient curse terrified her. If it were true, Evie could never be sure what else might happen, what other accidents or tragedies the ruby might bring about. And right now, Evie had no way to stop it. With the pressure on all sides mounting, and her cloak of secrets and lies lying heavy on her shoulders, tears spilled down Evie's cheeks. She thought about her father lying in the hospital bed and hugged her pillow tight, hoping exhaustion would soon send her to sleep.

CHAPTER THIRTY-FIVE

For the next two days, Evie didn't dare leave the house. Like the rest of the household, she waited anxiously to hear the latest news of her father. Professor Wells was doing well, Dr Elliott said, but he wanted to keep a close eye on him for a couple of days. He was in a room by himself, receiving excellent care. No one except Mrs Wells was allowed to visit, and the family was not to worry about him catching infection. He would be home as soon as the proper nursing care could be arranged in the Wells' home.

Matthew and Grace sent kind replies to Evie's letters, telling them about her father's stroke. Evie felt the old anxiety bubbling beneath the surface again. Having found a new determination and trying so hard to get on top of all she had to do, suddenly everything looked bleak. She felt shaken to the core and wondered if using the Black Ruby to destroy Olga meant the ruby was exacting some sort of payback as part of its curse. She chided herself for such wild imaginings, but the thought gnawed at her anyway.

Even the weather was awful. All the April showers seemed to arrive together, and it poured and poured. Evie struggled to remain hopeful about anything, frequently retreating to her bedroom and her music.

After a few difficult days – waiting for updates about her father, then for his return home, and finally having a new routine established in the house – Evie was delighted to see Matthew and Grace. They finally persuaded her to meet in one of the lovely tea rooms in the town. Her friends were anxious to know how Evie was doing and asked particularly after her father. She was glad of their company and grateful for their concern.

'Your life has been turned upside down this last year,' Grace said.

'Enough about me and my woes,' Evie said. 'What have you two been doing? Give me some good news.'

'Nothing strange or different for me,' Grace said.

'My father has been keeping me very busy with his new project,' Mathew said. 'A *secret* project.' He smiled at Evie. 'Now that we both have a secret, Evie, we must find one for Grace.'

'I'd like that,' Grace said. 'Then one day, we can share all our secrets and compare them!'

Evie gave a watery smile. She didn't want to talk about secrets, but a couple of things had been bothering her. She had to mention them, though it made her feel uncomfortable. 'Did either of you tell anyone about Charlie giving me that notebook?' she asked. 'You remember, the day we were in Branston for the concert.'

Grace and Matthew looked at each other, then back at Evie.

'Absolutely not,' Grace said. 'That was a private matter.'

'I gave you my promise,' Matthew said. 'And I kept it.'

'Someone else must have seen me,' Evie said. 'My father

questioned me about it shortly before he became ill. He said he thought I was behaving strangely.'

'Well, you have been, sort of,' Grace said quietly, dropping her gaze.

'I said I would explain when I could,' Evie said. 'But the time is not right. I'm sorry. Yet again.'

'What you really mean is that you haven't told your father about your secret either,' Matthew said. 'Or your mother. Though I'm not sure about Julia and Freddie.' He eyed her mischievously.

Evie stared at Matthew, unsure what to say. She didn't want to ruin the whole afternoon by getting into a row or creating any awkwardness between them.

'Perfectly understandable,' Matthew continued, rescuing the situation. 'I wouldn't tell my father any of my secrets either.'

'Does he have a secret too, Matthew?' Evie asked.

Silence.

'Does he?' Evie asked again.

'You mean the project?' Matthew asked. 'I simply can't tell you what it is just yet. I'm sworn to secrecy for another little while.'

Evie was looking at Matthew but she could feel Grace staring at her, no doubt wondering what Evie really meant. Then Evie took the plunge.

'How well did your father know the maestro, Mr Thorn?' Evie asked.

'The man who kidnapped you?' Grace shrieked.

'He, um, he mentioned him once or twice,' Matthew said, clearly uncomfortable. 'I didn't like to tell you as I thought it might upset you ... after what happened.'

'Yes, it does a bit,' Evie said. 'When did your father last see him?'

'Ah,' Matthew said, 'I was hoping you wouldn't ask me that.'

Evie felt instant alarm. Her pulse was racing, her hands were clammy, and all of a sudden, she felt betrayed too. Had she taken more of her friendships for granted without giving them a single sensible thought?

'When was it, Matthew? Was it when I was held prisoner?' Evie asked.

'Goodness, no!' Matthew said, his face showing as much alarm as Evie felt. 'He told me he knew Thorn some years ago – *years*, Evie, *decades*. They had met in college but lost touch, and then he heard that Thorn was living in Dower Hall. He called to the house once but was told to go away by a very rude housekeeper, apparently.'

'Could that have been the same housekeeper you met, Evie?' Grace asked.

'Probably,' Evie said.

'He tried once more after that, but no one answered the door,' Matthew said. 'He wrote a couple of letters, because he felt sure someone was in the house. He said he heard music, so someone must have been there.'

'It could have been Lucia,' Evie said. 'If he had tried harder to get in, he might have saved her!'

'Evie!' Grace whispered.

'Well, perhaps,' Matthew mumbled. 'I don't really know.'

Silence.

After a moment, Grace said, 'Or Mr Reid might have been kidnapped too, or even killed.'

'Yes, of course. I am sorry,' Evie said.

'Someone might have impersonated him,' Grace said. 'It might not have been the real Mr Thorn at all.'

My word! Evie thought. How insightful she is! It was a demon who possessed his body and kidnapped me, but I can't tell them about demons! I just wonder how much Mr Reid knew, if anything.

Another pause.

'Yes, I think Grace must be right,' Matthew said. 'How did you discover that they knew each other at all, Evie?'

'I saw Mr Thorn's name and address on one of your father's sheets of music,' Evie said. 'When he spilled them in the carriage after the last concert.'

'You should have told me right away,' Matthew said.

'I didn't like to,' Evie said. 'I didn't know how, and I was afraid that perhaps you had been friends too.'

'Certainly not!' Matthew said. 'I didn't mention their acquaintance simply because I didn't want to upset you. Really, Evie, you must believe me. My father had nothing to do with that man and his appalling behaviour. They met thirty years ago and then went their separate ways.'

'That's a relief, isn't it, Evie?' Grace said, trying to help.

'And they had no further contact?' Evie asked.

'None at all,' Matthew said. 'Clearly something dreadful must have happened during that time to turn Mr Thorn into some sort of monster.'

Evie squirmed.

'Are you all right, Evie?' Grace asked. 'Here, have some more tea.' She poured another cup for everyone.

'Evie, please don't hold this against my father, or me

for that matter,' Matthew said. 'He simply called to Dower Hall hoping to reconnect with a fellow musician. That's all. He wouldn't have gone near the place if he knew what was going on there, what sort of man Thorn had become.'

'But you never said that you knew Dower Hall,' Evie said. 'Even when we were talking about it.'

'Because I didn't! I don't!' Matthew said. 'I don't listen to half my father's mutterings. I didn't even recall the name Thorn until he explained to me what had happened to you.'

'And there's nothing left of Dower Hall now,' Grace said. 'It's gone. For good. And so is Mr Thorn.'

More silence.

'Please, Evie, tell me this hasn't spoiled our friendship,' Matthew said.

Evie could feel Grace's foot tapping hers under the table, an encouraging nudge-nudge.

The silence continued for another minute. It was unlike Evie to be so quiet, but she found it hard to know what to say, what to think. She wanted to believe Matthew's version of events, and somehow she just couldn't see Mr Reid being a part of any demon plan to kidnap and murder. They drank more tea, ate cake and as they chatted about other things, mostly music, Evie began to relax. Music was always a subject of interest and they steered clear of further mention of Mr Reid's and Mr Thorn's history.

After another hour passed, Evie felt more reassured by Matthew but still a bit uneasy about his father. Any connection to Dower Hall could also be a connection, however innocent or unwitting, to the demons.

When Evie returned home, Dr Elliott had just left and the news about Evie's father was mixed.

Everyone gathered in the parlour.

'First of all, I'm happy to tell you that Professor Wells is doing well,' Evie's mother said. 'Dr Elliott is pleased with his progress.'

There were sighs of relief and several expressions of 'Thank goodness!'

'However,' Evie's mother continued, 'he will have a number of challenges for a while, and this will mean some changes around the house. I would ask everyone to be as accommodating as possible. Dr Elliott has given us a strict regime for Professor Wells to follow.'

'Whatever the professor needs,' Hudson said.

'Thank you, Hudson,' Evie's mother said.

'What sort of challenges?' Evie asked.

'The doctors are not sure if he will make a *full* recovery,' Evie's mother said.

Evie cringed at the sharp intakes of breath around the room, eyes glancing nervously from one person to the next.

'Professor Wells is having difficulty with his speech as you will have noticed, and also some trouble walking, though both are expected to improve with special exercises. I will be relying on you, Hudson, to take on some additional care duties for my husband, and the day and night nurses will remain in place for as long as Henry needs them. He will be confined to his bedroom for some time, but as you all know, nothing keeps him cooped up for long. I expect he will want his entire study transferred upstairs.'

There was a trickle of laughter at the thought of such a scene. Everyone knew the professor liked to be busy and lived for his work.

'It sounds bad, Aunt Clara,' Freddie said. 'Will he really get better?'

'I admit it sounds dreadful right now, dear,' Evie's mother said. 'But the doctor said this often happens after a stroke, and your Uncle Henry was lucky. His recovery will take time. Time and lots of patience – from everyone, especially Uncle Henry himself.'

Tilly left the room briefly and reappeared with tea and scones. Everyone looked like they needed some refreshment.

'Thank you, Tilly,' Evie's mother said, taking the first cup of tea. 'My husband should be able to return to work in his study, in time,' she continued. 'Travel will be out of the question, of course, for the foreseeable future.'

Evie couldn't help it; she burst into tears.

'There, there, dear, he'll be all right,' her mother said. 'You've had too many frights these last few months. Perhaps you should get some fresh air. You're looking strained lately.'

'I'm afraid it has just started to rain again,' Hudson said.

'Has it?' Evie's mother groaned, and the room fell quiet. The enormity of the professor's illness was beginning to sink in, including what it might mean for the whole household.

'I'll look after Evie and Freddie,' Julia said, breaking the silence. 'We've lots of lessons to catch up on.'

'Are you sure you're feeling up to it, Julia?' Evie's mother asked.

'Certainly,' Julia said. 'We'll start with music and art, nothing too demanding.'

The servants went back to their routines, and Evie's mother went to lie down. Freddie got his paints out and Evie sat at the harp but didn't play.

'What is it, Evie?' Julia asked. 'Is there something else bothering you? You must believe Dr Elliott when he says your father is doing well.'

'I do,' Evie said. 'It's such a relief to hear he will recover, it's just …'

'You're not worrying about the sleeping draught, are you?' Julia whispered.

Evie looked at her.

'Absolutely not,' Julia said. 'It had nothing to do with his stroke. Everyone knows your father has been working too hard. He needs a good rest.'

'It's not that,' Evie said. 'Nala told me the Black Ruby may be cursed. What if it is? What if that's what caused his stroke?'

Julia sat down on the settle. 'It couldn't. Could it?' she said. 'I mean, does that sort of thing really happen? Curses? No, it's nonsense, Evie. It has to be a myth, a fairy tale, that's all.'

'A myth or a fairy tale?' Evie said. 'But we know magic exists and if it does, why not a curse?'

'I can't answer that,' Julia said. 'Come, we need a break from these awful thoughts. If you don't feel like playing, come and paint with me and Freddie. You might feel like playing the harp or the flute later. You've had a shock, we all have. You'll be able to think more clearly in a day or two. Things won't seem so catastrophic. Your father is getting the best of care. Your mother will make sure he does everything the doctor tells him.'

Evie nodded and joined Freddie at the table to paint. But not for long. Despite what Julia had said, she needed to think – and not to think. Her list of worries and concerns was growing. She felt like a fly ensnared in a spider's web, only there were several spiders all preparing to pounce. She left the parlour and went to her bedroom to play the flute. Playing the flute always soothed her, and after an hour, she felt ready to practise the fifth charm. When she returned to the parlour to get the harp, she saw that Freddie and Julia were reading.

'Freddie told me you had only one charm left on step one,' Julia said, looking up from her book. 'Are you going to play it now?'

'Yes,' Evie said. 'Then I move to step two of six. I wish I had already finished them all.'

'One at a time is what it takes,' Julia said.

'I should warn you,' Evie said. 'This one doesn't sound very musical at all.'

'It's snake-charm music,' Freddie said.

Julia smiled. 'He did tell me it was peculiar.'

'It is,' Evie said. 'It's Nala's music, so we shouldn't be surprised that it sounds different from what I usually play. I should have asked her where she came from. I should have asked her many things.'

'Perhaps she wanted you to discover them yourself,' Julia said.

'The answers to all your questions are probably in her notebook,' Freddie said.

'You may both be right,' Evie said. She sat down at the harp and opened the notebook beside her to read the music. Settling herself comfortably on a stool, she took a few slow, calming breaths, then loosened up her fingers with some practice strokes. She began the charm. It was indeed a strange, unmelodic tune but Evie played it slowly, carefully and perfectly. As soon as she finished, she turned the page to see the secret revealed. Julia and Freddie came to her side to watch.

> *Prepare to leave your home, your family, your friends – everyone you know and love – and dedicate your life entirely to the harp.*

Evie looked at Freddie, then at Julia. All three were silent as she closed the notebook and left the room.

CHAPTER THIRTY-SIX

A few days later, a note arrived from Matthew. He would be leaving a little sooner than expected as the work with his father was complete, and there was a suitable train later that evening. He was sorry they wouldn't have time for their walk and asked if he could call on Evie before he left. His father had asked if he might come too to see Evie's father. Mr Reid wanted to offer him his best wishes. Evie wrote back, saying yes. She would be happy to see Matthew, though disappointed he was leaving early, and hoped it had nothing to do with their last discussion. She felt a bit uncomfortable seeing Mr Reid, though her concerns about his involvement in any nasty business were all but gone.

Evie and Matthew sat together in the parlour chatting with Freddie and Julia. After some pleasant conversation, Julia ushered Freddie out of the room with an excuse about lessons, leaving Evie and Matthew alone for a while.

'I wanted to tell you my secret before I leave,' Matthew said. 'Actually, it's not going to be a secret much longer.'

Evie was instantly on edge, but it was good news.

'My father is going to put an announcement in the newspaper and a notice up in the town hall,' Matthew said.

'Really? What for?' Evie asked, bursting with curiosity.

'We are opening The Reid Academy of Music,' Matthew said, 'and I am going to become a music tutor.'

'That's wonderful!' Evie said. 'Where will it be?'

'We're converting the old Mulligan building,' Matthew said. 'It was once a sewing factory right on the edge of town. We hired an architect and a builder to advise us. It's in surprisingly good condition, despite lying idle for over two years now. It will need complete refurbishment inside, though. That's why I've been so busy. We had to make a lot of decisions quickly so the builder could get started right away.'

'That is such a big project,' Evie said. 'But your own academy! You must be thrilled, Matthew.'

'Yes, I'm very excited now that it's really happening,' Matthew said. 'We hope to have it ready before the end of the year. My father would like the Hartville Ensemble to hold a concert to open it formally.'

'Wonderful!' Evie said. 'I'm so happy for you.'

'He wants to organise a scholarship too,' Matthew continued. 'For musicians who show talent but can't afford tuition. He's already looking for sponsors.'

'That's such a good idea,' Evie said, though for a moment it reminded her of Mr Thorn's scholarship. 'It's a wonderful thing to bring music to so many more people. Will all our lessons be held at the new premises once it opens?'

'Yes, all of them,' Matthew said. 'No more visiting homes or having students come to our home. Everything will take place at the academy. We are going to advertise heavily in the new year, hopefully take on more students, and in time, more tutors. My father wants to have a private secretary too, to organise everything. He certainly needs one!' Matthew rolled his eyes; his father's disorganisation was as well-known as his talent for teaching and his enthusiasm.

'You will find it hard to concentrate on your studies with all this going on,' Evie said.

Matthew nodded. 'Once I finish school this summer, I will be taking further music studies, which luckily, my father is qualified to instruct. It will be so convenient – studying at the academy and tutoring at the academy, doing what I love forever.'

'It sounds so perfect,' Evie said.

'Now you know almost all of my secrets,' Matthew said, his eyes twinkling, daring Evie to tell him hers.

'You have more?' Evie asked.

'I do, but nothing you should worry about,' Matthew said. 'And I hope we can put that business about my father behind us. I asked him about it again, and he was horrified to think that anyone might suspect him of working with a madman! He asked me to apologise to you on his behalf for upsetting you in any way at all.'

'Oh, you didn't tell him what I said, did you?' Evie asked.

'Not exactly, just that you were surprised to hear that he once knew Mr Thorn,' Matthew said. 'I assure you, Evie, he is totally innocent of any wrongdoing. He remembers Thorn as a quiet young man who adored music.'

'Well,' Evie said, 'I'm glad he might have been normal at some point in his life.' But Evie couldn't tell Matthew that the real Mr Thorn was an innocent man who had been possessed by a demon.

A short silence.

'Anyway, I wanted to see you before I left, mostly to make sure we are still friends,' Matthew said. 'And we are, aren't we, Evie?'

Evie looked into his soft brown eyes. How could she not believe him, trust him?

'Yes, we are, Matthew,' she said. 'We most definitely are.'

'Excellent!'

In that moment, Evie longed to tell him all her secrets. She almost had to bite her tongue to stop herself. 'And congratulations, Matthew! I really mean it,' she said, trying to change the subject back to something safer. 'What a lovely career you will have.'

'At eighteen years of age, I will be on track to fulfil my life's goal,' Matthew said. 'A life filled with music. I am very lucky. Do you know what your life's goal is, Evie?'

Evie hesitated.

'Do I detect another secret, or the same secret that I still don't know?' Matthew asked good-naturedly.

Evie tried to avoid his gaze, as well as avoid answering.

'Perhaps you'll tell me someday,' Matthew said. 'It really is most intriguing, which makes me all the more desperate to know!'

'Grace said something like that to me too,' Evie said.

'Grace suspected you had a secret long before I did,' Matthew said. 'You should talk to her, Evie. She's worried about you.'

Evie felt herself blush, which she knew made her look guilty and childish. She wasn't sure which was worse, and almost groaned with embarrassment.

'I want you to know,' Matthew continued, politely

ignoring her discomfort, 'that even if it is a deep and dark secret, it might be good to share it with someone you trust. You can trust me and I believe you can trust Grace too. We are your friends. And my other secret isn't the easiest one to share either.'

'Only one more?' Evie said, cheekily. 'Or are you just teasing me?'

'Sorry, I simply can't answer that!' Matthew said.

They both laughed, but for the first time, Evie thought Matthew looked embarrassed. She was about to press him good-naturedly, but she let it go. How lucky she was to have kind and loyal friends. She needed Matthew and Grace in so many ways, but that need could endanger them too. It might be another sacrifice she would have to make some day, and she dreaded it.

'Then let us keep our secrets secret,' Evie said. 'For now.'

'Agreed,' Matthew said. 'But we must write, Evie. School finishes in July, but please write and tell me how you are, tell me all your news. Promise me you'll write, and I'll promise not to mention that you have a secret to anyone!'

'I promise, Matthew,' Evie said.

'Then I promise too.'

Matthew squeezed Evie's hand, and she felt herself blush again. Why, oh why did she behave so ridiculously in Matthew's company?

They heard voices in the hall. Mr Reid was taking leave of Mrs Wells.

'I'm glad to see the professor looking so well,' Mr Reid said.

'He is doing well,' Evie's mother said.

'And Evie is doing well too, after her ordeal,' Mr Reid said.

'Yes, she is keeping busy,' Evie's mother said. 'She finds great comfort in her music.'

'She is a wonderful student. I knew that maestro, you know. Lionel Thorn.'

Evie froze behind the parlour door, causing Matthew to bump into her.

'Oops, sorry!' Matthew whispered. 'Oh dear, now isn't the time for him to mention this.'

Evie and Matthew didn't know whether to interrupt or not. They stayed in the parlour listening to the conversation on the other side of the door.

'Were you actually friends with that awful man?' Mrs Wells asked, sounding quite appalled.

'More … minor acquaintances,' Mr Reid said awkwardly. 'We studied music together in our youth, then we lost touch. Thorn was always a bit of a recluse as I recall. Loved music, and very talented. Isn't it shocking how someone can change?'

'Indeed it is! That man was a monster!' Evie's mother snapped. 'Good day, Mr Reid. Thank you for calling to see my husband.'

'Time to go,' Matthew said. 'Please apologise to your mother. You know how my father can bumble on, and he rather made a mess of that. Do you still promise to write?'

Evie hesitated, still trying to understand how Mr Reid could have any possible connection to what had happened to her.

'Well, take care, Evie,' Matthew said, deflated.

Matthew went out to the hall. His father was already waiting outside.

'I will write, Matthew,' Evie cried, hurrying after him. They stood together at the hall door, alone, Evie's mother having gone upstairs in rather a hurry. 'You can understand this was quite a surprise for me and for Mother. But I'll explain it to her again, she'll understand. She has been very upset lately.'

'Of course,' Matthew said. 'But I assure you my father would never associate with anyone who would break the law, and so horribly too.'

'I know,' Evie said. 'I believe you, Matthew. And I believe your father too.'

'Really?' Matthew said, hope lighting up his face.

Evie nodded, and Matthew suddenly gave her a warm embrace. 'I am so very glad, Evie,' he said. 'Thank you.'

'Matthew, you'll miss your train,' Mr Reid called to him.

'I must go,' Matthew said, releasing Evie. 'Goodbye, Evie. Take care of yourself. And talk to Grace. She needs your friendship as much as I do. And write often!'

'I will, I will!' Evie cried, almost laughing with delight and relief. 'Goodbye, Matthew. And work hard, very hard indeed!'

Evie laughed at the funny face Matthew made, and waved him and his father off from the gate. She stood watching while they drove away. Matthew would be gone for almost three months. Suddenly, Evie wished she had told him everything.

CHAPTER THIRTY-SEVEN

A week later, Evie finally received a reply from Grace, telling her that Grace and her father were going away, and they would call on her before they left. Mr Finch was also keen to see Evie's father.

When Grace and her father arrived, Evie knew immediately that something was wrong. Assuming that Grace was upset with her, Evie decided to open her heart and tell her everything. At last, Evie thought, my best friend will understand why I've been behaving so oddly. It would be such a relief! But something told Evie she should wait until she heard Grace's news first. She would be glad she did.

Grace seemed uneasy, distant, not her usual self. Evie brought her into the parlour, while Evie's mother took Mr Finch upstairs to see her father.

'It's good of you to call, Grace,' Evie said. 'Things have been rather chaotic since my father came home from hospital. We've all had to adjust to his new routine.'

'I understand,' Grace said. 'We've had some troubles too.'

Evie stared at her. Oh, no, she thought, not the Black Ruby again. 'Um, I hoped we could have gone to the tearooms again, to talk, catch up on things. But that can wait until you return. By the way, when did you receive my letter?'

'I'm sorry for not replying right away,' Grace said, awkwardly. 'It was rude of me, but I wasn't sure when I could come.'

'What happened, Grace?' Evie asked. 'Is everything all right?'

'My father is still bothered that we had a connection with a murdered man,' Grace said. 'He keeps going on about it.'

'I see,' Evie said. 'It was awful what happened to poor Mr McGinn.'

'Samuel told me that the police think it was a violent robbery,' Grace said.

'Very likely,' Evie said.

'Do you think so?' Grace asked. 'I don't understand what the robbers thought they could steal. Mr McGinn didn't appear to be wealthy.'

'No,' Evie said softly.

'Do you think that missing housekeeper had something to do with it?' Grace asked. 'She's still on the run, isn't she? You said you saw her.'

'I, um, I'm not entirely sure,' Evie said, surprised again at how close Grace had come to the truth.

'The police said there's been no trace of a woman that fits her description,' Grace said. 'But perhaps she changed her appearance, or she could be part of some criminal gang.'

'It's possible,' Evie said.

'She must know the police are after her,' Grace said.

Evie was wondering where the conversation was going. 'You said you had some trouble, Grace. Tell me, what was it?'

'My father's eldest sister died,' Grace said. 'My Aunt Violet. I didn't know her well, and they weren't close in recent years. There was some sort of falling out.'

'I'm so sorry,' Evie said.

'My father is doubly upset because of it, wishing they had made up before it was too late,' Grace said. 'We're on our way to the funeral now. It's not for another two days, but it's quite a long journey. We're going to stay with some distant cousins for a while. Father will have things to take care of afterwards.'

Evie nodded.

'We'll be away for about ten days altogether,' Grace continued. 'He wanted me to go with him for the full time, not just the funeral. He thinks I need a change of scene.'

Evie quickly calculated that Grace wouldn't be back until after the next full moon on 21 May. She didn't want to chicken out, but it didn't seem to be the right time to tell her friend all her secrets. Again.

'What is it, Evie?' Grace said. 'For a moment, you looked far away. I'm sorry, I should have asked about your father as soon as I came in. You said in your letter that he still has some difficulties after the stroke. Is there any improvement?'

'The doctor says he's doing remarkably well. You know how determined he is,' Evie said. 'His speech is difficult, though he has recovered a lot of words now and it will improve with practice. The other problem is his legs. They are very stiff, so balance is tricky, and walking is hard but not impossible with some help. He hates taking medication too, as it makes him drowsy, but Hudson and the nurses are making sure he takes it, and they help him with his exercises every day. It's awful to see him so helpless. He must really hate it, and he can't even tell us properly.'

'Give him a pen and some paper,' Grace said. 'He will soon give you lots of instructions.' She smiled. 'You told me he has a library of books, that should help keep him occupied.'

'His books help a lot,' Evie said. 'He actually wants to get back to work. Can you believe it? We are hoping he'll get better at accepting the changes he will have to make, like not travelling so much. We have to accept it too. He may never be the same again.'

Evie felt her lip tremble and tears welled up in her eyes.

Grace broke the silence that followed.

'Could we take a little walk around your garden, Evie?' she asked. 'The flowers must be lovely after all the rain and now the warm sunshine. I hope this better weather continues.'

The walk in the garden cheered them both, but Evie didn't have the heart to tell Grace her story. It nagged at Evie's conscience. She wanted desperately to confide in Grace, but it was obviously not the right time. As soon as Grace returns from her aunt's funeral, Evie thought, I will tell her. Definitely. No later. They would meet for tea then go for a walk in the park, and Evie would tell Grace everything.

When they came inside, Grace's father was waiting for her.

'There you are,' he said. 'Time to begin our long journey, Grace. It was lovely to see you, Mrs Wells, and you too, Evie. Once again, my very best wishes to the professor for a speedy recovery.'

'Thank you for calling to see him, Mr Finch,' Evie's mother said. 'I think it did him the world of good.'

'Time is a great healer, Mrs Wells,' Mr Finch said.

'I hope so,' Evie's mother said softly. Evie noticed how sad she looked.

Harp Maiden

After Grace and her father left, Evie returned to her music. It was strange how she still didn't feel that the harp was truly hers yet, not like the flute. From the moment she first played it, the flute felt like a part of her. In contrast the harp was 'on loan', simply passing from one Harp Maiden to the next, never really belonging to anyone. Perhaps when Evie finished the charms, when she committed herself completely, she would feel different about it. The charms were bound to become more difficult as she climbed each step of the Ladder. After the charms, she would be endowed with magic, powerful enough to destroy the Black Ruby. What exactly would that mean for Evie? How would she do it and would it come at a cost?

Evie worked hard, devoting all her spare time to finishing step two quickly, and without a hitch. Once again, there were five charms on the second step of the Ladder. But this time the secrets that were revealed were rules of behaviour to be learned by heart, written on parchment and burned at the next full moon. In so doing, they would become a code of conduct that Evie must strive to live by. She wrote them down immediately and kept the sheet of parchment folded up inside Nala's notebook, ready for the next full moon. Evie recited them each night, quietly to herself before going to bed.

1. *Learn resilience: the role of the Harp Maiden is long and challenging*

2. *Foster calm and positive thoughts: you will face sadness, fear and despair*

3. Strive to be brave and fearless, but never reckless or vengeful

4. Be true to your heart; it will guide you through difficult decisions

5. Trust the harp; it chose you for a reason

Volok was never far from Evie's thoughts. The demon lord and his wife Madruga, the one to 'beware', still had to be defeated. But at least Olga was gone, thanks to Nala's knowledge of the Black Ruby and Evie's magical moment. Eventually there would be only Evie and Volok. 'Hopefully, I will find what I need in here,' she whispered to the notebook. 'When I'm ready.' She put the notebook away in her private drawer. There was nothing more she could do about Volok and Madruga until she finished the Ladder of Charms.

It wasn't long until the next full moon and Evie had already written the wish: good fortune for Charlie McGinn's family. It was the least she could do. Later, she would tell Grace her secret and how she could help her eyesight with a wish. That conversation would have to be handled with care, but she looked forward to finally helping her best friend.

Evie enjoyed exchanging letters with Matthew. Mr Reid was his usual self at her music lessons, and she would calm her mother's fears with regard to his acquaintance with Mr Thorn over time. She knew it must have been the real Lionel Thorn that Mr Reid had known, rather than the demon who later possessed him. One day Evie might like to learn about the real maestro, the unfortunate recluse who had come to such a bitter end.

Harp Maiden

From the middle of June, Evie and Freddie began riding lessons – a surprise Evie's father had arranged before he fell ill. Before long, they were galloping across fields, fearless Freddie hallooing with excitement, Evie feeling more confident in herself again, and finally getting used to riding side-saddle. With the wind in her thick, auburn hair flying out from under her riding hat and the summer sun shining on her face, Evie felt free as a bird. She knew that learning to ride would be a useful skill to have now that she had mastered the carriage. It would be a summer like no other, with many duties at home as well as those of a Harp Maiden intent on finishing a dangerous mission.

Nala's magic had tied Evie to an extraordinary destiny, a world of magic not without danger and sacrifice. But Evie was growing into her role now. Perhaps she was already endowed with some magic from the charms, magic that was helping her come to terms with all the extraordinary changes in her young life. Sometimes, she thought she felt the magic coursing through her veins, more often she dreamed of it. Perhaps, as Nala told her, she would become the most important Harp Maiden of all time, but such a lofty title was bound to come at a price. Evelyn Wells had only just begun to climb the Ladder of Charms. There were many steps ahead, and she had yet to discover precisely where that ladder would lead her.

THE END

ACKNOWLEDGEMENTS

Once again, a big thank you to all the special team: Rachel Corcoran (illustrator), Robert Doran (editor) and Chenile Keogh (Kazoo). I also want to particularly thank the bookstores, schools and libraries that continue to support my work, and all the enthusiastic young readers who enjoy my stories. A special mention always for my husband Angelo, my biggest supporter, wisest advisor and best friend.

The adventure continues …

HARP MAIDEN
Ladder of Charms

CHAPTER ONE

Even at two o'clock in the morning it was warm, too warm. Evie could feel beads of perspiration pricking at her temples, and one drop was annoyingly trickling slowly down the back of her neck. But her discomfort wasn't only because of the heat. She desperately wanted to reach the safety of her home, run inside, shut the door, bolt it tight and ensure the harp was safe. Then she could breathe a sigh of relief. But this night of the July full moon, something felt very wrong.

Evie had prepared for the ritual as usual, gathering everything she needed for her satchel in her bedroom in plenty of time. The parchment, the neatly tied bundle of dry twigs for the fire, the matches, and a new thick felt cover she had made for the harp – everything was ready.

It was another humid night. Recently the weather had been unusually hot and there had been no rain since the end of May. Everyone was worrying about a continuing drought, this year's crops and even some farmers' entire livelihoods. The looming crisis was on the front page of every newspaper for the last few weeks.

But Evie could fix that problem, or rather the magic in her harp could. She had already written this month's wish on the parchment: for enough rain to fall to fill the wells and reservoirs and save the farmers' crops. It was a good wish that would help so many people. The rain might even arrive the very next day, if not within hours.

That night, however, Evie's delight at being able to do so much good was interrupted. Once or twice as she prepared to play the harp, she thought she heard a rustle, a tiny twig crack, a leaf flutter. Something was moving nearby, behind the cover of bushes. She dismissed it at first, but the second time she couldn't. It was a ground noise, unlikely to be a bird. What would be out in this isolated little corner of the local park, where she came to play the harp for a few minutes at every full moon? Was it a mouse, a rabbit, a fox? Not with the fire lit. There should be no one, nothing, nearby at this hour of night.

As she put out the little fire with stones and some soil, Evie stiffened. There it was again, a noise and a definite movement this time, and it was coming from the thicket beside her. For a horrible moment Evie thought it might be Volok, the demon lord who she expected would sooner or later seek her out.

But Volok wouldn't skulk around, she thought. He would pounce and roar, grab her and the harp and run back to his cave, or wherever he was hiding now. Olga, the demon-ogress and Volok's servant, was dead, so it couldn't be her either. So who was watching her? Her thoughts raced through the possibility that it was just some vagrant. She should have considered that before, and must include some means of defending herself in future, bring a weapon of some sort, anything to fend off unwanted company.

Whoever it was, it was a pointed reminder of how much danger she and her family and all those close to her would soon be in. A confrontation with Volok was undoubtedly edging ever closer, and soon his search would inevitably lead him to Evie.

She slung her satchel over her shoulder, grabbed the harp and its cover and broke into a run. But she didn't run straight home. If someone is following me, she thought, I'm not leading them straight to those I love most in the world.

Evie hurried as best she could, but it was difficult. Her satchel bounced around uncomfortably, often slipping off her shoulder, and the harp, though small, was surprisingly heavy and awkward. At the same time, she was trying to lift the hem of her skirt to allow her to run at all. She soon grew tired and very hot, her blouse sticking to her back as she hurried through the park, down several narrow laneways, then circled around and eventually arrived at the back of her house. She stumbled through the back gate, not bothering to stop to close it, and finally arrived out of breath at the back door.

Evie's hand was trembling as she lifted the key to the lock.

In her haste, she dropped the keys. Letting out a groan of frustration at her carelessness, she bent down to pick it up and bumped the harp against the door with a whump, bumping her head at the same time.

Cross now, and fumbling with the key, Evie heard a tiny squeak. Was that the gate? She didn't look behind but tried the key again. Successful this time, she almost fell through the door once it opened. She whirled around the door and into the boot room behind the kitchen, almost forgetting to shut the door *quietly*, pausing just in time to prevent a loud bang that might wake half the household. Evie leaned against the door with relief but was startled by another sound. Footsteps. Is he really coming all the way up to the house? she asked herself in disbelief.

Tightly clutching the harp, Evie backed away from the door. Frantic thoughts raced through her head, wondering what she should do, yet not wanting to call out for help and put her family in danger.

But Evie couldn't just run and hide, and her well-known curiosity was burning. She stopped retreating and began to walk slowly towards the back door again. By the glow of the gas street light, Evie could make out a shape behind the muffled pane of glass on the upper half of the back door. A dark shape, not overly large – another reason it was unlikely to be Volok. She watched as a lighter patch moved closer to the glass – a face. First the nose pressed tight to the glass, then the mouth and stubbled chin. He's trying to see inside, Evie thought. He wants to get in, come after me and the harp, perhaps my entire family. Maybe murder us all!

Evie gritted her teeth, placed the harp carefully on the floor and let her satchel slide off her shoulder. Clenching her fists, Evie was just two steps away from her pursuer behind the door when she stopped abruptly. He was pressing the whole of his face hard against the window now and Evie could see his eyes. No! Not his *eyes*, just *one* eye, wild and staring.

Evie knew exactly who it was.